THE BROWN ENVELOPE CLUB

THE BROWN ENVELOPE CLUB

Charles Barker

Inkstone Books

THE BROWN ENVELOPE CLUB

ISBN 978-962-86740-0-8
© 2010 Charles Barker
http://www.charlesbarker.org

Inkstone Books
http://inkstone.chameleonpress.com
22nd Floor, 253–261 Hennessy Road, Hong Kong

Typeset in Adobe Garamond by Alan Sargent

Printed in Hong Kong by Regal Printing
First printing February 2010

Always forgive your enemies —
but never forget their names!

Dramatis personae

Brown Envelope Club

Bill Marshall	Founder of the Brown Envelope Club
Commander Brian Cooper	Ex-Kuwait Navy
Major Mike Newcombe	Ex-SAS (Special Air Service)
Nick Chater	Ex-regular soldier and adviser in Qatar
Jim Masterson	Ex-SBS (Special Boat Service)
Little George	Ex-Green Jackets and parachute instructor
Ian Scott	Ex-Omani Air Force
Ernst Gunter	Swiss financier and playboy
Tony Carson	Arms dealer

Gulf Co-operation Council states

Abdullah Bin-Abd-al-Aziz Al Saud	King of Saudi Arabia
General Zhuror	Military chief of staff, Abu Dhabi
Anthony Appleby	Internal Security, Abu Dhabi
Colonel Charles Wilmot	Chief of security for ruler of Abu Dhabi
The Minister	Minister for commerce and industry, Oman
General Paul Ashman	Head of security for the Saudi royal family
Brigadier Mahmoud Ayyad	Chief of intelligence, Bahrain
Colonel Ray Kenwright	Security advisor to Sultan Qaboos, Oman
Sheikh Salem Al Sabah	Emir of Kuwait
Sheikh Al Nahyan	Ruler of Abu Dhabi and president of the UAE
Qaboos bin Said Al Said	Sultan of Oman
Captain Ian Gascoigne	Royal Flight, Oman
Lawrence Beaumont	General manager, Al Bustan Palace Hotel, Oman
Sir Timothy Armitage	British ambassador to Oman

Antigua

Sheikh Yaya Awaida	Owner of the St Peter's Club
Lester Fish	Prime minister of Antigua
Eric Wilkinson	Manager, St Peter's Club
Nigel Elliott	Deputy manager, St Peter's Club
Russell	Part-owner of the Copper & Lumber Store Hotel
Hans Schwartz	Head of scuba diving centres, St Peter's Club and Copper & Lumber Store
Sandra Hardy	Guest relations manager, St Peter's Club and mistress of Lester Fish
Trevor Barton	Chief engineer, St Peter's Club

Mike Church	Skipper of the *Paladin*
Steve Hellerman	First mate, *Paladin*
Ann Fraser	Cook and hostess, *Paladin*
John Gavat	Yacht agent
Titi	Owner of Colombo's Bar & Restaurant

Iraq
Saddam Hussein	President of Iraq
Colonel Rousan	Chief of intelligence
Tariq Aziz	Deputy prime minister and foreign minister
General Musbah	Chief of staff

London
Sir William Hood	Director general of MI6
Crispin Steele	Assistant to Sir William Hood
Sir James Parsons	Cabinet secretary
Sarah Renard	Director general of MI5
Martin Henshaw	MI5 officer
Stuart Raber	Mossad officer

New York
Lord Douglas Styles	Secretary general of the United Nations
Chuck Campbell	Assistant to Lord Styles
'Joe' Yousef Al Khyumi	Omani ambassador to the United Nations

Israel
Brigadier Ari Diarra	Director general of Mossad
Shimon Peres	Prime minister

Porlock Weir
Charlie Bailey	Landlord of Anchor Inn
Jill Bailey	Daughter of Charlie
Major Bennett	Squire of Tytherleigh Manor
Dr Morton	Retired GP

Jordan
Oswald Prendergast	SIS chief of station, British embassy
Major Ibrahim	General Intelligence Department, Jordan
Rashid Masri	Mossad chief of station, Amman
Brigadier Samir Raslam	Chief security officer, InterContinental Hotel
Yacoub	Head receptionist, Hishan Hotel
Firas Al Rahman	Iraqi captain
Mustafa Ali Said	Saudi businessman and Iraqi spy
Mahmoud Kanaan	Director of sales, Amman Excelsior Hotel

Spain
Kate Lladro	Arms dealer
Alvarro, José, Carlos	Captain and crew of *Pila*

Prologue
The Seeds of Revenge

Baghdad, Iraq

He DID NOT WANT to die and leave his family. He was just a simple tradesman who had done nothing to hurt anyone, but someone must have spoken against him. He felt so completely sick with fear his legs could no longer support him, so his uniformed tormentors simply dragged him pitilessly through the sparse crowd to the unoccupied street lamp post. Two ropes were already slung over the post's crossbars, swaying limply in the wind and, below each, a rickety wooden box awaited another trembling victim.

He wanted to cry out but his terror froze the scream in his throat as he was manhandled onto the box, his bound hands now as useless as his legs. He was held upright while the noose was put over his head and tightened, then they let him go. They were laughing as one of the guards kicked the box from under him and he began to die. Another confused and innocent victim of a fearful regime had been executed.

Like all of the world's great tyrannies since the dawn of man, the people of Iraq toiled under the oppressive burden of the classical police state. Ruling by fear and terror, Saddam Hussein kept his diverse and turbulent people in order with a rod of iron, the rope and a pistol, the latter of which he carried with him always and used in earnest frequently.

Since being militarily vanquished by the combined might of science and the Western world in 1991, Hussein had vowed to avenge himself and his nation. His quarrel was not principally with the West, however, but with his neighbours in the Middle East who, with the exception of Jordan, he considered to be a bunch of despotic tribesmen and spoilt children. So, in much the same way as Germany had picked herself up from the Treaty of Versailles at the end of the First World War, Iraq too had learnt her lessons and was planning her revenge.

The first lesson learnt was that, while fearsome rhetoric and sabre rattling were all very well, a quiet, methodical and conventional military rebuilding programme was imperative. It was not so important to have huge legions, impossible to train discreetly, equip and supply, but rather to have smaller numbers whose quality and skills would make up for their numerical deficiency.

And so it was that, from the ranks of his Republican Guard, an elite special services regiment was formed.

The second lesson learnt was the need to select outstanding lieutenants and advisors and to listen to what they had to say. While this made him feel more vulnerable, Saddam recognised the need to create an environment in which his best strategists could feel able to contribute opinions and advice without fear of retribution.

The learning of these lessons, however, was more easily absorbed than their implementation but after a few years the nation was better prepared than ever before and, in the process, had attracted little concern and attention from the West. All that remained now was the right opportunity, and this time there would be no miscalculations, no stopping off in Kuwait. No, this time he would grip the entire Arabian Peninsula in a vice so strong and threatening that only diplomats and politicians would come to parley for peace and not the cursed American B-52s. It all depended on timing and seizing the moment.

Thumrait, Oman

THE LEADING JAGUAR was travelling at 450 knots through the Jebel Aktar mountain range – nothing remarkable except that it was below the level of the top of the canyon through which it was hurtling with less than thirty metres' clearance either side or below it.

The two novice Omani pilots following Wing Commander Ian Scott could not bring themselves to follow what they considered to be such a suicidal flight path. They lurked uncertainly behind and overhead and watched in misery as their leader performed manoeuvres they could not believe these fighter aircraft were meant to make, or humans to imagine. They were particularly miserable because they knew that at any moment they too would be made to sink down into the abyss and perform like their crazed commander.

Suddenly, Scott's Jaguar pulled into a vertical climb up the sheer side of Jebel Shams and rocketed into the sky. Before they knew it, he was on the tail of his apprentices, very good ones he conceded, and was issuing the instructions they dreaded.

'Right Ahmed, Mohammed, get your asses down there and let's see if you really know how to fly. And if you bend those planes there'll be trouble.' Ahmed dutifully obeyed and was followed by his partner from the Flying Academy shortly after.

Although surrounded by a plethora of information on dials and digital monitors, the most critical data were projected onto the inside of the Jaguar's cockpit canopy in a punchy green read out – the head up display. This reduced the need for pilots to constantly be looking down and concentrate instead on not hitting things like mountains during fast, low-level flying.

The exercise did not last long and both pilots felt a mixture of elation and exhaustion at having completed the test without obliterating themselves. They had not even had to pull more than a couple of GS the whole flight, but for all that they felt drained. As they rejoined Scott in formation for the flight back to their base in Thumrait, he was laughing.

'There's nothing like a mountain to help improve your steering,' he chuckled, 'Anyway lads, that was well done. Let's go home.'

The flight back was uneventful and Scott wondered how much longer he would be able to keep this job. He was forty-three and having a ball he knew could not last. The latest Omanisation efforts in the Sultan's Armed Forces had already taken their toll of many of his friends and colleagues and he realised it was only a matter of time. Still, the role he had was a very complex and demanding one and there certainly weren't any Omanis anywhere near capable of taking over from him for at least a couple of years.

After the flight debriefing, Scott went to his office to work on some administration, his least favourite activity. Ali, an elderly and decrepit survivor of the Dhofar wars, who performed various odd jobs around the base, from messenger 'boy' to coffee man, was hovering anxiously in the doorway.

'What is it Ali?' demanded Scott.

'Sorry boss, big chief visit while you gone.' Ali seemed unusually nervous.

'Which big chief, Ali?'

'Al Raisi, boss'

'You're kidding,' said Scott uneasily. 'He never mentioned a visit and anyway, why didn't he stay?'

'He told me give you this.' Ali, looking more dejected than ever, almost threw something onto Scott's desk and fled the room.

Wing Commander Ian Scott looked at the small brown envelope and the air went out of him. He couldn't believe it but as he ripped open the courier his worst fear was confirmed. After almost ten years in Oman's Air Force his contract was terminated. No explanation, no thanks, and delivered by the bloody office boy. Disbelief turned to anger and he swept the papers off his desk with an oath and stormed out of the office for the mess. The bastards had even chosen Christmas as his last working day.

Abu Dhabi, United Arab Emirates

'MERCHANTS OF DEATH' are a tough and ruthless breed of people by necessity. Although often respectable themselves and operating within international legal boundaries, those with whom the arms dealers do their business are at best frequently bending laws and much of the time totally disregarding them.

Tony Carson was one such merchant. He had worked for years for a reputable British arms manufacturer following a very respectable career in the army. Buyers liked dealing with Carson because he was not only a salesman but a practical demonstrator as well. He really knew his weapons and their capabilities, not just their prices, and so he was very successful in this highly competitive field.

Although his employers recognised his ability, they were very traditional, however, in their approach to remuneration and, in Carson's view, were downright stingy when it came to paying him. He had very few commitments, being a confirmed bachelor and preferring a militarily austere style of life, but it was a matter of principle. Accordingly, Tony Carson had a perfectly clear conscience in performing deals between other interested parties, and sometimes not in his company's clients' best interests.

Carson's game, however, was a dangerous one. Several Third World countries now had him on their black lists and his world was getting smaller. At the end of December 1994, it shrank still further.

He was staying at the Forte Grand Hotel and working on the final stages of a deal with Abu Dhabi's military chief, General Zhuror. Lightweight, surface-to-air, shoulder-launched guided missiles were something of a speciality with Carson, and he had been promoting his company's latest such weapon now for many months with the general. At last it seemed success was in sight, particularly since the last 'inducement' had been handed over. While the company knew such actions were sometimes necessary they did not officially recognise them, although a certain leniency was allowed to their sales representative's budgets and expense accounts.

Luck, however, was not on Carson's side. He had a meeting set up with the general at his office for noon on the 30th and was hoping for a contract to celebrate the New Year with. He arrived punctually and, unusually, was shown into his office by an armed sergeant. The soldier did not leave and instead of finding the general at his desk, there brooding ominously was the mysterious and sinister spectre of Mr Anthony Appleby.

No one really knew who Appleby was or what his real role was. It was without question, though, that his power and influence in Abu Dhabi's internal security services was without parallel. Seated opposite Appleby was another heavyweight Carson recognised, Colonel Charles Wilmot. Wilmot was chief of security for Abu Dhabi's ruler, Sheikh Al Nahyan, and had just returned from the Gulf Co-operation Council conference in Qatar.

Without preamble or any courtesies, Appleby opened the proceedings.

'The general is no longer with us Mr Carson. We understand that you have been involved with him in an unauthorised arms contract which has included certain private payments. Do you have any comments?'

Still standing, Carson felt like a schoolboy about to be thrashed by his headmaster. There was that sinking, hollow feeling in the pit of his stomach for he knew that the men before him could inflict far worse punishments than a caning.

'The contract is a perfectly legitimate one, fully documented and approved by the authorities in the UK. If General Zhuror was not authorised to contract such a deal, I am sorry, but as he is head of the army. . . .'

'Was!' interrupted Wilmot.

'Very well,' continued Carson cautiously, 'as he was head of the army, and as we had dealt with him before, it seemed not un-reasonable that we should consider him your country's bona fide decision maker.'

'Tell me, Carson,' snapped Wilmot, 'do you also consider it reasonable to bribe this country's representatives to achieve your own ends?'

Carson was feeling distinctly uncomfortable by now and, despite the air conditioning, could feel the sweat breaking out all over him.

'Certain ex-gratia payments have always been necessary. . . .'

'Oh, for God's sake, spare us the bullshit,' bawled Wilmot, inter-rupting again. Appleby took up for the prosecution.

'However you wish to justify your conduct, it is quite unacceptable here. We have made our views known to your government. The company you represent have been advised that they and their representatives are no longer welcome in the United Arab Emirates. I imagine your time with them is also over.' He paused, steepled his long thin fingers and glowered menacingly. 'As for you, well, there are two options.'

'Look,' said Carson, feeling decidedly sick by this stage, 'there must be some mistake. . . .'

'Yes, and you've made it,' broke in Wilmot.

'I mean, my company and I have traded with you on various occasions and we have always enjoyed an excellent relationship. Why has it suddenly gone wrong?'

'The general, it seems, has been pursuing his own agenda,' Appleby replied. 'Your conduct and association with him thus incriminate and implicate you.'

'But that's ridiculous,' said Carson, realising that actually it wasn't but there was nothing he could now say or do in his defence.

'Ridiculous or not, I spoke of two options. Colonel Wilmot here would like to keep you as our guest for a couple of years in Al Sadr Jail and make an example of you to your, er, fellow tradesmen.'

A sadistic sneer (it couldn't be called a smile) had spread over Wilmot's face and Carson was now really frightened.

'And the other option?'

'The other option,' replied Appleby, 'is that you are taken from this room,' he paused again for effect, staring mercilessly into Carson's eyes, 'and deported from the airport forthwith, never to return to the United Arab Emirates. Fortunately, for you, it has been decided to adopt the latter option.'

Carson tried not to show his relief and could hardly wait to leave these two monsters. He heard Appleby continue.

'We know of the other contract officers who have been involved over this affair and they too will be leaving the country. Unfortunately, the local officers involved will not be so kindly treated. Good day, Carson.'

He looked over to the soldier who had remained at silent attention throughout the interview.

'Sergeant – see that Mr Carson is taken to the airport and departs on the next plane as we discussed.' With that, the sergeant opened the door and indicated for Carson to precede him. As he was leaving, he heard Appleby saying to Wilmot, 'Colonel, would you please see that these are distributed,' and saw being passed over the desk a small pile of brown envelopes.

Kuwait City, Kuwait

THE LARGE BLACK DESERT cobra lay immobile in its burrow, all its senses fully tuned to the campers a few metres away. At just four feet long, with its distinctive gun-metal colouring, it was an aggressive snake which attacked its prey with two short, fixed, tubular fangs injecting a neurotoxic venom. Once absorbed, the motor nerves become affected leading to paralysis in all muscles. Three such drops of venom can kill a man.

Although usually nocturnal, the cobra had been disturbed by the arrival of a four-wheel-drive Pajero in the late afternoon and the raucous noise that always accompanies the making of a camp. It was now fully alert and it was angry, fearing to stay yet fearing to escape. So, glowering malevolently, it watched and waited.

The people making camp were two off-duty contract naval officers with their wives. Since the Gulf conflict, Kuwait had spent a fortune on developing a navy that could defend its shores and patrol its territorial waters. With the ever-continuing cutback in the British armed forces, there was no shortage of willing and qualified officers to take these lucrative contracts, and Commander Brian Cooper was one such.

A large, grey-bearded, middle-aged and piratical looking man, Cooper had spent much of his distinguished career on aircraft carriers, both as a pilot and then as a flight controller, the man to whom pilots entrust their lives with every carrier landing. Then, inevitably, he'd been obliged to take on desk duties but had been fortunate to secure a couple of naval- and air-attaché jobs in Dubai and then Oman before retirement.

He had started with a predominantly administrative job in Kuwait's navy within two months of leaving Muscat and, although the work was unexciting, it paid well and kept him occupied.

Cooper and his colleagues frequently camped out in the arid and more remote parts of the country. They enjoyed the open spaces in much the same way they did the vast expanses of ocean, with which they had been more familiar. More particularly, they all liked to get out of Kuwait City as often as they could and leave that oppressive and self-centred community behind them, if only for the weekend.

However, like his friends when ashore, Cooper was still, at heart, an old sea dog, and so as dusk was approaching and he walked a few paces away from the camp to relieve himself, he was unconcerned and incautious to the possible dangers that lurked out there in the scrub.

The cobra struck with such speed that, at first, Cooper did not realise he had been bitten. In the split second of the attack, he thought perhaps he had pierced his bare calf with a thorn. However, the sight of a long, shiny, black reptile retreating into the gloom with astonishing speed brought on a wave of nausea and initial shock.

He had a dazed expression when he rejoined his fellow campers and his breathing was coming in gasps and was clearly strained.

'Whatever's the matter?' his wife Sue asked. 'You look like you've seen a ghost.'

Cooper felt he was choking. He wanted to say what had happened but everything was becoming difficult – concentration, breathing, speaking.

'Black snake . . . bit me,' he whispered hoarsely. The others had come round by now to see what the problem was and a near panic greeted Cooper's croaked announcement. They made him lie down and started examining him for signs of the bite. Sue, who despite her own acute alarm, was trying to calm her husband, found a single puncture mark just above his right ankle. There was no swelling or bruising.

'We've got to get him to hospital fast,' said Stuart Russell, a former Royal Navy captain who, along with his wife Jane, were long-time friends of the Coopers. 'Sue, you and Jane bandage then immobilise his leg and keep talking to him and comfort him. If his breathing becomes any worse, massage his heart. I'll get the truck ready – come on, let's move it.'

They quickly settled Cooper into the back of the Pajero and with Sue and Jane beside him, they raced back the way they had just come. With luck, they'd be at the main Al Sabah hospital in about an hour and a half.

By the time they reached the hospital, Cooper was in a bad way. His breathing had become very laboured and shallow, his eyelids were closed and a bluish hue discoloured his face. Sue was frantic and went with him as far as she was allowed into the emergency and casualty department.

Russell described to the American casualty officer on duty what had happened and the party was then left to wait for what seemed like an eternity. However, after a while, the doctor emerged with a pleased look on his face.

'He's going to be okay,' he announced. 'You said it was a black snake, so with these symptoms we reckon it was a cobra. Mrs Cooper, your husband's a lucky man 'cause it only nicked him on the leg. A proper bite with full penetration and, well . . .' he paused, realising he was becoming morbid, 'Well, anyway, we have a good prognosis. Your husband will need to stay here for a few days, but he's going to be fine.'

The 'few days' turned out to be a couple of weeks and it was almost a month before Cooper was back at work.

He was warmly greeted by his colleagues but met a distinctly hostile Admiral Mustafa Al Sabah, the Kuwaiti naval chief of staff, who summoned him to his office shortly after his arrival.

The admiral was, inevitably, closely related to the Emir. His rank was totally unearned and unmerited but his appointment some years ago ensured that, like all other key positions in the country, everything remained comfortably in the family. He was short and fat with over-indulgence, and sported the small goatee beard similarly favoured by the ruler. He was constantly perspiring and had an unpleasantly high-pitched, squeaky voice. His equally odious deputy was also in the room, another example of nepotism at its most effective.

'Commander Cooper,' he began, not inviting the senior officer the courtesy of a seat, 'we have been most displeased by all the fuss and attention over your accident. Frankly we find it incredible that a senior naval officer should let such a stupid thing happen in the first place and it has led us to question your abilities for the role you presently have with us.'

'Now wait a minute, I almost died out there. There is no connection whatever between my professional competence and getting bitten by a snake.'

'You have been brought here to work and help develop our armed forces, commander, not to spend weeks convalescing after picnicking in the desert.'

'I can't believe I'm hearing this. . . .'

'I don't care what you believe, commander,' squeaked the admiral. 'The fact is, we are looking to reduce our dependency, throughout all the armed services, on officers such as you and, accordingly, have decided to conclude your contract.'

Cooper was speechless and was having to exercise considerable self control not to hit the repugnant little slob in front of him.

'You will hand over your duties to my deputy here, and leave by the end of the month. You will find all the relevant details in this,' and he tossed contemptuously a thick brown manila envelope across his desk. Cooper took it and left without another word.

Part I
Terms of Engagement

Winter 1994/1995

Hereford, England

THE MONTHLY MEETING of the Brown Envelope Club started in its usual, rather morose way and became gloomier as the evening wore on.

Membership of the club demanded rather particular and unusual qualifications. To begin with, a background in the armed services, whether conventional army, navy and air force, or less conventional in a variety of 'special' or related services. Service overseas as a contracted officer to one of the many nations requiring expertise, training and development for their various armed forces. Such nations were typically African and Middle Eastern, but most were now pursuing policies of nationalisation; 'expats out' was definitely in fashion, even though in most cases this would lead to economic and military degeneration.

The other qualification was to have received a brown envelope at work one day, the curt contents of which advised the recipient that his employment had been terminated.

The majority of members were no spring chickens. Many were in their late forties or early fifties and so, when the axe had fallen, they had had neither the resourcefulness, contacts, resolve nor indeed the ability to start anew. Thus, the highlight of their lives was the monthly meeting where they would meet up with old cronies, exchange oft-repeated anecdotes, and soak up large quantities of gin.

However, not all were like this. There were some who, although still down on their luck, kept themselves fit and trim and, most importantly, actively sought work in whatever form it might take.

These were the really tough ones, the resourceful and tireless ones. They were also the ones who wanted to get even!

The club was run by Bill Marshall, one of the few people to have left 'The Regiment' for another career and landed well on his feet. But many of his colleagues had not done as well. Accordingly, a principal aim of the club was to try and help members find work when they left their previous employment.

Marshall owned a couple of small but lucrative estate agency shops in the area and had a share in a sports club in the Caribbean at which he pursued his two passions in life, black girls and scuba diving. He had recently converted an outbuilding of his beautifully appointed farmhouse on the outskirts of Hereford to a large bar and games room. It was here that the members of the Brown Envelope Club met and monthly considered their fortune.

Riyadh, Saudi Arabia

THE DESIRE TO INGRATIATE ONESELF with those in high office is one which certain Middle Eastern nations have refined to an art form and Sheikh Yaya Awaida was one of its greatest practitioners.

Although of considerable rank and influence in his own right, he was not of the ruling family. Since he was from Saudi Arabia, therefore, his survival and success depended absolutely upon his ability to please the royals of that prosperous, technologically advanced yet culturally retarded nation. This was no mean feat, for a more hypocritical and self-interested group of people was not to be found on the planet.

Since the old King Fahd had been overthrown and butchered by one of his many cousins, Prince Abdullah, the country had regressed in the eyes of the world and lost much of the respect it had once commanded. Although the religious police kept the nation in a state of primeval subjugation, the leaders of the country dissipated their wealth in orgiastic displays and many of Saudi's smaller but equally prosperous neighbours were becoming just as self-indulgent.

In 1981 there had been formed in the Arabian Peninsula a loose economic bonding between six countries called the Gulf Co-operation Council. Consisting of Saudi Arabia, Oman, Kuwait, Bahrain, the United Arab Emirates and Qatar, the GCC was still in existence. How or why it did was a matter of complete mystery to anyone interested in analysing the issue, for most assuredly, no individual or group benefit was now derived by the association.

However, every year in December, the six leaders of the GCC met for a conference. Initially, this served as an venue to agree on regional policies, both economic and military, and to pronounce these to the world in a spirit of solidarity and brotherhood. Each nation took its turn to act as host and each tried to outdo the previous year's host in terms of extravagance, pomp and ceremony. But after eleven years, there were only so many new palaces that could be built to house and impress the guests and their entourages. The various monarchs were then left searching for new ways to inspire their colleagues and so it was that Sheikh Awaida sought this opportunity.

For many years Yaya Awaida had owned a fabulous hotel and club, the St Peter's Club, on the Caribbean island of Antigua. Located on a peninsula at the southern tip of the island, it was not only a beautiful setting but also afforded ideal security arrangements. Awaida owned all the land approaches to the peninsula and, perhaps more importantly, he owned the corrupt and mercenary government of the island, led as it had been for years by the Fish dynasty.

Awaida knew that the recently held GCC conference in Qatar had been a monumental bore and, since the following year it would be Saudi Arabia's turn to host the meeting, he laid his plans and sought an audience with the new King.

Brecon, Wales

MAJOR MIKE NEWCOMBE walked into the King's Head on the out-skirts of Brecon and cursed the weather, his luck, his job and the world in general. By the time he reached the bar, his usual frothing pint was waiting for him and he drank half of it down in a long gulp before taking in his surroundings and exchanging greetings with other regulars, many of whom hailed from a military background.

Although still using his rank and title, Newcombe had left the army a couple of years previously in the latest round of cutbacks. His commanding officer had been as helpful as possible but Newcombe was bitter about being 'put out to grass', as he saw it.

He had had a very distinguished army career, serving with the 22nd Regiment of the Special Air Service for his last six years. He had received the Military Cross for his actions in Iraq during the Gulf Crisis in 1991 and a string of other decorations for various, less publicised, actions around the world subsequently.

Newcombe was a man of action who was highly skilled and trained for a role in life which it seemed was no longer required or needed. His current job of taking parties of school children for outward-bound courses on the Brecon Beacons thrilled him not at all, and the inactivity was building up frustration inside him like a time bomb. Still, it was at least a job and he was grateful to Bill Marshall at the Brown Envelope Club for fixing him up with it.

Newcombe was on his third pint when the landlord, Owen Davies, pointed out a big, bluff, middle-aged man in the corner of the bar, drinking large gin and tonics like they were going out of fashion.

'You were in the Middle East, weren't you Mike? That chap's just been thrown out of somewhere called *Catter* or some such place. Been cursing the Arabs something rotten, he has. Says he was in the army there, teaching them which way round to hold their guns.'

At that moment the man in question stood up and came over to the bar for another drink. Newcombe had not really noticed him until now and saw just how huge he was. He also walked square shouldered and erect and had the proud bearing of a traditional old soldier.

'Let me get it,' invited Newcombe, ordering another for himself. 'I did a spell in the Gulf and hear you've just come back from Qatar; name's Mike Newcombe.'

'Nick Chater,' said the giant, proffering a huge slab of a hand in greeting. 'And which bunch of rag heads did you hang out with?' His voice was deep and gritty, but he was obviously well spoken and educated.

'Cheers!' Newcombe replied as the drinks came. 'Well, I was here and there, you know. Did a bit in Desert Storm, then a spell in Kuwait building armies for them. What about yourself?'

'Been a contract officer for twenty years; Oman, Bahrain, Saudi then Qatar. Same old story – give 'em your all, then they think they can do the job better than you can. Sling you out without so much as a thank you, let alone a decent pay off.'

'When did you leave Qatar?'

'Humph! Just a couple a days back. They had their annual GCC bash, my bunch hosting, and the only thing they could decide on was a mutual desire to reduce the number of expats. "Too much dependency on foreigners, especially from the West", they said. They've said it before, but this time they really went in with the knife. 'Course, they'll keep on all the fucking jinglies otherwise the whole country'll collapse! God almighty, what a bunch, eh?'

Chater returned morosely to his gin and tonic and they both drank for a while in silence. Newcombe finished off his beer and said, 'Well, you know what they say, "Don't get mad, get even". Look, there's a place some of us go to down Hereford way – first Friday of each month. We call it the Brown Envelope Club and you've got to have had one to be a member. Come down with me next week. You might meet up with some old mates.'

'Less of the "old", thanks.' Chater gave a crooked grin and fingered his glass. 'Yes, why not? I've nothing else to do and my sister's already driving me to drink.'

'Okay, I'll pick you up here at 1300 hours.' With which formal military salutation, they parted.

Hereford, England

T HERE WAS SOMETHING noticeably different about the year's first club meeting that wet, windy January afternoon. Bill Marshall was doing the rounds and greeting familiar faces, but there were several new people he hadn't met before. They were being introduced around the members and there was an extra spark of interest in the air. The big fellow that Newcombe had brought down seemed a curious sort – big bastard, too, thought Marshall. He positively emanated a mixture of animal forcefulness and anger. Not someone to be on the wrong side of.

At that moment, the big man was holding forth to a small group and Marshall hovered on its edges and listened in.

'. . . It was Mike who made me start thinking about it – "Don't get mad, get even" he said. Seemed pretty ridiculous at the time. I mean, how can one "get even" against a whole bloody country, 'specially if you don't live in it and need visas and God knows what, even to go for a crap!'

There was some subdued laughter, but everyone seemed to be thinking the same thoughts – wouldn't it be nice to get even. More people had come over to join the group and listen in. One chap, a sandy haired, very fit looking man who had been in the Special Boat Service, Jim Masterson, took up Chater's idea.

'Sounds great, but you need a clearly focused plan. What do you want to do anyway? I mean you can't just kill half the Qatar Military Command 'cause they gave you the shove.'

'It's not just Qatar, but everywhere in the Middle East,' said another newcomer, apparently a Jaguar squadron wing commander, recently out of Oman. 'The bastards are kicking people like us around all over the place. It really would be magic to teach them all a lesson and put the boot on the other foot.'

A chorus of 'Hear! Hear!' ran round the room. By now, everyone was listening in on the debate.

'So, what we gonna do?' This from Little George, a civilian parachute instructor at Shoreham since his ejection from the Green Jackets for one bar room brawl too many. A humorous cockney, Little George was only just over five feet tall but as he was also almost five feet wide and tough as nails, he commanded everyone's respect wherever he went.

'Me, I'm bloody for it,' he continued. 'Teachin' clowns to jump at Shoreham's drivin' me bloody crazy anyway. I could do with some serious bloody action.'

A chorus of 'Yeh!' and 'Me too!' and 'Let's do it!' greeted this last call to arms and Marshall felt it was time to establish some sense of order before the Brown Envelope Club declared war on the entire Arabian Peninsula.

'Okay guys, so you want to take out the Arabs?' he asked, pushing his way to the front of the group. The earnest and positive chorus in reply sounded like a bunch of mischievous school boys.

'So, like Jim here says, we'll need a plan and if you lot can't put one together, no one can. As president of the club, therefore, I nominate Major Newcombe. . . .' several snorts of amusement interrupted this last remark as no one present was ever addressed by their previous rank. With tongue in cheek, Marshall continued. 'As I was saying, Major Newcombe will act as chief planning officer for Operation Brown Envelope.'

A round of cheers and applause greeted this announcement and then Marshall went on. 'Major, please gather a team around you and present your proposals at the club's next meeting.'

''s sir,' snapped Newcombe coming to attention. Everyone laughed and broke up into small groups, talking excitedly and, for the most part, heading back for the bar.

Marshall shook his head and thought again that this was like a bunch of naughty school boys. Still, they were enjoying themselves for a change and there was no harm in that . . . was there?

Muscat, Oman

THE ONLY PLACE TO HAVE a serious chat with the minister was in the hairdressing salon at the Al Bustan Palace Hotel. Actually, the Al Bustan was less of a hotel than a magnificent palace that took paying guests when it suited it. Otherwise it was first and foremost a government hospitality facility, designed and built to host one of the earlier GCC Summit Conferences in the mid-eighties.

The Al Bustan's general manager was an Englishman in his late thirties. Suave and polished, yet with a thoroughly ruthless streak in him, Lawrence Beaumont was nothing if not an opportunist. The minister's weekly visits to the salon were a great time to network on what was going at the very heart of the political scene and generally exchange information and that most valuable of all commodities, gossip.

Unlike many of his colleagues, the minister in question was a no-nonsense, straight talking, ex-military man. He was direct in his dealings, refreshingly lacking in deviousness and had no time for intrigue.

The two men were friends and enjoyed their weekly constitutionals although it had been some time since they had last met. The minister had been in Qatar with the Sultan of Oman at the GCC Summit Conference while Beaumont had been on holiday. They had some catching up to do.

'How was the conference, your excellency?' Beaumont asked the minister as the scissors went to work.

'To tell you the truth Lawrence, it was a complete waste of time. Those Qataris are nothing but a bunch of squabbling tribesmen. They and the Saudis make me sick, always arguing and bickering and yet pretending they do so much good. I wish His Majesty would take us out of the GCC once and for all.'

'Why doesn't he?' probed the hotelier.

'He'd like to but it would make too many waves and we really should try to hold this region together if we can.'

The Omanis are fiercely nationalistic, and rightly consider themselves to be a race apart from their neighbours on the Arabian Peninsula. Although not as rich as others in the region, they see themselves occupying a leadership role and never fail to recognise their global strategic value both politically and geographically.

'Anyway,' continued the minister, 'whatever our desires, I doubt much it will change. What about you and the family, did you have a good holiday?'

'Yes, we had a great time. We went to the Caribbean. You may remember I used to run the St Peter's Club in Antigua and we enjoy going back each year around New Year. The weather's perfect and the scuba diving is great – it's a fabulous holiday.'

'Well, don't make any plans for next year because between you and me, King Abdullah is planning to take over that place for the next GCC conference. His Majesty has just told us about it. Apparently Abdullah thinks it will make a nice change and for once, I think he's probably right.'

'He certainly is – there are some stunning villas on a hill overlooking the main complex – it's a perfect place. Mind you, they'll have to work on the food and service a bit.' And that, thought Beaumont, was an understatement. He also reflected that certain rulers might feel very much out of their depth, not being able to deport or imprison unruly subcontinent staff at will! The idea rather amused him.

The conversation then switched on to local business, how the hotel was doing and the latest saga on whether or not the nearby InterContinental Hotel was really going to collapse or was structurally sound after all, a debate that had been raging to everyone's amusement, except perhaps the management's, for years.

The grooming over, the minister took his leave and Beaumont went off to make some phone calls. Maybe next winter they'd go skiing instead.

Antigua, Leeward Islands

THE MANAGER OF THE ST PETER'S CLUB was a particularly half-witted, inexperienced but very inoffensive Englishman called Eric Wilkinson. Most usually referred to as 'Wilky', he had large buck teeth, a usually vacant expression and had the habit of driving into ditches, posts, other cars, grazing animals and almost anything his car took a fancy to. In short, he was a hopeless driver, a useless hotelier but a genial host and a totally obedient puppet to the absent owner of the club, Sheikh Yaya Awaida of Saudi Arabia.

Strangely enough, the club worked quite well, mainly due to the tireless efforts and energies of Wilkinson's deputy, Nigel Elliott. Elliott had come from Jordan and decided that, of the two, the Caribbean was definitely the place to be where his extra-curricular requirements could more easily be satisfied. His sexual appetite and prowess was as legendary on the island as was his dedication and involvement with the St Peter's Club and he was a popular figure, both on and off duty.

The club was in its usual state of pandemonium when expecting the imminent arrival of its illustrious owner. He had not visited for many months and Wilkinson was in a state of apoplexy trying to ensure that everything was going to be okay. He would have had the old local battleaxe housekeeper, Mrs Richards, vacuum the front lawn if Elliott had not chucked a large gin and tonic down him to calm his nerves.

Eventually the convoy transporting Awaida and his entourage arrived and the Sheikh, free of his Islamic constraints, jumped from the car with a massive cigar wedged between his teeth and met his manager with a slap on the back that made his huge teeth clatter. He bellowed effusive greetings to all in sight, which included a scattering of bewildered guests, and strolled purposefully into the spacious and open lobby of the club. His favourite wife, gangs of children of all ages and a gaggle of wretched nannies and servants followed, in that order. The owner had most definitely arrived.

Although Wilkinson hated these visits, locals and 'yachties' from miles around loved it when Awaida hit the island. His hospitality knew no bounds and, if you were within sight or earshot, you were invited to his table to feast. The club had learned long ago that the table had a habit of growing as the evenings wore on, so plenty of space was always left at both ends for expansion, at which would be placed the endless succession of freeloaders, managers and tarts that were inexorably drawn into Awaida's web.

The atmosphere around the pool on these evenings was always exuberant. Sucking pigs, roasting on spits; steel bandsmen beating their oil drums in drug-induced stupors; warm trade winds beating the surf onto the rocks below and a constant cacophony of laughter and bawdy banter emanating from the host's mouth. He loved everything to excess and revelled in the attention he received from all and sundry.

Wilkinson and Elliott were always present at these gastronomic orgies at the owner's insistence. In Wilkinson's case it was because Awaida enjoyed making him drunk, while Elliott's presence was needed to procure appropriate playthings for the Sheikh's second bedroom later.

Not everyone, however, shared in the partying, that first night of the owner's return. Ernst Gunter was an enormously wealthy Swiss-German playboy who spent much of his time at the club. He travelled extensively throughout Europe when engaged in his business activities, at which he was most astute, and would then return to the club, often with a stunning girl in tow. He was enormously conceited, very mischievous with a wicked sense of humour and liked always to be the centre of attention. Awaida's behaviour, therefore, pleased him not at all, and after a couple of drinks he dragged his current bimbo off to nearby English Harbour for a meal at the Copper & Lumber Store. This was a magnificently restored building, once a part of Admiral Nelson's dockyard, and was now run as a small hotel, restaurant and sports club.

Russell, the ever-grinning Antiguan who part-owned the place, was in his usual place behind the bar and had opened a couple of Red Stripes by the time Gunter reached it.

'Pace too much for you up the club?' teased Russell, laughing at the grimace on Gunter's face. 'Hear old Sheikhy's back in town, so if you want a room here for a while,' he eyed up enviously the luxuriously bosomed redhead that Gunter had brought in, 'we should be able to squeeze you in.'

'I might just do that.' Gunter replied in his crisp and clipped accent. 'The place becomes a real bore when that lunatic gets in. Everyone fawning all over him and grovelling and scraping. It makes me sick.'

'You're just jealous,' said Russell. 'Anyway, Bill's coming over for a few days next week.' He was referring to his partner, Bill Marshall, who had put up the money to purchase the hotel. 'You can take your mind off things and get stuck into some serious diving.'

'Scuba or muff?' leered Gunter and the redhead giggled, slipped her hand over his crotch and started to bite his ear.

'Hey,' said Russell with mock indignation, 'this is a respectable joint.'

'Now who's jealous?' grinned Gunter pressing the redhead's hand. He sighed with anticipation and said, 'I think, Russell, I'd better have that room.'

The following morning, everyone at the club was feeling distinctly the worse for wear. Wilkinson thought his head would explode and actually rather hoped it would in order to end his misery. He had been sick as a dog during the night and still felt decidedly ill. Even Elliott was not his usual ebullient self and, as the various managers congregated for their morning operations meeting, a spirit of lethargy seemed to pervade under a haze of brandy fumes and bad breath.

They were just starting the meeting when a hearty roar was heard from the outer office and Sheikh Awaida burst through the door, jovial and fresh. Elliott thought it incredible that anyone could be so fit and healthy having just the night before consumed at least two bottles of Cognac and then been treated by arrangement to the special talents of Velma, who, he remembered with a tinge of jealousy, had once left even him weak at the knees.

Sheikh Awaida acknowledged each in turn, warmly pumping their hands and billowing smoke from yet another of his huge Havana cigars.

'Eric, how are you? Looking a little frail I think.' He bellowed with laughter, obviously finding Wilkinson's discomfort highly amusing. 'Nigel,' he winked, 'I'll see you later.' He grinned conspiratorially. 'Hans, how's that gorgeous wife of yours? Fay, isn't it? Didn't see her last night.'

Hans Schwartz ran the Scuba Diving Centre at the club as well as another diving operation from the Copper & Lumber Store. He had drifted over to the Caribbean years ago from his native Germany and had been captivated by a beautiful Antiguan girl, Fay, to whom he was now married. Fay, like her brother Russell, wore a perpetual bright smile on her face and seemed to radiate happiness wherever she went. Hans had earned many a local man's envy.

Awaida was continuing his round. 'Johnny – keeping the rooms full I hope and Mrs Richards, how are you dear?' Johnny Harris and Mrs Richards were both locals who had been with the club for years and who were by now part of the furniture. 'And the lovely Sandra. . . .' He gave the fat guest relations manager a hug and a squeeze, not so much out of lechery but politics. Sandra Hardy was the mistress to the island's prime minister and virtual dictator, Lester Fish, and she was a useful conduit of information.

'Trevor, good to see you again.' This last greeting was to Trevor Barton, the chief engineer. Barton was reserved and quiet but highly competent and resourceful on an island where supplies and spares were so hard to come by. He had been a senior submariner, leaving the Royal Navy at the end of the Falklands conflict in 1982. Although he never spoke of it, his was the submarine which had sunk the *Belgrano* and the experience had clearly had a profound effect upon him.

His greetings completed, Awaida sat down and, without any preamble, dropped his bombshell on the assembled company.

'I've got some exciting news for you all. Later this year, we're going to have a very special gathering here at the club. I'm sure you know of the GCC. Well, each year there's a summit conference for the leaders of the six member countries and this year it's going to be held here.' He paused for effect and was not surprised that it was Elliott who commented first.

'That's usually in December, isn't it? Do you know the exact dates yet because, as you know, it's our busiest time of year?'

'Don't worry about that.' Awaida waved his hand dismissively. 'This will make more money and be a bigger event than any sort of business you'll get from your usual New York bunch.'

'But. . . .' started Wilkinson, only to be interrupted.

'But nothing, Eric – don't be negative. It'll be a great event and bring prestige to all of you.' Prestige to you, more like aggravation and grief to us, thought Wilkinson truculently. 'Anyway,' continued the Sheikh, 'if you've got any bookings, cancel them and keep the whole of December clear. There'll be a lot of preparation needed. I'll be sending somebody over soon who'll co-ordinate the whole thing. Right, I must be going. I'm meeting with Lester Fish to discuss the plans with him. We'll talk more about it all later.'

Apparently satisfied with himself, he bounced up and left the office for his car, leaving a bewildered and mind-boggled group behind him.

'Love a duck,' moaned Wilkinson, 'that's all we bloody needed.'

London, England

SINCE ITS OPENING IN THE MID-SEVENTIES, the InterContinental Hotel at Hyde Park Corner had become known in certain circles as a place for the procurement or disposal of arms contracts. Bill Marshall, who had stayed there on a number of occasions, reckoned it was exactly the right place for the meeting he had convened. It was international, with plenty of bustle and activity, had a great restaurant and was close to Shepherd Market, the red light district off Park Lane, from which he could quickly obtain satisfaction for his lustful urges. He had booked a large suite overlooking Apsley House, home to that old warhorse, the Duke of Wellington. A fitting backdrop for the meeting to come, he thought.

The doorbell rang and he welcomed in the first of his guests, Mike Newcombe, accompanied by his giant companion, Nick Chater. Greetings were exchanged and shortly two others had arrived, Ian Scott and Jim Masterson. They were all curious to know why they had been invited by Marshall and even more puzzled to find that all present constituted the planning team for Operation Brown Envelope. Several weeks had passed since the club had met and enthusiastically declared war on the Middle East, but little had happened since and the idea had been all but forgotten.

Marshall was pouring out drinks when the last guest arrived, an immaculately dressed stranger to the group.

'Gentlemen, I'd like you to meet Mr Ernst Gunter.' Introductions were effected, drinks freshened and the meeting began.

'A couple of months ago,' began Marshall, 'an idea was put forward at the club to get even with some of our previous employers. This idea was heartily received but we all realised it was an overwhelmingly difficult task even to come up with a plan, let alone execute it.'

Except for Gunter, each was nodding his assent.

'As some of you know, I spend a bit of time in Antigua in the Caribbean, which is where I know Ernst from. We were over there a couple of weeks back and heard some news we thought you might like to know about.'

He paused for effect and most certainly had their complete attention.

'This year's GCC Summit Conference is going to take place in Antigua.'

Incredulity was written on the group's faces. Knowing the passion for security that each Arabian monarch had, it was extraordinary that they would consider such a trip. But incredulity was soon replaced by sly and wolfish grins and each bent forward with anticipation, the better to hear Marshall as he continued.

'There is a place called the St Peter's Club on the south side of the island. It's owned by a Saudi by the name of Sheikh Yaya Awaida who is trying to score brownie points with King Abdullah. As it's the

Saudis' turn to host the summit this year, he came up with the idea of using the club as the venue and it's been accepted. So what do you think of that?'

Forceful and brash as ever, it was Chater who spoke first. 'Bloody great – we can go in and blow up the whole let of 'em.'

'Well, steady on, is that really what you want to do?' asked Marshall.

'Don't see why not,' replied Chater, but he was already feeling a bit stupid. Of course they couldn't do that. He went to the bar and poured himself another drink.

Masterson asked, 'What sort of coastline is it around the club? What access for boats and what cover?'

Marshall smiled and produced two maps, one a large marine chart of the area and, the second, an ordnance survey map of the island. The men poured over the maps, their military minds searching and analysing, scheming and planning.

After a few minutes and having answered the odd question, Marshall asked, 'What do you actually want to do chaps? That's the point. All this talk of getting even has been just so much hot air. But now there's an opportunity. What are you going to do with it?'

There was silence. These men had all been trained to the very highest standards to fight and kill a given target or enemy. They were professionals, not criminals and murderers and, now that they were faced with the prospect, they felt uncomfortable to a man.

'I should have thought it was obvious.' Everyone looked at Gunter, who had said virtually nothing since his arrival but for the next half hour he outlined to them his idea. Pleased with the effect this had on the assembled company he continued. 'People with your resourcefulness should have little difficulty in pulling it off; all you need is a fast boat, the right equipment and support. Then you can all retire in extreme comfort for the rest of your lives. The authorities will take a dim view but I doubt they'll be too bothered. There's little love lost between the international community and the GCC nowadays and the Arab's security apparatus stops at their borders. I think most of the world would actually be rather pleased to see them getting a dose of their own medicine.'

There was more silence for a while then Newcombe asked, 'Excuse me for asking, Mr Gunter, but why are you involved in this scheme? We all have a common interest, as I imagine Bill has told you, but how do you fit in?'

'Fair question – I can't stand Awaida and I think it would be rather fun.' He beamed at the simplicity of his involvement.

'That's one helluva strange reason to embark on this sort of venture,' said Scott. 'Is there anything else you'd like to tell us?'

Marshall spoke up. 'Ernst is one of life's great adventurers and, knowing him as I do, really does want to be involved for the fun of it. However, more importantly, if we do decide to go ahead with a caper, we're going to need a lot of money. Ernst has offered to bankroll us.'

No one had thought that far but now the enormity of what they were considering started to dawn on them. Drinks were refilled, stronger than the previous ones, and the planning began in earnest.

The time passed rapidly and, after a few hours, they had the makings of a viable operation. Marshall wrapped up the meeting.

'Well gentlemen, we've each got some work to do and I need hardly say that secrecy is paramount. Nothing, but nothing, goes outside this room. I'll contact you again shortly and we'll all go over there and have ourselves a little holiday in the sun.'

The meeting broke up and a very pensive but excited group of men left Bill Marshall's suite. Many plots, and even coups, had been planned within the walls of the InterContinental but the audacity of the scheme hatched that February evening was going to rock the world.

Riyadh, Saudi Arabia

AT THE SAME TIME BILL MARSHALL and his team were hatching their plans in London, another group were engaged in a far stormier meeting in Riyadh at the palatial Security Service headquarters on the outskirts of the city.

General Paul Ashman was feeling acutely uncomfortable, for it was he who was responsible for the personal safety and security of the upper echelons of Saudi Arabia's royal family. He had been informed only a few days previously of the monarch's intention to host the next GCC Summit Conference in the Caribbean and he was very unhappy. He had immediately requested his opposite numbers from the remaining five GCC countries to convene for a briefing, along with their key staff and other concerned parties.

They were a mixture of high-ranking contract expatriate officers, loan service officers (all British), local nationals who'd done well and a mixture of ministerial advisors and henchmen from the GCC. All of them knew the real meaning of bureaucracy and had long ago perfected the art of obstacle raising and non-decision making.

The meeting had only been going for five minutes yet already it was in uproar. Everyone was talking at once, pounding the table with their fists, gesticulating wildly with their canes, staffs, fingers, pencils and anything else that came to hand. Inevitably, they were getting nowhere. Ashman thought of Lawrence in Damascus all those years ago and shared a momentary empathy with that strangest of men in his quest to unite these diverse peoples.

'Gentlemen, gentlemen, please,' shouted the general above the din, 'We will get nowhere if we all shout and scream at each other.' This made little impression on the assembled company, so he sat back and allowed the ranting to continue until it finally exhausted itself and then petered out altogether. Patience was a virtue, he had learned long ago, and an absolute necessity for survival in these turbulent desert regions.

'Thank you. Now perhaps we can get started,' he continued in a rather superior manner. Colonel Wilmot, the general's opposite number in the Emirates and long-time acquaintance, exchanged a knowing look with him, thanking his Maker meanwhile that he was not in his shoes.

'As I was saying, His Majesty has elected to host next year's summit in the Caribbean. Although this breaks with tradition, His Majesty has suggested that this would be a refreshing change for everyone. Furthermore, I am advised by His Majesty that he has discussed the matter on a personal basis with your respective leaders and all have agreed in principle to attend. Accordingly, it is now up to us to proceed on a practical basis and ensure the smooth running of the whole affair.'

'Can you tell us something about the place His Majesty has in mind?' This came from Brigadier Mahmoud Ayyad, chief of intelligence for the Kingdom of Bahrain. He was young for such a position, in his early forties, and enjoyed good living. However, his flabby and soft appearance hid a ruthless individual who, in the name of nationalisation, had mercilessly hacked his way to the top, generally to the detriment of the state.

General Ashman rose and, at a touch of a button, revealed several maps and diagrams on a back-projected screen behind him. There was first a map of the Caribbean, with the island of Antigua circled at the top of the Leeward Islands. A map of the island itself came next, followed by detailed plans and pictures of the St Peter's Club and its environs. While these were being shown, Ashman described the set-up and ownership of the club, the political arrangements on the island and as much background information as he had been able to amass in the short time since being advised of His Majesty's pleasure.

Those from military backgrounds were now absorbing the information analytically and for the most part, keeping their own counsel. The rest of the group, meanwhile, were beginning to forget the logistical obstacles facing them and were seeing instead a paradise holiday island and a chance to enjoy themselves. There was no table thumping now but rather a buzz of excited chatter and big grins.

'And who, may I ask, general, will have the dubious honour of co-ordinating this adventure?' So far Colonel Ray Kenwright had remained silent and unflinching. He was the archetypal British officer – blue eyes, stiff upper lip, iron grey hair, humourless but coldly efficient and effective. He was personal advisor to Sultan Qaboos of Oman on all matters of security and was held in high esteem by his peers throughout the Middle East for his astuteness and balanced and unemotional judgement.

'We rather thought you might have the answer to that one, Colonel Kenwright. There happens to be a chap working in Muscat at the Al Bustan Palace Hotel who was in charge when you last hosted the GCC Summit.'

'Of course, Lawrence Beaumont, the general manager – yes he also worked in the Caribbean as I recall. My word general, you have been scanning your computer files thoroughly.' Ashman permitted himself a smile of satisfaction at this compliment. During his time in Saudi Arabia, he had amassed an awesome amount of data in his computer banks and had been given the money and manpower to make them work well for him.

'So you'd like to second Beaumont to co-ordinate the show?' continued Kenwright. 'I don't suppose that'd be too much trouble – he's a mercenary beggar but a good hotelier. More important, he's also a first class administrator and organiser and as you say, he's already got one GCC conference successfully under his belt. Yes, I think he'd do you very well.'

'Do you think you could have a word with him then?' Kenwright nodded while the general continued. 'We'll need to see him over here of course, and then make the necessary arrangements with his current bosses and the owner of the club.' The general's manner indicated that there was no question of Beaumont refusing such an assignment. In his experience, every one had his price, so one way or another, the man would be his.

'Speaking for myself, I'd like to arrange a recce of the island at the earliest opportunity, general.' Colonel Wilmot was anxious to establish an agenda. He knew just how quickly the time would fly and he did not want to waste another minute of it.

'Naturally, colonel, and I'm sure we all do. There are, however, certain niceties to be observed with the Antiguan government which are presently being sorted out. A full familiarisation trip will be arranged as soon as these discussions are concluded.'

'Yes, but when will that be? Can't we just pay off the appropriate powers that be and get on with it?'

That's rich coming from Wilmot, Kenwright thought to himself, but actually asked, 'When do we anticipate the conclusion of the discussions?'

'It should only take a couple of weeks. Sheikh Awaida's over there now sealing the arrangements.' The general paused and looked around him. 'I've no doubt you'll wish to discuss this matter with your colleagues, so I propose we reconvene here again three weeks from today. We'll have more information by then and will be able to present an agenda and timetable for the whole show. Are there any more questions?'

There were many more questions as it turned out, most of which were unanswerable at the time. General Ashman fielded them as best he could and the meeting eventually broke up. Fleets of new Mercedes drove the delegates back to their smart hotels or to the airport, all of them excited but the more experienced ones nervous and apprehensive. In their own fiefdoms security was a relatively easy matter but beyond their borders they knew just how exposed they and their charges were. It was because of this vulnerability that few of them travelled at all, being as concerned by outside threats as they were by internal opportunistic ones. Coup attempts were an ever-present possibility where the power, wealth and greed were the prime motivators in a land of spoilt tribesmen.

Ashman signalled to Kenwright as he was leaving, and the two left together for the general's home quarters.

'I'm going to need your help on this one Ray.' They toasted each other with large, stiff drinks, which like everything else in Saudi Arabia, was part and parcel of the double standard enjoyed by the well placed. 'What amazes me is how young Abdullah managed to persuade the others to agree to go to the bloody island in the first place. Your chief I can understand. He's worldly and sophisticated, but the others . . . I don't know. It beats me.'

'It probably was simply a matter of face,' answered Kenwright. 'One of them proposes something and the others follow the lead or feel weakened by non-supportiveness. You know what they're like; they hate confrontation.'

'Yes, I know.' The general paused and then changing the subject asked, 'Do you know this chap Beaumont well? A lot could hinge on him doing a good job. Obviously he won't have much to do with the security organisation but his local knowledge could be invaluable.'

'Actually, I do know him quite well. He even helps out with the odd job for us. Nothing sensitive mind you, but he's pretty switched on. In fact, I'd involve him quite a lot on the security side. The co-ordination of the event in administration terms is tightly linked to the security side anyway; to keep him out of it would merely hamper him.'

'Mmm, well we'll have to see,' said the general non-committally. 'Anyway, if you can start the ball rolling with him at your end that'd be a great help. I'd like to have had a full session with him before the next gathering of our illustrious partners, maybe even a visit to the island, and then have him give them a presentation.'

'Okay, John, no problem, leave it with me.' Kenwright looked at his watch and put his glass down. 'I think I'll be getting along now if you don't mind. I've got a Royal Flight plane on standby and I want to get cracking on this one ASAP.'

'Absolutely; please keep me informed constantly on this one, Ray. Frankly, the whole thing is scaring the shit out of me.'

'Don't worry, old boy. If it's any consolation it does me too!'

They clapped each other on the back and Kenwright departed into the night.

Muscat, Oman

THE 'MOTHERS AND LOVERS' TELEPHONE rang loudly on the desk of the general manager of the Al Bustan Palace Hotel. He had two telephones, one for general administration purposes and the other, as the name suggested, for more limited and private use. The number of this was given to only a select few and bypassed the switchboard along with its snoopers. Not that Beaumont was naïve enough to imagine the line as being fully secure. On the contrary, he acted continuously on the basis that everything he said and did would be known about by all or as many interested parties as wanted or needed to know.

This was a necessary technique for those wishing to live comfortably in Third World environments, where all too often a good expatriate could become an object for bureaucratic target practice and rapidly end up on an aeroplane home.

'Hello!' he said noncommittally into the mouthpiece.

'Lawrence, is that you? It's Ray Kenwright here.'

'Hello Ray, how are you?' Slightly disappointed that the call was not from one of the categories for which the telephone had been christened, this seemed likely to be a request for one of the security chief's 'special interview' rooms.

'Not too bad thanks. Look, don't want to talk on the blower. Can I come round and see you, say in about half an hour?'

Although most days were occupied by a pretty tight schedule, Beaumont was accustomed to the need for constant change in his diary, especially when bigwigs issued what were, effectively, royal commands.

'Not a problem, Ray, look forward to seeing you around eleven then.'

The calls from Kenwright were not unusual but it was rare for him personally to venture out and want a chat. Anyway, no point speculating, he'd know what was up soon enough.

Thirty minutes later exactly, Colonel Kenwright presented himself at the front of the hotel where Beaumont was waiting for him. They shook hands, exchanged greetings and Beaumont invited his visitor to the office.

'Tell you what, why don't we walk outside instead? Nice to be able to before the really hot weather starts, eh? Besides, I love looking around the gardens anyway.'

It was true, the hotel's gardens were magnificent, the more so because of their barren, stark and mountainous backdrop. At the base of the mountain was the hotel itself, quite breathtaking in its design and structure, surrounded by 200 acres of palm gardens, immaculate lawns, hedges of bougainvillaea and multitudes of colourful tropical flowers. These all ended abruptly at a golden beach that stretched around the hotel's own crescent bay. For those fortunate enough to bask in the luxury of this splendid place, lounge idly around its pool or dive off its shore, this was surely a sample of heaven.

Beaumont, however, was not appreciating the beauty of his surroundings. His cynicism about being constantly bugged and monitored was endorsed on such occasions, for clearly his guest's desire was not to walk in the garden so much as ensure no one overheard them.

Kenwright began his pitch: 'There's a little project coming up soon which we believe you may be able to help us with. Naturally, this is strictly confidential, but it concerns the next GCC Summit Conference.'

Being of a somewhat perverse nature and always enjoying an opportunity to score points, Beaumont replied, 'Oh yes, the one at the St Peter's Club in Antigua.'

Kenwright stopped dead. He did not often show his feelings, but this really shook him. 'How the hell did you know about that?' he asked, scowling.

'I like to keep myself up to date on things.' Beaumont replied, mysteriously, pleased with the effect he had had.

'Apparently! Well, anyway, as you can perhaps imagine, there is a high level of concern by all parties involved in this event. We're particularly worried by the administration, security and co-ordination of this next summit. It's all a bit out of our territory, you see.'

'Why should you be so concerned? Surely it's mainly the Saudi's problem.'

'That's true up to a point but the management of the event itself worries us and especially my opposite number in Saudi, General Ashman, whom you may recall. He's asked me for some help and is aware of, shall we say, your curriculum vitae.'

'I see,' replied Beaumont, ignoring the reference to a euphemistic cv. 'Well, naturally, if there's anything I can do, I'd be delighted to help. Do you want me to meet with the general or do you have something else in mind?'

'Well, actually, we do have a proposal for you. We want you to co-ordinate the whole event for us in Antigua.' Now it was Beaumont's turn to stop dead in his tracks.

Kenwright continued unabashed. 'You did such a super job running the last GCC conference here and you've worked at the St Peter's and know the people and the territory there. You see, you're uniquely qualified.'

'Yes maybe, but this sort of thing takes months of preparation and planning and that's with a hardworking, experienced labour force. The St Peter's is a wonderful holiday place but to hope to bring it up to the standard of a GCC Summit is, frankly, pushing one's luck a bit.'

'Exactly; you're the one person who knows what'll be required and so if anyone can make it work, you can.'

'Let's go down to the beach bar – I need a beer.'

When they were both seated in the shade, still only thirty degrees Celsius at this time of year and not too humid, with ice-cool glasses of draught lager in front of them, Beaumont continued.

'I presume the date will be the usual time, around Christmas.'

'Correct.'

'Then whoever is going to run it will need to get started immediately. I was over there just over a month back and there's a ton of refurbishment necessary if nothing else. Honestly, Ray, logistically it'll be a nightmare. I've done the Caribbean once already and now I'm in this fabulous palace, with, I might add, a very pressing agenda here for the coming months, I really just don't need the grief.'

'I quite understand all that but these problems are surmountable. This hotel's requirements can be delegated to your deputy or held up until your return.'

'If I return – the chance of a complete nervous breakdown is high over there, even without a GCC Summit!'

'Nonsense. Anyway, you'll have complete *carte blanche* and needless to say, money will be no object. You'll be able to get anything you want and need from labour to materials, expertise and so forth.'

'Things must have changed then, because that hasn't been the case up till now.'

'Oh, I think you'll find a lot has changed. Sheikh Awaida, whom I'm sure you know, has made an arrangement with Lester Fish so there'll be no nonsense on this one.'

'Lucky Lester and his Swiss bank account,' replied Beaumont cynically. 'Talking of Swiss bank accounts, what "arrangements" are you proposing to make this worth my while?'

'I thought you'd never ask. Let's finish off this and discuss it on the way back.'

They downed the beers and strolled slowly back through the gardens. Kenwright continued, 'The Saudis are particularly anxious for this to go well and want to ensure they get the right man for the job and that he's fully on side. Accordingly, they're offering a contract package of a hundred thousand dollars plus all expenses and a further hundred thousand bonus on the summit's successful completion. Meanwhile, as our gesture of support, you'll retain your full position, benefits and remuneration here, and if your family want to stay on, that'll be no problem – probably easier for all of you actually.'

'Well, it's certainly nice to be appreciated! My God, you weren't kidding when you said they were anxious. I imagine you've already discussed this with the ministry?'

Kenwright nodded. 'Yes, everything's fixed. All you have to do is say "yes", sign the dotted line with the general – he'll be over here tomorrow by the way – then pop over to the Caribbean and get started.'

By the time they reached the lobby, Beaumont had decided to go for it. The package was great but also the idea of getting stuck into the St Peter's Club again with full support was appealing. The big problem had always been lack of adequate funding and back-up to make the place really special. This time, though, it could be done, and if the government were on side, he could really crack a few heads and make things happen.

But he knew that he would really earn the money. There would be monumental obstacles and aggravation to overcome but balancing everything up, he reckoned this adventure might be quite fun.

'Okay,' he said to Kenwright. 'I'm in. When will you be around with the general?'

'Good show!' grinned Kenwright, showing one of his rare displays of emotions and pumping Beaumont's hand up and down. 'Jolly good show. Knew you'd go for it. We'll all feel a lot better knowing our man will be in charge. I'll get things rolling immediately. You'll obviously need to discuss this with certain people, but try to keep it on a need-to-know basis if you can.'

'Ray, I reckon half Muscat probably knows about it. Cocktail party speculation and gossip is as insatiable here as it is everywhere else in the Gulf, you know that. But, don't worry, I shall be discreet.'

'I know you will. Anyway, I must dash. I'll see you tomorrow with the general 'bout the same time. I may also have a surprise visitor with us, old friend of yours actually. I can't say more right now.'

Beaumont did not push it and saw Kenwright into his car. ''Bye Ray, see you tomorrow.'

'Goodbye Lawrence and many thanks.'

The chauffeur eased the large armoured Mercedes away from the forecourt and a rather amazed general manager returned to his office. A mass of messages and papers had accumulated during his relatively brief absence, all of which now seemed rather mundane. He chucked them all back at his reliable workhorse, Nadine, who had been his and his predecessors' secretary for years. She could handle most of it or find someone else to.

'Take care of the shop,' he said to her. 'I'm taking the rest of the day off.'

A bewildered Nadine watched him leave the office. This was really strange behaviour. 'He's either been fired or promoted,' she thought. Either way, she also knew he would tell her soon enough and so she executed his instructions with her usual ruthless efficiency and ensured that the Al Bustan Palace Hotel continued functioning in its normal and well-lubricated fashion.

At eleven o'clock precisely the following morning the big Mercedes again pulled up at the front of the hotel and Colonel Kenwright emerged with another soldierly figure, that of General Ashman. Both were dressed in civvies, however, so their rank and status could only really be deduced from the car number plates, for those in the know.

Immediately behind them, a very smart new BMW screeched to a halt and out from the driver's seat jumped a muscular, bearded and grinning Omani. He charged over to Beaumont, placed him in a bear hug and kissed him three times on the cheeks.

'Lawrence, my old friend, how are you? Long time no see.'

'Joe, it's good to see you. I didn't know you were in town. Why didn't you call?'

'Joe's full name was Yousef Chauki bin Sultan Al Khyumi, but back at school where they had first met and become friends, this had proven a bit of a mouthful, and anyway, no one had then been quite sure which bit of the name to use, including its owner. So he had been called Joe, which was much easier for all concerned.

'I only just got the summons. Come on let's go in, I can't stand this heat.'

By now all the visitors had converged, so it seemed greetings and introductions were in order.

'Er, do you know Colonel Kenwright? Morning Ray, may I introduce you to His Excellency Yousef Al Khyumi, Oman's ambassador to France.'

'Hello Lawrence, yes we do know each other. Actually he's the surprise visitor I mentioned yesterday.' Turning to the other man, Kenwright introduced the general and the four of them went inside to Beaumont's office. Kenwright, it seemed, was less concerned with security today, presumably since he felt that the main issues had been covered already. 'Either that or I'm just getting paranoid,' thought Beaumont.

They settled down over a coffee and for a few minutes exchanged appropriate and idle banter as is customary in the region. Then they got down to business. The general started the ball rolling.

'Well I must say, Mr Beaumont, we're extremely glad you've taken on this assignment. You really are quite uniquely qualified for the task and we're all enormously relieved to have you on board.'

'Thank you very much, sir.'

'You're probably wondering what his excellency is doing here,' took up Kenwright. 'Actually he's no longer Oman's ambassador to France, but takes up his duties shortly in the same role at the United Nations.'

'That's tremendous – well done Yousef, many congratulations.' Beaumont and he shook hands, with Al Khyumi appreciating the switch to his Arabic name. 'Joe' was fine between themselves but he felt uncomfortable with its use in unknown company, particularly on his home territory.

Kenwright continued. 'The Saudi Arabian ambassador to the United States will actually co-ordinate most activities related to the summit on the political and diplomatic front. However, in view of the circumstances, we felt it might be useful for you to have your own diplomatic channel, as it were. If there's any tangle or anything you need, the ambassador here will be able to help and arrange necessary assistance.'

'Well thank you very much. I am sure it won't be necessary to bother you, but it'll be good to know you're there.' Beaumont could not think off-hand what a United Nations ambassador could help with in this scenario, however friendly they might be, but kept his counsel on this.

'We also thought it might be helpful to provide you with a diplomatic status yourself.' This now came from the general. 'Makes things so much easier to get about, you know. We had a word with your ambassador here, Sir Timothy Armitage, and he's been good enough to provide you with this.' He handed Beaumont over a bright red new passport, which when opened, he noted had been issued a full seven days previously. 'They have been busy,' he thought, but again said nothing.

The general was continuing. 'Colonel Kenwright explained the package arrangements to you yesterday, which I understand met with your approval. So, if you would be kind enough to sign this contract, then we can discuss the specifics of the job in hand.' He proffered two identical sheets from a rather battered briefcase and Beaumont read them through quickly.

'There is just one point we didn't cover yesterday,' Beaumont said. 'My family will stay on here for the duration. The schooling's better and frankly I'm going to be charging around so much, they won't see much of me anyway. Can we please confirm some personal travel arrangements?'

'Oh absolutely,' replied the general, 'just put in the bills along with your other expenses. First-class travel whenever you or the family need it. Make no mistake; this is going to be a tough assignment so we want you taken care of.'

The contract seemed fine, so Beaumont signed and committed.

'Excellent, excellent,' said the general taking back one copy. 'Right, now I'll want to do your main briefing at the St Peter's itself. We'll all have a better feel for it that way and Sheikh Awaida can then endorse your position there with the staff and so forth at the same time. How soon do you think you could be over there?'

'Well, I'll need to check travel schedules, but say in about a week.'

'No need for that,' said Kenwright. 'Both Oman and Saudi Arabia are working closely on this one. There'll be a Royal Flight aircraft to take you over as soon as you can make it. You can get your friend Captain Ian Gascoigne to teach you to fly a 747 on the way over.'

''Strewth, is there anything you don't know?' asked Beaumont. This, of course, was the highest of compliments to those in intelligence circles, so with beams all over everyone's faces, dates were established and the meeting was over. The elder men declined lunch so Al Khyumi and Beaumont indulged in a magnificent meal at the Al Mahjan restaurant, washed down with copious quantities of extremely expensive claret and Cognac. It wasn't every day that one's favourite Pauillac could be justified, but this was certainly one of them.

Antigua, Leeward Islands

T HE TRIP OVER FROM OMAN was nothing if not luxurious. The Royal Flight 747 stopped in at Riyadh to pick up General Ashman and the two men, when they were not snoozing, drinking or eating mouth-watering delights prepared and served with enviable mastery and perfection, spent the time discussing the main agenda for the summit. Al Khyumi was not with them but had promised to visit as soon as he was able.

They approached the island around noontime, so Beaumont suggested a low-level pass over of the island, particularly the southern part.

'Capital idea,' said the general, and Ian Gascoigne received immediate approval from air traffic control.

They crossed the coast at Half Moon Bay, slightly to the east of the club. Antigua boasts 365 beaches but, of them all, Half Moon is surely the most idyllic, reached either by sea or a decrepit old road from the island's interior through old abandoned sugar-cane fields. They were soon over Willoughby Bay with its deep anchorages, provided you knew your way around the coral reef at its entrance. Then over a hill and there was the St Peter's Club, resting on its peninsula with its own private Mamora Bay, almost a lake so small is its mouth, and then the endless expanse of the South Atlantic. However, the glimpse of the club, its outbuildings and private villas was all too brief, even though the great plane was throttled back close to stalling speed. They then passed over Shirley Heights and saw the breathtaking views of English and Falmouth Harbours where the British had headquartered their fleets as one of the Caribbean's permanent naval stations since the early 1700s. Admiral Nelson made his base here for a number of years and much of the area is as it was then, a thoroughly well-defendable naval centre.

The terrain then became more mountainous showing off its volcanic ancestry. The lush vegetation of the tropical rain forest covering it thrust itself up to the clear sky and the passing jumbo. A succession of glorious bays, all uninhabited, fringed the forest and the coral reefs formed a colourful and foam-flecked breakwater in the deep blue of the ocean.

The sea itself was a mass of colour and activity, for everywhere there seemed to be yachts of all sizes and descriptions. They were coming from all directions, spinnakers billowing in the warm trade winds from the northeast, and were headed one and all for English Harbour, where the annual sailing week regatta would soon begin.

At Curtain Bluff, Gascoigne turned about and the great plane flew out to sea again, past the small but aptly named Green Island just offshore, making a final sweeping turn to the northwest, over Long Island and in to VC Bird International Airport.

As befitted the airplane, a full VIP welcome was at hand to greet them, with no lesser personage than the huge and imposing bulk of Lester Fish himself. He was accompanied by a posse of ministers, assorted busybodies and press and the ever-ebullient Sheikh Awaida, who was clearly enjoying himself enormously. Introductions were made all around and the party moved rapidly through an arrival area, specially reserved for such occasions, and passed outside to the club's principal transport, a large four-wheel-drive Cherokee, which was ideal for the appalling island roads. The reception committee took their leave and headed back to the capital, St John's, while the Cherokee took its valuable cargo to the St Peter's Club.

Inevitably, this had been noticed by everyone at the airport, especially the usual hive of disgruntled passengers queuing for the dubious honour of being glowered at by Antigua's more usual welcome committee, the customs officers. Among this sweaty and disgruntled throng was Bill Marshall and his current girlfriend,

Kerry, a beautiful black girl from Trinidad with designs on a permanent residence in Hereford.

'I wonder who that was?' asked Marshall. 'Must be pretty top-notch to get old Lester out.'

'Well, we'll probably see in the papers tomorrow,' replied Kerry. 'They had enough press men there to cover a royal visit.'

'Maybe they *are* royals. Did you see that crest on the jumbo they came in on? It was even emblazoned on the engines. Maybe some Arab potentate, huh?'

'Oh no,' replied Kerry positively, 'they were a couple of honkies, just like you baby.' She laughed engagingly as Marshall pulled a face, but further conversation was quelled by an aggressive bellow from a mammoth customs lady who seemed determined to crush the unfortunate chair on which she was perched.

'I said, NEXT,' she shouted, and although they'd both been through the procedure a hundred times, they approached the awesome harridan with trepidation and loathing. 'Welcome to Antigua, to you too,' thought Marshall as she glowered at him, then smashed his passport with such force he thought it must surely disintegrate.

Another lovely spell in paradise had begun.

The journey to the St Peter's Club passed without incident. For Beaumont there was a mixed feeling of excitement and anxiety. As the old Cherokee bumped and swerved its way along the island's pothole-scarred roads, the enormity of what he was embarking upon was gradually sinking in. Although quaint, picturesque and peaceful, Antigua was still firmly placed in the Third World and the idea of running a GCC Summit Conference here was becoming increasingly daunting by the minute.

The general was clearly thinking the same thoughts. He wore a perpetual frown as his military and analytical mind surveyed the environment through which they were passing. The only person who seemed remotely relaxed was Awaida who was thoroughly enjoying himself, pointing at places of interest as the small convoy passed along and generally exuding an air of relaxed bonhomie.

At Cobb's Cross, they forked off to the left and proceeded along the final few miles to the club. Soon they crested the brow of a small hill and there before them lay the gin-clear waters of Mamora Bay and, surrounding half of it, the villas, club house, rooms and restaurants of the St Peter's Club. It was a beautiful scene, encircled by small red, cactus-covered green hills, blue seas speckled with coral reefs and a kaleidoscope of flowers of all types and colours imaginable. Several boats of different sizes were moored stern-to on the club's jetty and a few larger yachts were riding gently at anchor in the bay, safely out of reach of the Atlantic rollers that constantly barraged these idyllic islands. A lovely sight to be sure and one that uplifted the spirits of the island's most recent arrivals.

As they came into the club, two security officers snapped to attention in a guardhouse which much resembled an old sugar mill. They had to stop to allow six large Texas Quarter Horses, returning from a ride with some guests, to pass and then they were pulling up at the main entrance to be greeted by Awaida's usual welcoming committee.

Warm and friendly greetings were extended to all and as registration procedures were attended to, the general was taken off to his beachfront villa in one of a fleet of electric carts. Beaumont arranged to meet him and Awaida for a drink and late lunch at the Docksider Café at two-thirty. Meanwhile, he exchanged gossip and chatter with some of his old colleagues, many of whom he had last seen a couple of months earlier. The only person who seemed distinctly unwelcoming was Wilkinson, but then that was only to be expected. The bush telegraph being what it was, everyone seemed to know that Beaumont had come back to work amongst them, and for the most part, they were looking forward to it.

Beaumont just had time for a quick shower and change before joining Awaida and the general at the Docksider. Of all the clubs, restaurants and bars, this had always been his favourite. It looked out over a jetty on the one side and a long crescent beach on the other, while between, a myriad of coloured sails on windsurfers, Lasers, Hobie Cats and Sunfish jostled for position in the bay. Built out into the water, the Docksider was relaxed and casual, friendly and cheerful and the ideal place to unwind after a long journey.

After ordering drinks and food, Awaida opened the discussion.

'I suggest this afternoon we have an orientation trip of the club and grounds. Sandra Hardy, the guest relations manager, will show you around and update you on all the club and island gossip.'

He paused to light another of his huge cigars and order a fresh round of drinks before continuing.

'In the evening, I think it would be a good idea to meet all the department heads over a drink and I can then formally outline the plan and clarify Lawrence's role.'

'Have you discussed it yet with Eric?' asked Beaumont. 'He didn't seem overjoyed to see me today, but if I'm to be free to set up and run this show, I want him to stay and be on-side. Although he's a bit dim-witted, he's good with the staff and guests and can certainly be trusted to keep the basic operation ticking over.'

'Well, yes I did mention it, but not in too much detail.' Awaida looked away to sea, and therefore, knowing the Arabic dislike for confrontation, Beaumont realised that Wilkinson probably knew very little and surely felt threatened. Here was a bridge to be built, and fast.

'What about Nigel Elliott? I'll be relying heavily on him and of course Trevor Barton.'

'Oh, they're fine,' replied Awaida, 'I've taken good care of them recently and they both seem quite excited by the whole thing.'

'What about the rest of the island, Sheikh Awaida?' This was the first time the general had said anything. 'How do they feel? I mean, from their point of view this will be a pretty major event. Will they be supportive or is there likely to be aggravation between rival clubs and hotels?'

Very astute, thought Beaumont, aware that the latter option was the likely scenario. Awaida, however, thought differently. 'Oh, it'll all be fine,' he enthused, 'and everyone will help and pitch in from all over the place.' He winked conspiratorially and leant forward. 'Besides, everything's taken care of with old Lester, so if anyone gives you a problem, we just call him up.'

The general and Beaumont were exchanging glances just as the lunch came. They talked for a while about the island and were soon joined by Sandra Hardy, ready to take them for their tour.

Sandra positively gushed with life and hardly a minute passed without her quaking with a deep throaty laugh which sent ripples spreading over her fat, large and curvaceous body.

Awaida announced that he was going to take a rest and left his two guests in the capable care of Sandra.

'Well, when you two gen'men are ready, we can get started on the grand tour.' A somewhat bemused Ashman and Beaumont followed her to an electric cart, the principal means of transport around the club, and off they went.

That evening there was an air of expectancy on the balcony of Sheikh Awaida's suite, where the department heads had been summoned. Beaumont had bumped into most of them during the afternoon except for Wilkinson, who was still noticeable by his absence.

He eventually turned up rather flustered only to be shouted at by his host and boss. 'Where the hell have you been Eric, we're all waiting for you!'

'I'm sorry Sheikh Awaida, but the car wouldn't start and then I hit a cat on the way in. It's been one of those days.'

His slightly north-country accent coupled with his lugubrious manner made these unfortunate experiences merely sound comical and everyone roared with laughter, led, as always, by their ebullient master. Beaumont, however, took Wilkinson aside, gave him a large gin and tonic and introduced him once again to the general. They chatted briefly until Awaida called for the silence they had all been waiting for and began.

'Ladies and gentlemen, I would like to introduce you to General Ashman. Lawrence Beaumont here naturally needs no introduction. As you all by now know, the St Peter's Club will this year be host to the Gulf Co-operation Council's annual summit conference, taking place in late December. This will be the first time that this summit will have been held outside of the Middle East and so I cannot overstress the importance for us and indeed the honour.'

He paused and surveyed his audience, beaming proudly and puffing his cigar the while and taking another large gulp of Cognac. Assured of everyone's rapt attention, he continued.

'The GCC consists of six member states: Saudi Arabia, Bahrain, the UAE, Oman and . . .' he paused, showing distaste, 'Kuwait and Qatar. It will be the rulers of these countries that will be coming here in just nine months time and it will be my own country, Saudi Arabia, which will be host to this great event.'

He paused again and draining his Cognac, took a replacement glass proffered by a knowing waiter.

'General Ashman represents the Saudi Arabian royal family. He is the gentleman responsible for their security and all related affairs. He has complete autonomy over all matters relating to the summit here and essentially has full control over the club from now on.'

Everyone was looking at the General almost furtively, who nodded gravely back, and muttered an inaudible 'Good evening' through clenched teeth.

'Lawrence Beaumont is here to co-ordinate the entire affair and is answerable directly to the General. Since leaving us some years ago, Lawrence has been working in the Middle East and has already organised one such summit conference in Oman. As he knows Antigua and of course the club as well, he is uniquely qualified for the job and I know he will be able to count on all of you for your fullest support. Effective immediately, therefore, Lawrence is appointed chief executive of the St Peter's Club with my total authority to act in any way he chooses, in every regard, with all personnel reporting to him. I should add that this arrangement is purely until all matters relating to the summit are over, at which time he will once again be leaving us.'

All eyes were now locked on to Beaumont's, who like the general, nodded slowly around the assembled company.

'Eric will continue his duties as general manager,' went on Awaida, 'and continue being responsible for the day-to-day operations of the club.' He paused for some more Cognac, all the formal speech making clearly not being his strong point. 'There's not much more I want to say now so perhaps General Ashman would like to say a few words.'

'Thank you, Sheikh Awaida, for the introductions and thanks to all of you for your warm welcome. I am sure that with such gracious hospitality, we need have no concern whatever for the inevitable success of the summit.' He paused, thinking that a little flattery never hurt, even if not always sincerely meant. 'I shall be coming in and out over the next few months with various people, so I'll look forward to getting to know you all. Sadly, though, this visit will be very brief but we'll have lots more to tell you about over the coming weeks. I wonder, Lawrence, can you add anything at this stage?'

'Certainly. I shan't be going back with the general so we will all get reacquainted in the next day or so and start into the detailed planning straight away. This is going to be a very tough job for all of us, make no mistake. However, it's good to be back once again and I know I can count on your support.' He paused, remembering that the best speeches were the shortest ones, so wrapped it up quickly. 'Good luck to all of us – we're going to need it!'

With that he raised his glass and everyone toasted the summit that lay ahead.

Later that evening, Beaumont bumped into an old scuba-diving friend at the bar.

'Bill! How the hell are you?'

'Lawrence my old mate, good to see you. May I introduce my friend Kerry?'

'Nice to meet you,' said Beaumont, almost overcome by the dazzle of perfect teeth and heart-stopping smile. Bill was really excelling himself this time.

'So what brings you to this neck of the woods?' enquired Marshall. 'Word in the harbour is you've come to take over again – that'll please Wilky.'

'Word travels fast, but yes, that's basically it, only it's a short-term project for Awaida, nothing permanent.'

'A GCC Summit sort of project?' asked Marshall with a grin. 'Come on, you know there are no secrets here.'

'Yeh, I guess I'd forgotten. Anyway, how are you keeping? Done any good shark riding lately?'

They exchanged news for a while after which Marshall took Kerry back to English Harbour, leaving Beaumont to catch up with other old acquaintances.

It was, however, a very pensive Marshall who walked in to the Copper & Lumber Store later that night. With Wilky in charge of the place, Operation Brown Envelope would have been relatively easy. Beaumont's presence, however, added a new dimension and even the later ministrations of Kerry could not brush away a sense of foreboding.

Porlock Weir, England

BY LATE MARCH, THE PLOTTERS of the Brown Envelope Club were well advanced with their plans and a meeting had been convened in the tiny north Devon coast village of Porlock Weir.

For Marshall, who had just flown in from the balmy Caribbean, the cold and rain-laden north wind lashing in off the Bristol Channel was a very unpleasant change. The remainder of the party, however, seemed oblivious to discomfort as they arrived one by one at the bar in the Anchor Inn.

It had been Jim Masterson's idea to come to Porlock Weir. He was very familiar with this coastline and knew that this small, old smugglers' haunt would be perfect for their requirements. It was remote and in winter seldom visited, and had the endless exposure of Exmoor's hills as its backdrop.

The landlord of the Anchor Inn was a jovial and hearty fellow with a huge pot belly and a never-ending patter of inane jokes, all of which he laughed at uproariously regardless of other peoples' appreciation of them. Charlie Bailey had been in the British army for most of his life and had spent much of that time as a loan service officer with the Trucial Scouts of Muscat and Oman, in the days when all of the Gulf states had been warring factions of marauding tribesman. He had never been high ranking but was content to have reached junior officer status and had always been in at the sharp end when there was action to be had. When he eventually retired, he held various odd civilian jobs throughout the region, the latter of which had been as the general manager of a small chain of supermarkets in Muscat. This assignment was as mystifying to him as it was to everyone else who knew him and, as he used to say, 'It's bloody ridiculous – I've shot 'em, killed 'em, buried 'em and now I'm bloody feeding 'em!'

On returning home, he had looked around and been happy enough to find the Anchor Inn where he had settled down with his wife Brigitte and daughter Jill. They had had Jill late in life and she was a much pampered nineteen-year-old whose passions in life were horses, closely followed by boys, for whom she had a voracious appetite. Although not particularly lovely, the sight of her striding out in her tight jodhpurs and provocatively clinging roll-neck, drove most of the local would-be studs into frenzies. The queue for Jill's favours was as long as the list of fights and brawls inspired by them and she loved it.

The parents seemed to notice none of this and Bailey himself was merely content to see out his days telling his endless yarns to all who would listen. Jim had heard them often, having known him for many years, and knew that although garrulous when it didn't matter, Bailey was fully trustworthy and discreet when it did.

There were two other men in the bar that gloomy morning, sitting at separate tables and keeping their own counsel. One was a big, grey-bearded and extremely capable looking man with clear blue and penetrating eyes. He was in his mid-fifties and had about him an air of restlessness as he nursed a half-pint of local scrumpy.

The other man was very much older, now in his early nineties. He was very thin and slight and had a black patch over his left eye. He limped slightly as he left his place by the log fire to freshen his glass and he winced with the pain of old wounds, never properly healed, as he moved.

'Same again, major?' asked Bailey, knowing the answer and already pouring his most regular customer's second pink gin of the day.

'If you please, Charlie – thanks.' His gnarled and arthritic hand reached stiffly up to the bar, passed over the cash, then he took a sip before returning to the fire. Although a generation apart, Major Bennett and Bailey had much in common as old campaigners. The major had started his military career in India and worked his way through two World Wars, the latter of which had cost him his eye and nearly his life to a German sniper. After leaving the army, he had used a timely inheritance to buy an old manor house on the hill above Porlock Weir and had become squire of the village. He had been a gentleman sheep farmer ever since, scratching a living from a tough land and forever wondering how the next bills would be paid.

The last of the club members involved in Operation Brown Envelope arrived, collected his drink and joined his companions, now in the small private room at the back of the bar. After exchanging greetings and pleasantries, Marshall bought the meeting to order and began providing a résumé of the plan they had conceived and updating them on his recent island recce.

'This man Beaumont,' asked Newcombe when Marshall had finished, 'is there any possibility of bringing him in? It would certainly be great to have someone on the inside.'

'There's a possibility, but I don't want to make any move there just yet. Besides, as we're buddies, I might be able to get a fair bit out of him without having to spill the beans.'

'Trouble with that is he'll be able to finger you afterwards, Bill.' Ian Scott took up the idea. 'I reckon you've either got to keep him at arm's length or bring him in completely – there's no half measures on this one.'

'Okay,' said Marshall, 'we'll leave him out for the time being and play it by ear. Now, Jim, what's happening from your side?'

'Well, gentlemen, I've made a fair bit of progress but I'm going to need some help from the navy.' There were grins of approval all round. 'As it happens, I bumped into an old chum on the Isle of Wight recently who fits the bill perfectly. He's ex-navy and actually qualifies for club membership since he's just been thrown out of Kuwait.'

'Who is he, Jim?' asked Newcombe. Everyone's basic survival instincts were against outsiders, and having dealt first with Beaumont's possible involvement, another unknown member of the team was not a particularly welcome idea.

Masterson described his proposed new recruit and his background, and, more importantly, the need to involve him. 'You see, I've got exactly the right boat in mind for the job but I'm going to need help with her. In fact, you'll get on well with him Ian, as he's been a flyer for most of his career.'

'When could we meet up with him and suss him out?' asked Marshall.

Masterson gave a rather shifty grin and said, 'Well as a matter of fact he's here now. I haven't told him anything at all except that there's a possible job for him if he turned up here for an interview. Poor chap was climbing the walls in Great Yarmouth and jumped at it.'

'Well then, you better get him in,' said Newcombe.

A moment later, Masterson returned with the big man from the bar and introduced him. 'Gentlemen, this is Commander Brian Cooper.'

Chater had been keeping fairly quiet for most of the meeting as the sharp end of the plan was being ironed out. He contributed concisely when appropriate but otherwise was keeping his own counsel. The others noted the change in him and were glad to see the emergence of the professional soldier he undoubtedly was. When he spoke now, he voiced a concern they all had. 'We seem to be fairly clear about what we're going to do in Antigua, but I really feel we haven't thought through this end of things carefully enough.' There were nods of agreement. 'Most importantly, where exactly is going to be our bolt-hole over here?'

'Well I've got an idea about that.' Jim Masterson again seemed to have the answer. 'Did you all see that old soldier in the bar, Major Bennett? He's a bit like the squire of the village round here and certainly has the largest house. There's tons of space and he could certainly do with the money. Besides, he'd probably love the whole thing.'

'You may well be right Jim,' said Marshall, 'and I think we're all beginning to realise that an operation of this size requires far more people being involved than we'd imagined. The thing is we have to be very careful with our selection of outsiders, no disrespect intended Brian, and ensure that only those who are absolutely necessary to the operation are involved.'

'Agreed,' said Newcombe flatly, 'and on the subject of which, we still haven't determined who our procurement officer will be. Personally, I don't know anyone in the club who can lay their hands on what I need.'

Cooper, who had been briefed on the plan after his introduction to the group, now spoke up for the first time. 'There was a chap we dealt with in Kuwait just after the war. He was ostensibly with Short Brothers, one of the official government arms suppliers, but he also did a lot of dealing on the side. He was an odd fellow but he really produced the goods. I could try and run him to earth if you like.'

'Good idea,' said Newcombe. 'Why don't you and Nick work on that side of things?'

They were all by now dry and hungry and so they adjourned to the bar for a late pub lunch served up by Jill. She helped out from time to time when she was not chasing foxes or men. Her gaze lingered on Chater whose huge size intrigued her and when he winked back she determined that she would definitely like to add him to her collection. The major had left by now to be replaced by a sprinkling of locals. The group of strangers attracted some curious looks but the locals soon got bored and considered more important things, like cribbage and skittles and fantasies involving Jill.

A long walk and recce was on the agenda and as they left the pub for the cold and pouring rain, they heard the laughter flowing from Bailey behind the bar accompanied by a series of groans from the locals.

Without a doubt, Porlock Weir would do the Brown Envelope Club ideally.

Farnborough/London, England

Tony CARSON LIVED AT THE END of an uninspiring row of terraced houses on the outskirts of Farnborough. When he wasn't travelling, this location suited him perfectly as he was able to keep in touch with all the news in the military. This was the heart of Britain's army and aeronautical research and development operations and Carson had often been able to familiarise himself on new technology here, especially when his employers were not in the picture.

Since his return from Abu Dhabi and Short's harsh and rapid termination of his services, Carson had been laying low and planning his future. He was well off from his private trading activities, although his house and standard of living disguised this fact admirably, so he was in no hurry to find another permanent job. In any case, it would be hard to find another respectable company who would give him one after the last debacle. He decided to make some phone calls to some of his more shady acquaintances in the morning and, meanwhile, go down to his local pub and have a few beers with some of the chaps from the airbase.

He was just leaving when the telephone rang. As was his habit, he merely lifted the receiver and waited for the caller to speak.

'Good evening . . . is this Mr Carson's residence?' asked a remotely familiar voice. 'This is Commander Brian Cooper speaking.'

'Good evening commander,' replied Carson, remembering the amiable naval officer from Kuwait. 'What can I do for you?'

'Well, I'd like to meet up with you and have a chat.'

'Where are you calling from?' asked Carson.

'I'm staying in London at the Portman Hotel with a colleague. Any chance of meeting there?'

'Sure, when would suit? I've got a pretty open programme at the moment. Could come up to town now if you like and you could buy me dinner.'

They agreed to meet at seven which just gave Carson time to chuck a few items into a large briefcase and catch the train.

They met in the pub of that most cosy and clubby of hotels and Cooper introduced Chater then ordered drinks. For a while they exchanged small talk until Carson brought them round to business.

'Well, gentlemen, you haven't asked me here just to talk about Kuwaiti cobras. Why did you call me?'

Cooper and Chater had agreed that it would be the latter who conducted most of the briefing, so Chater answered. 'We represent a small group who will be conducting a private military exercise later this year. I have a list here of our requirements and Brian here suggested you may be able to supply us.'

He handed several sheets of paper over to Carson who studied it for a while then said, 'Whew! Are you sure it's only a small group? This lot looks like you're going to war.'

'Yes, well, er, shall we say, small but warlike group,' replied Chater a little shiftily. 'Do you think you can help us?'

'Oh yes, I could help you, but whether I will or not I'm not so sure.' Cooper and Chater exchanged worried glances. It hadn't actually occurred to them what to do either in the event of Carson's inability to help or indeed his refusal. 'Before we go any further, I'm going to want far more details on the mission, especially its timing, destination for delivery and targets. Strangely enough, I do have certain values and the wrong targets could permanently damage my health. Perhaps most importantly, though, I need to know how you're going to pay for this little lot. Including the boats, the tab for this will go over the million mark and, with respect, I doubt your pensions will stretch that far!'

'Everything you say sounds fair enough but I'm afraid we'll have to seek guidance on how to proceed from our . . . er . . . colleagues,' said Cooper. 'Our main objective today was to determine your ability and willingness to procure the items in the first place.'

'Well, then I suppose your mission is almost complete.'

'Almost?' asked Cooper guardedly.

'Yes! You still have to buy me dinner and I'm famished.'

They went upstairs to the fabulous Truffles Restaurant and had an excellent meal washed down with good wine and old army and navy talk. As they were leaving Carson said, 'Why not leave that list with me? I can start sniffing around now which might save us all a bit of time later.'

'Seems fair enough,' said Chater. 'We should be in touch in a couple of days though. Can we get you at the same number?'

'Sure, but if I have to go I'll leave a message on the answerphone where you can reach me.'

After he'd gone, Cooper and Chater had a nightcap and considered how the encounter had gone.

'Seems to me he's a prime candidate for club membership himself,' said Chater, sipping a Rémy Martin. 'That incident in Abu Dhabi must have really shaken him up a bit.'

'Still, he seemed pretty confident about getting the gear,' replied Cooper. 'I suppose it was okay letting him take the list. I'm sure he can be trusted but you never know.'

Cooper thought Chater was more confident than his naval colleague, or maybe he had just had more to drink. 'No problem at all,' Chater said. 'There's no identifying marks on the paper and if anything did backfire at this stage, we can just deny having had anything to do with him. Anyway, what's done is done. I'm off to bed.'

They parted company and both retired via reception, collecting their keys as they went.

Intelligence and security services worldwide dislike and mistrust rogue agents and although not strictly one from their ranks, people such as Tony Carson were kept under close scrutiny. Following his departure from Short Brothers and his known private enterprises, more than one such service was keeping a very close eye on him indeed.

The first and most obvious was the British Internal Security Service, or MI5 as it is known. Martin Henshaw was the officer charged with amassing data on Carson, principally through a very elaborate bugging system at his house. The gadgetry at Henshaw's disposal was awesome and, although relatively fresh out of Cambridge, he had already proved himself an efficient and highly effective operator. He rarely worked in the field; however the mysterious call to Farnborough arranging a rendezvous had triggered alarm bells and so he had followed up on it personally.

Considering Carson's regular stamping grounds in the Middle East, the other organisation particularly interested in his activities was Israel's Mossad. Although elaborate bugging systems were less easy to organise and monitor on foreign soil, they were past masters at surveillance and Stuart Raber was one of their best in Britain. Born and bred a Londoner of Jewish parents in Golders Green, he had become a member of the Mossad whilst working on a kibbutz one summer holiday in his late teens and had never looked back. He loved the thrill and excitement of his job which, although seldom dangerous, provided him with a great sense of purpose and satisfaction.

As soon as Cooper and Chater had collected their keys, Raber had gone up to the concierge desk and, proffering a ten-pound note, had asked the elegant white-haired gentleman behind the desk for a photocopy of their registration cards. Bristling with rage and right-eous indignation, the concierge was on the point of calling security when Raber upped the ante and produced a fifty-pound note. The concierge visibly exhaled, looked around and advised the enquirer that one such note for each card would be acceptable. Raber's natural inclination, born of generations of bargainers, was to argue but instead he produced the extra note and within minutes was gone with the two copies.

'Now that,' mused Henshaw, who was sitting at a plush leather armchair reading a paper but just within earshot, 'was very interesting. Must find out who that chappie is also.'

A few minutes later, the night shift came on duty and to Henshaw's relief, the duty receptionist was far less principled on disclosing confidential hotel information. The photocopy machine whirred and Henshaw too departed into the night. He grinned to himself with a childish sense of triumph. It had only cost him twenty pounds.

Riyadh, Saudi Arabia

AT THE VERY END OF MARCH, Beaumont was ready to brief Ashman on his requirements to make the St Peter's Club fit for not just one, but six kings. Based on his previous GCC Summit in Oman, he knew pretty well what would be required and the list was mind-boggling. However, as he pointed out to the general, it was not an insurmountable task and much of the inventories that would be needed could all come from the Saudi Royal Palace.

The real brainwave that the hotelier presented was regarding accommodation. The general was particularly concerned over this point as security balanced with comfort was going to be a nightmare.

'Our suggestion,' said Beaumont, 'is to have all the leader's royal yachts dispatched to the island in advance and let them all stay aboard them. There are good anchorages both sides of the club here in Willoughby Bay and here,' he was pointing to a large sea chart, 'in Falmouth and English Harbours. I know at least three of the yachts can take helicopters. This way, everyone takes care of his own security to a great extent and the burden on the club living up to the required standards is reduced.'

'I think the idea is fantastic – well done. You can put it to the big shots tomorrow when we make the presentation. I'm sure they'll all be delighted.'

They talked through other issues and logistics and the general finally left Beaumont to finalise his presentation. This was going to be crucial as the need to inspire confidence in the participants' security representatives was critical. If they were not they'd make life intolerable, as Beaumont knew from experience.

The meeting the following day started early and was smaller than the initial briefing. Ashman had only invited the key personnel and told them in no uncertain terms that the political advisors and lackeys were not wanted. This made for a very much more ordered and civilised affair and they went straight down to business.

Beaumont knew most of the attendees from his previous summit in Oman, so introductions were brief and the general began by summarising the programme for the summit.

The yacht idea was well received although it was felt advisable to maintain a land option in any case. Beaumont had envisioned this and had already been in touch with the owners of the ten stunning villas on the hill overlooking the club. Although all wealthy in their own rights, the compensation promised soon persuaded even the most belligerent of them to make their homes available.

The usual plethora of journalists would be housed in the main accommodation blocks while the member nations' staff and support teams would be well catered for in the main club village. This consisted of seventy two- and three-bedroom villas with dedicated catering and entertainment facilities. The whole set-up was really ideal for everyone.

Transport was a concern but fleets of Mercedes and golf carts would be shipped over for the event, so that was another problem out of the way.

The order and contents of the meetings were then aired at some length. This was always difficult, for in reality very little was actually ever discussed, let alone achieved. Rather, any positive steps would be taken by the respective foreign ministers in advance and the resultant statements of intent would then be ratified by their leaders. However, there had to be a respectable amount of time in conference, if only for all concerned to feel a sense of accomplishment.

After a short break for a late and light lunch, there followed detailed discussion regarding dining arrangements and finally, yet for Beaumont the most complex, the plans for recreation and entertainment were presented. These, however, were to be an inspiration and a definite departure from the usual massed military parades and camel-mounted bagpipe troops, so incongruous to Western eyes.

The group eventually broke up in the late evening. Without exception, they were now feeling more positive about the whole summit and their combined sense of dread was rapidly receding. They still all had significant security reservations, which were only to be expected, but in essence it was a part of their jobs to worry over this, regardless of the circumstances.

The general's and Beaumont's proposals were fully endorsed and the latter briefed to proceed with the plans put forward. Although there would be several liaison and updating meetings over the coming months, Beaumont proposed they all come over to the island at the end of August. This would give him time to consolidate the plans, provide the group with a chance for a detailed recce and at the same time enjoy Antigua's annual Carnival.

This too was agreed and the party broke up.

'Well,' said the general, gathering his papers together after everyone had left, 'that couldn't have gone better if we'd paid them to agree. Well done Lawrence, that was bloody good. Keep this up and the whole thing will be a doddle.'

'That's as maybe, general, but remember this is the Caribbean we're talking about and converting plans into action is usually harder than you think.'

'Nonsense, dear boy, I know you'll manage it just fine. Now, we'd better get a shift on if we're to meet up with that lot again in time for dinner.'

They left the conference room with Beaumont feeling a distinct sense of unease. Nothing could go this smoothly for long, particularly bearing in mind who he was dealing with. He was definitely going to need more help, particularly on the recreation side – someone who knew the island well and had good communications and clout. Maybe someone like Bill Marshall? Yes, he'd be just the man, thought Beaumont. I'll give him and call and see if he's interested.

And with that idea easing his peace of mind, he followed General Ashman out to the waiting car. Maybe the whole thing could work well after all.

Spring 1995
Amman, Jordan

JUST AS IRAQ WAS RIDDLED WITH SPIES and informers for the Alliance countries before, during and after the Gulf War, so too Iraq had an extensive network of spies throughout the Middle East.

As Jordan was the only country through which Iraqis could freely travel, she thus became the principal conduit nation for information, both incoming and outgoing. The number of networks and clandestine activities taking place in Amman would have put the old Cold War protagonists to shame and, although a poor country, many people were making great profit from the sanctions still imposed by a recalcitrant and obstinate United Nations.

The Saudi Arabian occupying the Royal Suite of the Marriott Hotel in Shmeisani, the more well-to-do part of Amman, was thoroughly enjoying himself. Like many of his compatriots when released from the oppressive shackles of their homeland, he indulged himself lavishly in women and Black Label, both of which he consumed with a seemingly unquenchable appetite. Even the senior Palestinian receptionist, who supplied Mr Mustafa Ali Said with his requirements, was finding himself quite hard pressed to keep up with his benefactor's needs, which were constant throughout the day as well as night. This never ceased to amaze him for Mr Ali Said must have weighed at least 140 kilograms and puffed and sweated profusely at the slightest exertion. He was bald, with a shiny round face and podgy, fat fingers which would occasionally come together for a 'wet fish' handshake. He was not a nice creature.

Mr Ali Said also entertained other guests and business associates, who were similarly treated to the exotic delights of their host. He was generously extravagant to those he favoured.

It was almost midday and the receptionist at the front desk was daydreaming when an immaculately dressed man came up and asked for Mr Ali Said's room. 'He's expecting me,' said the stranger in perfect English, although his features were dark and suggested a southern Mediterranean or Middle Eastern heritage.

'What name shall I give, sir?' the receptionist asked, also in English, raising the telephone and dialling the suite.

'Tell him . . . "Mohammed". He'll know me,' replied the stranger.

'That doesn't help much,' thought the receptionist but after a brief word on the telephone said, 'Mr Ali Said has asked me to escort you up, sir.'

Taking the lift to the twelfth floor, they ascended in silence and the knock on the door was immediately answered by a young woman, perhaps in her early twenties. She was plump, dishevelled and completely naked, aside from her smudged thick make up. She held a drink in one hand and crooking her free index finger, silently invited Mohammed in. As she closed the door, she winked and mouthed a kiss at the receptionist who blushed and fled.

The whore put an arm around Mohammed's neck, pushed her body against him and tried to kiss him. Mohammed pushed her back with a force that sent her sprawling on to a sofa, spilling her drink onto her flabby body. He heard the beginning of a curse as he walked out of the room in search of the bedroom where he knew he would find Ali Said.

He opened the door to find his would-be host flat on his back, naked on the king-size bed, purple in the face, wheezing and groaning and generally giving all the indications of a major heart attack. The cause, however, was not the state of his heart but another creature, similar to the first, straddled over his loins facing him and moving up and down in mock ecstasy, moaning and sighing dramatically as she rocked on his extended member. Her huge, pendulous breasts swung tantalisingly in front of her customer's stubby outstretched fingers, which she brushed occasionally with her large and erect nipples.

Switching to Arabic the visitor said disgustedly, 'For the love of Allah, get that slut off you and let's talk – I don't have long.' He retreated back into the lounge only to be met by the first girl again. She dropped to her knees in front of him and reached for his zip, her mouth open and her tongue wetting her lips.

He hit her then, hard across the side of her head and she fell sideways, upturning a small glass coffee table which broke under the force. Blood came from her mouth as she looked up to see the violent stranger approach her with a long, thin stiletto. She was about to scream and he hit her again, back-handed, stifling the cry that was to have come. He held the knife at her nose and she was so terrified she could hardly hear his snake-like hiss.

'When I need filth like you I'll call you. Until then you get out of here fast and never tell anyone what you have seen. If you do, I will know, and next time I will not be so gentle.' He moved the knife threateningly down between her legs and the fear made her almost choke.

At that moment, Ali Said came in, wrapped in a towelling robe and surveyed the scene before him. 'What ever is going on here?' he asked, somewhat nervously. 'I only asked her to look after you.'

'Get these filth out of here, NOW – then get dressed and we'll talk, you oversized son of a goatherd.'

The girls needed no persuasion and within minutes had left. Their fat client soon re-emerged and sat down opposite his guest. He was shaken by the violence and anger in the man and more than a little frightened. 'Well Colonel Rousan, how can I be of service to you this time?'

Colonel Rousan, alias 'Mohammed', was one of Iraq's most senior officers in that country's feared intelligence service. His loyalty to

Saddam Hussein was absolute and his cruelty and total disregard for human life was as legendary as was that of his master. He travelled extensively under many guises and ran networks of agents, both voluntary and coerced, throughout the world.

Ali Said had been co-opted when copies of some very compromising film of him indulging in his more extreme sexual preferences had been sent to him. He was close to many senior and influential people in the kingdom of Saudi Arabia and so could be a highly useful source of information. The springing of the honey trap two years previously had ensured his service to Iraq and he was now completely and hopelessly ensnared by Rousan.

'We understand that the GCC Summit Conference this year, which your country will be hosting, will be taking on a different format than usual. We want the exact details of the plan.'

Ali Said had heard talk of some Caribbean island playing host but he knew little and, so far, had cared even less. But now, the nature of the colonel's question filled him with a deep sense of dread. He got up and reached for a half empty bottle of Black Label at the bar. He poured a large shot into a glass and drank it down neat, then refilled it.

'May I ask the purpose of your enquiry?' He knew the answer before he had completed the question.

'Don't be ridiculous,' snapped the colonel. 'We just need to know what's going on and you're going to help us. I need hardly remind you of the consequences if you fail me and I don't imagine your own people would be very lenient if you confessed all and told them of our, shall we say, arrangement. Knowing their delight in chopping things off, in your case they'll probably start with your prick and work up.' He gave a slight laugh then continued on his tormented victim. 'I shall expect a preliminary report two weeks from today and full details by the end of the month. We'll meet again in Amman but different hotels next time. First the Regency, then the Philadelphia. They have a lower profile and the receptionists are less ingratiating and . . . er . . . more trustworthy.'

'Very well,' sighed Ali Said, 'I'll do my best, but I can't promise anything. These things are very closely guarded you know.'

Colonel Rousan smiled dangerously, produced his stiletto and held it hard against the obese man's stomach, so that the skin was just pierced through his shirt and blood spread brightly over the white silk.

'I said, we want everything, my friend,' he replied softly. 'I'm sure it's not necessary for me to point out the consequence of failure for you, but there are those in my country with a less pleasant and forgiving nature than I. Frankly, you cannot imagine the suffering that would be inflicted on you, and your family, should you let us down, so I suggest you help. Anyway, it's just a little bit of information we're after, so there's no need for us to fall out – is there?' He slowly wiped the knife clean on Ali Said's shirt and, still smiling, made for the door. 'See you in a fortnight,' he said, and was gone.

Ali Said went to the bathroom and threw up. Tears of frustration and fear coursed down his cheeks. The Iraqi desire for vengeance was so obvious; he could not believe the summit would go ahead. But what could he do? So he had another drink and pondered the afternoon's carnal schedule.

Oswald Prendergast was the personification of a classic British public-schoolboy twit. He worked in the Commercial Department of the British embassy in Jordan as a cultural liaison officer, whatever that was. He was rather vague and whimsical and treated almost with disdain by most of those with whom he came into contact. He was, however, well acquainted with the Middle East, fluent in Arabic and gave excellent parties. As such, he was good humouredly tolerated and was on most senior community member's invitation lists, both local and expatriate.

The apparent urbanity, however, disguised his real role in life. He was actually an officer in the British Secret Intelligence Service and in fact the most senior in the region, a fact known only to a very few.

In this role, he had established an extensive intelligence-gathering network throughout Jordan and its neighbours and fed to the mandarins of Whitehall constant and valuable information. His network also included a complex and highly sophisticated bugging operation, which included the major suites and many rooms of Amman's top hotels.

The operations meeting on the morning following Colonel Rousan's visit to the Marriott was electric with anxiety. A few telephone calls established that both Rousan and Ali Said had left the country so they now had two weeks to mount an intensive surveillance exercise for their return visits.

The excitement in Prendergast's office was mirrored in a small and rather dingy office in Cambridge Circus in London, where his boss ran the Middle East Desk in the Secret Intelligence Service headquarters, or MI6 as it is more commonly known. After reading the decoded dispatch he pulled on his jacket and headed straight for the deputy director's office, muttering to himself as he went.

'Bloody hell, this is all we need. Killing off that lot will make Desert Storm look like a sodding Sunday school picnic.'

Antigua, Leeward Islands

IT WAS SAILING WEEK IN ENGLISH HARBOUR, an annual event in early April that brought together thousands of people from all over the Caribbean for racing, raucous revelry and Red Stripe.

Some of the finest yachts in the world came to compete in this boating extravaganza. It was not just the magnificent setting that lured the sailors; nor was it the outstanding sailing conditions – a constant, warm trade wind blowing at a steady ten knots from the northeast over huge dark-blue Atlantic rollers; it certainly wasn't the prize money, probably the least to be had in the entire global yachting calendar; but it was the sheer fun of the place, the backdrop of Nelson's Dockyard, the parties at the Copper & Lumber Store and Mrs Phillips's conch chowders at the Admiral's Inn. It was magical and an unforgettable experience for anyone who was there.

There were many other events also taking place. Visitors could watch the races from Shirley Heights or 'The Lookout', as Nelson had called it, high above the harbour entrance, with sizzling barbecues competing with steel bands for supremacy of attention. Here was to be found a truly eclectic gathering of people. There were strolling minstrels, conjurors, drug pushers, painters, conch-shell sellers and palm-leaf model makers. There were tourists and locals, yacht charterers and orgy organisers, all multi-coloured like the coral reef fishes, mixing and frolicking in the sun with garlands of hibiscus, yellow bells and bougainvillea around their heads and necks.

The local yacht club had long since given up trying to organise serious events, leaving that to a separate Race Week Committee, and concentrated on less-solemn pursuits such as wet T-shirt and greasy pole contests, make-it-yourself boat races and parties galore.

With so many strangers in the area, therefore, the small party of men who checked into the St Peter's Club on one of their scuba-diving packages aroused no curiosity whatever. Marshall had booked them into two three-bedroom villas side by side on the beach and had taken some friendly ribbing from Johnny Harris at reception when they had arrived.

'Wha's the matter Misser Bill, your hotel no' good 'nuf fo' your frens?'

Marshall smiled back. 'That's right Johnny, they insisted on a classy joint and since they didn't want to share their room with a couple of dozen yachties each, I figured you might do the honours! Besides, they've promised to stay at my pad next time, which is why I'm looking after them.'

'Sure thing, Misser Bill, anything you say. Evelyn, will you take these gen'men down to their villas. Have a good time now.'

The group consisted of the complete Brown Envelope operations team, the first time in fact that they had all assembled together. There was Bill Marshall of course, who was staying in his own place at the Copper & Lumber Store in English Harbour, just a short drive away. Then there was Ernst Gunter, who'd checked into the club some days earlier with a stunning blond Scandinavian girl. Sharing the two villas were Mike Newcombe, Nick Chater and Ian Scott in one and Jim Masterson and Brian Cooper in the other. There was also the most recently co-opted member of the team, Tony Carson.

They had discussed his inclusion at some length but felt in the end that he basically qualified for club membership and could prove more useful being fully involved than kept on the periphery. Since they had no experience in dealing with illicit arms procurement, it seemed likely that their venture could be doomed from the start if Carson was not completely included.

Newcombe, however, was uneasy about it. He knew, more than any of them, the need for secrecy above all else, an instinct bred into him on many a clandestine operation. He had ultimately bowed to group pressure but determined to keep an extra close eye on Tony Carson.

The British Airways flight had arrived very late so they had a couple of drinks and a meal together in the club's village restaurant and went their various ways, arranging to meet back there for breakfast at eight o'clock the next morning.

Marshall had arranged a detailed familiarisation of the island which included aerial, land and sea reconnaissance, both above and below water. Over the following week, they blended with the crowds and came to know the island well.

Scott chartered a small, single-engine Warrior aircraft from the airport and, using Carson for reconnaissance, spent much of his time learning the relief of the island and its neighbours. He became familiar with the quality and standards of the various airfields on the islands in general and was soon fully acquainted with the region.

Newcombe and Chater partnered up to study the island's geography, particularly in the southern part, and intimately in the club's environs. They also studied the coastline and assessed the efficiency of the island's police service and coastguard. And they checked up on Antigua's principal communications arrangements, which actually amounted to a simple and lightly guarded installation on the island's highest point, Boggy Peak. Scott, too, had surveyed this area and been happy with his findings. Telephones around the island were next to useless and everyone seemed to possess radios and handheld mobile sets. This too suited the group admirably.

Masterson and Cooper spent most of their time at sea. They chartered one of Hans Schwartz's boats and one of his boatmen for top cover and local knowledge, and they soon knew well the reefs and shoals, deep-water channels and hazards surrounding the club.

Finally, Gunter idled his days away around his favourite haunts, thoroughly enjoying himself and his beautiful companion. She really was rather special, he thought, and had a keen brain as well as her other more obvious attributes. He'd have to be careful with this one or he'd end up marrying her and that would never do!

Meanwhile, Marshall too was busy intelligence gathering and networking with his friends. All the local gossip centred on the big event up at St Peter's that coming winter. As agreed, though, no direct approaches were being made to the club itself for information at this stage. So it was a stroke of luck when he received a call from Beaumont suggesting they go for a dive. 'I need to get out of the place for a while, Bill, and besides, I've got a proposition for you.'

They agreed to meet Hans at his mooring at the Copper & Lumber Store at nine the next day and greetings exchanged, they set off for the Cathedral, a spire of rock which guarded the entrance to Indian Creek just near the St Peter's. It was only just submerged at the top and the single and mysterious pinnacle went down eighty fathoms. The three of them had dived on the site many times, for there was an abundance of fish there and the rock formation itself and its inhabitants were endlessly fascinating.

As neither had dived for a while, Hans kept it short and relatively shallow. Thirty minutes later they surfaced, dismantled their gear and had a coffee, basking in the sun and watching the day's first sailing race beat past.

'So what's this proposition you've got for me?' asked Marshall, unable to contain his curiosity any longer.

'I'm sure you know what's going on here in December, Bill – most of the island does. But the specific details and schedules we're keeping close to our chest, so I'd appreciate your discretion on what I'm about to say.'

'Absolutely, mate, fire away.' Beaumont proceeded to sketch in the idea of the summit conferences, their purpose and then, in detail, the recreational needs to make the event truly memorable.

'Sounds like one sod of a tough assignment you've got yourself there mate. How can I help though?'

'Well, I wondered if you'd like to be in charge of recreation and entertainment. You've got excellent contacts with the government and basically I need someone I can trust to get on with that side of things, while I set the rest of the show in order. Hans here is going to have his hands full co-ordinating with all the ships and their tenders and comings and goings, so I really need a free agent like you.'

Marshall could hardly believe his ears. 'Tell you what Hans, this coffee's boring. How about some Red Stripe?' They each opened a bottle and he continued. 'Let's go through this again. You're proposing an island tour for them all on the morning of the second day, probably by helicopter, and the main event on the third day being serious sailing and powerboat races watched from a grand stand at Shirley Heights.'

'Right,' said Beaumont, picking up the thread. 'We'll lay on a magnificent lunch up there too. Then in the evening, after the final ceremonial dinner, a huge firework display in the bay. I figure we could fix up a stand and refreshments for locals on the other side so they can feel involved. Afterwards, they all go back to their yachts and that'll be that.'

'It's quite a plan but I would think it's relatively straightforward. Particularly as you say you've got Lester Fish's co-operation. Maybe if we went to see him together, we could get the ball rolling pretty fast.'

He paused and considered a moment. 'I'd also involve the Nicholsons at the Dockyard. They'd have all the right contacts for organising the racing, like they do for Sailing Week now. I would think you'd also need pretty good prize money and trophies to lure them all over, especially the powerboats. Any chance of old Awaida producing the goods on that one?'

'Tell you the truth, I hadn't thought of it but it's a good idea and I'm sure he'll go for it. Anyway, do I take it you're interested in joining up? It'll be a lot of work Bill, but I'll see you get well looked after for it.'

'You can count me in for sure mate,' replied Marshall popping another Red Stripe. 'I wouldn't miss this little junket for the world.'

Each evening, the whole group met up in Newcombe's villa and pooled the data they had gathered that day. By the end of the week they had a very thorough composite picture of the St Peter's Club and the island in general. Their thirst for adventure and action was now truly wetted and their excitement was mounting rapidly.

When Marshall finally contributed his bombshell about Beaumont's invitation to join up with the organisation, they could hardly believe their luck, and so it was then that detailed planning for Operation Brown Envelope began in earnest.

London, England

THERE ARE FOUR PRINCIPAL COMMITTEES for handling the analysis and review of intelligence data, and the subsequent policy making and implementation. Three of these are made up of key cabinet ministers, two including the prime minister as chairman, and the fourth is the Joint Intelligence Committee consisting of senior representatives of MI5, MI6, Defence Intelligence Staff and Government Communications Headquarters. The reporting lines from one committee to another are tortuous in the extreme, particularly as each service chief is first obliged to go through his respective cabinet minister.

Sir William Hood was head of MI6, a job he had held for many years and through two prime ministers and their respective transient cabinet ministers. He was highly respected, both in the intelligence community and in Whitehall, for his balanced and reasonable judgements and his quiet and understated forcefulness.

Reporting directly to the prime minister was the cabinet secretary, Sir James Parsons, the most senior Whitehall mandarin. Among his many duties was oversight of the intelligence community. He too was a veteran in his field and it was directly to him, as was often the case, that Sir William brought the information from Amman.

'This is very worrying,' observed Sir James. 'What do you make of it, William?'

'Frankly, we've been expecting Saddam to do something for ages. He's been keeping a lower than usual profile recently and with him that's always a concern. I must say, though, that an interest in all the GCC leaders seems rather ominous. Kuwait certainly and maybe Saudi, but the whole lot of them would appear ambitious to say the least.'

'How do you think we should play it?'

'Well for a start, I'd like the prime minister briefed and the subject discussed at an OPD meeting as soon as possible.' Sir William was referring to the Cabinet Office Committee for Overseas Policy and Defence. This group was responsible for all intelligence, security, defence and counter-terrorism policy. Chaired by the prime minister, its permanent membership consisted of the foreign and defence secretaries, the chancellor of the exchequer, the attorney general and the president of the Board of Trade. 'I think it would also be useful for me to be there along with Renard.' Sarah Renard was the rather controversial director general of MI5, Sir William Hood's opposite number, whose service was responsible for the gathering, analysing and co-ordination of intelligence on mainland Britain and Northern Ireland. 'If there is something brewing,' continued the director general of MI6, 'we all need to be involved at an early stage.'

'Okay, I agree and I'll get it set up. What else?'

'I'm going to increase our assets in the whole region. If Iraq's really planning another nonsense, we need to nip it in the bud, and fast, particularly now that the US is completely adrift on foreign policy. In fact, that's probably what Saddam's banking on.'

'Yes, but be careful there,' continued the cabinet secretary. 'We've nearly come to grief with our American cousins over the Balkans and we don't need another rift opening up on this one.'

'Fair enough; anyway, the other thing to do is get full details of the GCC leader's schedules for the next few months, and particularly what the Saudis have got in mind for their next summit in December.'

'What about the Israelis? Should we talk to them yet – pool resources and all that? Could be helpful.'

'I don't think so for the moment. Knowing them, they probably know all about it anyway! Let's dig around a bit first and get our facts together before we involve anyone else.'

'Right you are – I'll fix up the meetings and keep you posted. By the way,' continued Sir James less formally, 'it really is time we had a spot of lunch together. It's been simply ages.'

'Capital idea,' replied Sir William beaming, 'especially as I recall it's your turn to buy! Shall we say the Causerie at Claridge's, Wednesday, one o'clock? Haven't been there for a while.'

'Certainly, and by then we should have some facts to exchange.' Sir James became serious again as he rose from his chair to see his guest out. 'Well done William; I need hardly tell you, of all people, that this is critically important, but give it everything you've got. We've got to nail that bastard once and for all.'

With that economic statement of foreign policy, they parted.

Hereford, England

Following the successful antiguan trip, Newcombe insisted they all convene immediately at home base to determine exactly how they were each to proceed over the coming weeks.

Now that they were all focused on the objective, they had do the ground work with care and precision. One slip-up at this stage and the whole exercise would be jeopardised.

Since a major element of the operation was going to involve the sea, Masterson and Cooper were given the task of acquiring the boats needed and all related logistics. This was also going to involve Scott.

Chater was briefed to establish the set-up at Porlock and liaise as needed with Carson. They had all agreed that they should establish the base and convene there as soon as possible, so this now became a priority. Newcombe would be principal co-ordinator of their various activities.

Marshall, meanwhile, was going to develop the operation from the Antiguan end. Now that he had the brief from Beaumont, he had a bona fide excuse for being fully involved.

The last member of the group, Gunter, had the task of arranging lines of credit for everyone. It was necessary to do this in such a manner as to be untraceable back to him. Being an astute business-man, he also needed to keep a controlling hand on the disposal of these funds, so the task was not as simple as it seemed.

After the meeting, Newcombe decided to go through the plan again and refine some modifications they had agreed to. However, when the others had all gone, there was a knock on the door and Little George appeared.

Newcombe invited him to sit down and said, 'Thanks for coming George. Want a drink? This'll take a while.'

'No probs, major, what can I do for you?' said George, helping himself to a beer and sitting.

'You remember a couple of months ago we talked about an operation to bash the Arabs?'

'Yeh, sure – but I thought that was just booze talkin'. You got a plan then, major?'

'Yes we have, George, and I'd like you to be part of it. But I have to know before the briefing if you want in or not. It's certainly going to be dangerous but you could make a fair bit of dough and, probably for you more important, have a hell of a lot of fun.'

'With respect, just you bloody try keepin' me out … sir!' Little George was a fireball for sure, thought Newcombe, and was glad the little cockney was on side.

'Okay, here's what we're going to do;' and Newcombe proceeded to brief another recruit on Operation Brown Envelope.

When he finished, George was ecstatic. 'That's bloody marvellous. Gawd, we'll be like somefink out of a bloody book. I love it, major. What can I be doin'?'

'Well, as a matter of fact George, there is something I want you to do. I need you to keep an eye on someone for me and keep me posted.' He then briefed George on his assignment and when all was done, they parted company.

Tamariu, Spain

T HE EXQUISITE VILLA WAS SET HIGH UP on the hill overlooking the bay and small fishing village below. It was surrounded by a lush garden, pools of fish and lilies and, at its centre, a series of three irregularly shaped swimming pools were interconnected with small water channels and cascades.

For anyone who strayed into this little village on the Costa Brava, it was a miracle that it was not highly developed, with an abundance of hotels, squalid fish-and-chip restaurants, noisy speedboats and skiers and the ubiquitous stench of oil, whether it be from cooking, sunning bodies or engines.

Most such places on the Spanish coast had long since been gobbled up by the developers, but not Tamariu. For those in the know, this was not so much a miracle as the result of the concerted financial manoeuvrings of the village's protector and benefactor, the owner of the big villa on the hill, whose privacy was guarded as jealously as was her personal patronage sought.

Tony Carson sat by the largest of the pools at the villa and sipped appreciatively at a large Pimm's. He was admiring his surroundings and even considering that it was perhaps time he himself settled down to such luxury. After all, he could probably afford it by now, he told himself, certainly after this current caper.

His thoughts were interrupted by the appearance from the villa of a particularly striking blonde. He had long ago given up trying to assess her age but knew that she must be at least in her late forties, and if one judged her by her business acumen, at least another ten years on top of that.

'Tony, how lovely to see you again.' Her English was accentless and she gave Carson a light kiss on each cheek and they sat down, a servant bringing her a Perrier and Carson a fresh Pimm's.

'Kate, you look more stunning than ever,' replied Carson, 'how are you keeping?'

'A lot better than you, from what I gather. Honestly, Tony, surely you must have known that old crook Zhuror was up to no good.'

Carson was as always mystified by his hostess's intelligence data, but realised for the hundredth time that she was not top of her profession for nothing. For Kate Lladro, widow and international business woman, was one of the world's leading private arms suppliers and a principal source for many of Carson's 'private' enterprises.

They exchanged trade gossip for a while then over lunch got down to business. Carson produced the list of his requirements and then explained the operation. Lladro, he knew, would not even supply a peashooter unless she was fully acquainted with the objective, and unless she approved, would then not do business. He felt this was probably a borderline case and had considered a couple of other less reputable and inquisitive suppliers. However, Lladro when committed, was the most reliable he had ever worked with and, besides, he told himself, he liked her and wanted to see her again.

Lladro was somewhat sceptical. 'This seems a very wild adventure you're involved in Tony. I'm not sure I wholly approve of small private armies out for revenge. I mean, what will they do next, that is if any of them survive? Start killing off government officials in Europe because they don't agree with the latest traffic legislation?'

'No way, this is definitely a one off,' replied Carson. 'Anyway, they'll all be too busy keeping a low profile and spending the loot, if the plan works out, to consider other projects.'

'What will they do with the weapons afterwards?'

'I haven't a clue,' said Carson, never having considered what any of his clients did with their supplies. If he had started being concerned about that, he thought, he could never have stayed in the business.

'I'll tell you what,' said Lladro, arriving speedily at a decision. 'I will supply you completely – I've no love whatever for your, er, targets. But there's a condition. I want the full names of everyone involved in the Operation. It will not do me any good if it becomes known that I have been the principal arms supplier for a new terrorist organisation. So, if they get out of control in the future, I'll shop them.'

"Strewth!'

'I'll also want full prepayment – well, you know the usual terms. Deal?'

'That's a bit of a tall order. I'll have to check with my,' he paused, 'er . . . my principals.'

'Nonsense,' said Lladro, 'if they've got the funds for the project in the first place, this isn't going to worry them and there's no need for them to know of the other condition, is there? It's not a particularly big order, anyway. And presumably, as you're the expert, they trust you to do the right thing . . . don't they Tony?'

'Well, yes, I suppose so,' Carson wished he felt surer. 'I just didn't expect an answer so quickly. Can you give me a couple of days?'

'No,' said Lladro with finality. 'With your schedule, you frankly have no time whatever to lose. Not all of this shopping list comes off the shelf, you know. Decide now or no deal. You know you can trust me and I'll deliver. Can you say the same about your other contacts, like that slimy little South American you seem to be so fond of, Salinas?'

'Is there anything you don't know?' asked Carson incredulously. He couldn't believe anyone knew about that particular contact, he'd been so careful.

'I hope not.' She smiled and got up. 'Now, I have a busy schedule this afternoon Tony, so you'll have to excuse me. Do we shake on it?'

'Yes, sure,' said Carson resignedly and smiling, offered his hand. They shook, and as she retreated back into the coolness of the villa, said, 'I'll contact you in the usual way and we'll set up the payment and delivery arrangements. Take care, Tony.' She waved over her shoulder and was gone.

The squat little man in the beach café below finished his San Miguel, put away his camera and binoculars, and climbed uncomfortably into his boiling-hot hire car. Although still early in the season, the temperature was higher than he liked it and he cursed all places hot.

He drove off up the hill and pulled into the side of the road where a glorious panorama provided him with an excuse to stop and wait. It was not long, however, before the man he was watching came out of the wrought-iron gates of the villa he had just passed and drove away in the direction of Barcelona and, hopefully, the airport. He waited a moment, and then followed at a discreet distance.

Back in the café, strangers were always noticed and tough stocky men with cameras and binoculars particularly so. As was the custom, the proprietor placed a call to the Señora's residence and passed on his information to her house manager and general assistant, the ever-capable Lauro.

Amman, Jordan

Mr Mustafa Ali Said had spent over three weeks at the Regency Hotel waiting for the accursed Colonel Rousan to appear. He had not exactly been idle and had been further researching the plentiful supply of what he considered to be Jordan's prime natural resource. However, he did not at all like the Regency, which he found lacked the style and quality of the international chain hotels. The service was hopeless, the food, at best, unimaginative and the suite itself hideous. He was sorely tempted to check out and let that bastard

Rousan find him. The Marriott or InterContinental were certainly closer to his needs and infinitely more pleasant. But the thought of that repulsive stiletto and the hand that held it deterred any such rebellion, so he suffered silently and, when really frustrated, took his feelings out upon the hapless slut with whom he happened to be at the time.

However, although not a brave man, he was feeling very pleased with himself and almost looking forward to his next encounter with the principal of Iraq's intelligence apparatus. For he had managed, frankly to his amazement, to find out the entire details of the next GCC Summit Conference plan without any difficulty whatever. He had met the plan's garrulous instigator at a reception and Sheikh Awaida, who was busy proving how clever he was, had made it easy for him to glean the entire programme. With any luck, Rousan would leave him alone after this, or at least start paying him for his information. Yes, he'd see what he could get out of him.

When Rousan finally did make contact, Ali Said made sure he was fully dressed and alone.

'Sorry to have kept you waiting so long, my dear Mustafa,' Rousan began with elaborate false courtesy. 'I've been simply too tied up back home.'

Ali Said similarly greeted Rousan with protestations of affection, thinking the while that it was more likely someone else who was tied up, probably by the wrists and hanging from his pain-racked shoulders.

'So, my friend, what news do you have for me?'

'I think I have all the information you require,' said Ali Said more confidently than he actually felt.

'Excellent! Excellent! Tell me about it,' coached Rousan.

'Well, first, I'd like to make a proposal – well, er, trade, if you like.' Ali Said was sweating heavily now and felt most uneasy. The colonel stared back impassively at the trembling bulk in front of him and said nothing. This merely heightened Ali Said's anxiety, so after a moment he carried on.

'I thought, maybe, you could see your way to either letting me off the hook after this, or, er, perhaps – well, paying me something. I mean, whatever you've got in mind must be pretty big and my information is, well, shall we say most valuable. . . .'

He petered out and glanced at the colonel, who hadn't moved. However, the colonel had been thinking the same as many who had run informers before him: the most unreliable were those recruited through blackmail. Eventually, they always became a liability and it seemed Ali Said was rapidly approaching the end of his usefulness. Anyway, let's assess his information and play it by ear, he thought.

'Mustafa, my friend, relax. Of course we can come to an accommodation. Tell me what you know and I'll see what we can arrange.' He smiled encouragingly at Ali Said, who was now feeling a measure of relief. So he told the colonel everything he had learnt from Awaida and watched hopefully as the smile spread slowly across his face.

'Mustafa, you have done well. This is first-class information and as a gesture of good will, I shall send a messenger around later today with a token of our appreciation. He'll be a young man, Mustafa, so please don't have any distractions around, if you know what I mean. I'll contact you in the next day or so, and we'll discuss how best to proceed from there. Okay?'

Ali Said could hardly believe his ears. He so wanted to be out of the grasp of this monster but had never expected this reversal. As he saw Colonel Rousan out, and downed a large Black Label, he felt for the first time a ray of hope.

The afternoon traffic in Amman is loud and boisterous and aggressive. Nobody looks left or right as they drive and certainly never above. So no one saw or heard the grotesque and screaming fat man as he fell in a shower of glass from the top floor of the Regency Hotel onto the bonnet of an old Toyota, then slid lifelessly below its tyres as it swerved into a passing taxi. Also unseen was a strong young man with a briefcase who left the hotel shortly afterwards by the fire exit and melted into the rush-hour crowds to report yet another successful mission to his boss.

Cowes, Isle of Wight

THE MAIN HANGAR OF VOSPER THORNYCROFT had seen better and busier days but was still used for a variety of development and boat-servicing activities, mainly for patrol boats. In the days before RAF Wessex helicopters took on the role of coastal air-sea rescue services, this function was performed largely by Vosper's large, all-weather motor launches, similar in design to the famous World War II motor torpedo boats of the Royal Navy. They were fast and highly man-oeuvrable, capable of speeds in excess of thirty-five knots, extremely tough and able to handle themselves in any seas. They could carry at a pinch up to twenty people and there was space for supplies and extra fuel to power their two large supercharged diesel engines.

Resting idly at an old wharf by the hangar in which it was built forty-five years previously, unused, unloved and unwanted, decaying and dying, was one such old Vosper motor launch. The small inflatable with the little outboard motor was dwarfed by the old rusting hull as it chugged slowly around it. The two men aboard the inflatable studied the old launch keenly and objectively but it seemed to be perfect for their requirements.

'What do you think?' asked Masterson.

Cooper was feeling positively choked with emotion. 'You know, just after I started flying, I was on a training flight with a couple of other chaps in some of the first Phantoms. We were all novices based on *Ark Royal* and on manoeuvres in Lyme Bay. My engine blew up on me and I had to ditch on the return leg just out by Fastnet. I was in the water for about four hours. I'd given up all hope, was freezing my bollocks off and suddenly out of the grey sea came one of these beauties. It'd come all the way from Lyme Regis. I tell you Jim, mission or not, I want to have that boat.'

'I think someone's in love,' teased Masterson, but he knew the deep sentimental attachments that could be wrought in combat. 'Anyway, we've an appointment with the boss here to see over her in half an hour. He's an old pal of mine actually. She's certainly going to need a lot of work but on the face of it, I reckon she'll do great. We should also be able to get a good deal on her and save having to get some expensive gin palace, which would be less seaworthy anyway and then not have enough fuel.'

'Let's get at her Jim – I really want this baby and I'll buy her back after the mission.'

'Seems good to me,' said Masterson as he eased the inflatable up to the main jetty by the hangar, tied up and together they went in search of the manager.

Porlock Weir, England

CHARLIE BAILEY RECOGNISED the large bulk of Nick Chater the minute he walked through the door of the Anchor Inn. There were more people around this time, the early summer visitors beginning to make their forays to this quaint and scenic coastline.

Chater looked round the room and noted the old major was in his position of honour beside the now dormant fireplace. He went up to the bar and greeted Bailey.

'Nice to see you again,' said Bailey amiably. 'Friend of Jim Masterson as I recall. How are you?'

'Fine, thanks. Nick Chater's the name.' He proffered a huge hand and they shook. Just then Jill appeared from a door opening to the back of the pub marked 'Private'. She was dressed in riding gear and seemed in a hurry.

'Bye Dad – can't stop, I'm late for the meet.' She pecked her father on the cheek and was rushing off when she noticed Chater. She stopped and came over to him, offering her hand.

'Hello, I'm Jill – always nice to see a customer back. Staying long?' Her eyes fell briefly to below Chater's waist and he felt somewhat uncomfortable.

'Er, Nick Chater, how do you do.'

'I thought you were in a hurry? Go on, hop it Jill,' her father mock scolded. She smiled mischievously and left.

Bailey was smiling. 'I don't know,' he said, shaking his head, 'that girl will be the death of me. Now, what'll it be?'

'Half a bitter please and have one for yourself. Well, with any luck, I'm planning on becoming a very regular customer.' Jim Masterson had briefed him on an opening gambit and also had given him a letter of introduction should it be necessary. 'There's a few of us thinking of setting up an adventure training centre around these parts and we're looking for a place to rent for a few months while we recce the area and do a feasibility study. You have any ideas?'

Bailey passed his drink over and they toasted each other. 'This group – was that the gang that was in here a couple of months back?'

'Yes, some of us, why?'

'Well you all looked a pretty capable bunch – all ex-services I'd say.' He paused for reflection then continued. 'The old boy over by the fireplace is Major Bennett, sort of squire of these parts. He's got bags of space and would probably love to help out. Give him something to do, anyway, instead of drowning himself in pink gins.'

'Will you introduce me – he sounds ideal.'

At that moment, the major wandered over for a fill-up and Bailey performed the introductions. They shook hands and Chater bought Bennett a drink. Bailey followed up the thread.

'This gentleman's looking to rent some rooms for a few months, major. Planning on setting up an adventure training centre with that old chum of yours, Jim Masterson. I wondered if you'd be game for a few old soldiers extra.'

Major Bennett seemed delighted at the idea and showed a rare crooked grin.

'Sounds like a capital idea. Come on over and tell me all about it.'

So Chater refilled his glass and joined the major by the fireplace. They had all agreed previously to stick to the cover but now the time had come, Chater felt this to be unworthy. 'Never lie, if the truth will do as well,' his long dead mother had often told him, and now was a time for the truth. So that was what he told Major Bennett and the old Middlesex Regiment soldier loved every word of it.

'I think you had better come round and see the place,' he said when Chater had finished. 'There'll need to be a bit of sharing and doubling up but I'm sure that'll be no problem.' He paused and chuckled. 'Actually, the idea of it all is rather fun, what?'

They left the Anchor and walked a short distance up a footpath from behind the Inn. It was steep but the old soldier seemed undaunted by it. They came to a massive stone archway with a long, white five-bar gate guarding a driveway. The manor and main gardens were surrounded by a high stone wall covered in lichen and ivy. They went through the gate and a hundred metres in found a large three-storeyed house, a couple of barns and some unidentifiable outhouses. There was an orchard over to the right of the buildings and a beautifully kept garden in the foreground. All the buildings were covered in the same creepers and mosses as the outside walls and even the old slate roof was looking as though nature was winning the battle for repossession.

They entered the house through a heavy iron-studded oak door and walked over old worn stone slabs, occasionally covered by threadbare rugs from Persia, Pakistan and the Orient. The furniture was old and tired, like its solitary inhabitant, but homely nonetheless and the wood panelling around many of the walls gave a sense of comfort and old-world charm. The glowing embers in a huge fireplace were soon ablaze as the major shoved on another log, which crackled behind them as they began a tour of seventeenth-century Tytherleigh Manor.

When that was over, Chater was in no doubt as to the suitability of the place. The cellars were large and completely secure, affording plenty of space for their ordinance and other secret cargoes. The house itself was well concealed from the village by woods and sufficiently off the beaten track not to garner unsolicited attention from casual passers by. Also, should it come to it, the place was well defendable.

'It's perfect,' said Chater as they returned to the drawing room, the fire and another drink, 'absolutely perfect. Tell me, have you any idea what you'd like to charge us? Naturally, all provisions, victualling and so forth will be down to us. Any other expenses involving modifications, like security and so forth, we'll get your approval on first. But certainly a rental of some sort for your trouble is in order and please let us know what else you'd like.'

'Nonsense, old boy, this'll be the best fun I'll have had for years. Don't even think about it.'

'Well, I'm sure we can manage some sort of contribution for the upkeep of the place. Here's a small, shall we say, deposit, in case any other "adventure training" group has the same idea.' He handed the major over an envelope containing a thousand pounds. 'Naturally major, mum's very much the word, eh!'

'My dear chap, there's no need even to mention it,' replied Bennett somewhat haughtily.

'Sorry, of course not. How about a spot of lunch? We could go wherever you suggest.'

'Well actually, I'm due round for lunch at the Lorna Doone Hotel in Porlock. Meet up there once a week with old Doctor Morton. He's retired now, of course, but he keeps an eye on me and he's a good chum. Why don't you join us? You may even find you need him at some time when you're all down here.'

So they left the house, walked back down to the Weir to collect Chater's car, then drove the few minutes into Porlock Village, where an excellent lunch of fresh trout and venison was washed down with scrumpy and port. They said nothing to the kind and amiable doctor of their plans, but Chater took to him well and felt the major's foresight as to the need for discreet but uncommitted medical services to be more than a likely necessity.

When Chater exuberantly reported his success to Newcombe, he found that he too was in an upbeat mood.

'Jim and Brian have just confirmed they've got the boat plus a couple of fast inflatables, so we're really making progress. I'd like us to get settled in with Bennett as soon as possible and give ourselves plenty of time to really blend in down there. Tony's due to check in with us in a day or two, so we'll need to have a group get-together very soon now.'

'Fine, well I'll set up shop in Porlock with old Bennett and will wait till I hear from you.' He gave the manor's telephone number and ended with a cheerful, 'Good luck!'

'Bloody hell,' thought Newcombe, 'this sodding thing's really coming together. Amazing!'

London, England

THE NEWS FROM JORDAN had met with considerable consternation in the corridors of power in Whitehall and the various security services. The OPD meeting Sir William Hood had requested had taken longer to convene than anticipated and it was only now, near the end of May, that it was eventually sitting. Also in attendance was Oswald Prendergast, who had brought the news of Colonel Rousan and

Awaida over personally and whose regional expertise was considered necessary to the gathering.

The meeting itself was quite short. All had received a detailed briefing paper prepared by Prendergast along with his assessment of the affair. After a brief open forum discussion, the prime minister asked Sir William for a summary and proposals for action.

'We believe, prime minister, that there exists a serious threat here. Assassination of all GCC heads of state in Antigua seems to be the objective. However, Iraq's ability to mount an overseas operation of that scale seems highly questionable. Therefore, an alternative plot is more likely. Exactly what this could be we are currently unable to project but a high level of regional agitation, both in physical and morale terms, would seem a more likely and achievable possibility in the absence of their leaders. Mr Prendergast will be returning to the area forthwith, tasked with determining exactly what is being planned. Meanwhile, we would ask all branches of the intelligence community to place their assets on full alert and, through the Joint Intelligence Committee, ensure we communicate fully with each other on all possible leads.'

'Right you are, carry on and we will meet one month from today unless anything of consequence manifests itself sooner. Please liaise on this through Sir James here until further notice and not a word to any outside organisation at this stage, understood. Is there anything else? Very well, madam, gentlemen, thank you for your time.'

The prime minister stood to leave and on his way out took Prendergast by the elbow. 'There could be a lot riding on this Mr Prendergast. I must say, I don't envy you your task but, for God's sake, bring us good quality information and sharp about it. We want the lunatic run out this time, okay?'

'Leave it to me, prime minister,' said Prendergast with his most charming and urbane smile, thinking that 'running the lunatic out' was going to take a lot more time and effort than the last 'cricket match'!

The various section chiefs briefed their deputies the following morning and by the day's end the word was out to all field operators and officers wherever Britain had usable assets in place.

When Martin Henshaw received the news, he dug up the file on Carson and his associates, who by now had been identified, and read through the transcripts of his telephone calls since his last 'listen in'. At this stage, no one else in the service was particularly interested in the file and since there was nothing of substance to report, he took it home with him to study further. Although this was strictly against the rules of MI5, such regulations were weakly adhered to at best and, in any case, he told himself, it wasn't even a classified file.

Poring over the transcripts at home, he found little of interest except the frequently used telephone number of a place which he quickly established as an address in Hereford. He dialled the number and listened, hearing as a background the telltale noise of a boisterous and male dominated pub.

'Brown Envelope Club,' announced a slightly drink-tainted voice.

Henshaw hung up, found out the address and decided to check up on the place the next day and at the same time see what Carson was up to. He thought about it all for a while, reached no conclusion and so went out for a McDonalds and a beer. He'd start early in the morning.

Hereford, England

HENSHAW HAD BARELY ARRIVED outside Carson's house in Farnborough when the man in question came out and drove away. He had no time to check out the ground before following in pursuit so did not notice the other car, which at a more discreet distance, made up a convoy and followed both vehicles ahead to Hereford.

As they closed on Marshall's home, Henshaw anticipated that this would be the Brown Envelope Club as identified the previous evening. He drove past, turned and backtracked to a lay-by from which he could just see the house and drive. The third vehicle drove past the house and then him and headed on towards town where it parked. The driver then walked across country the couple of miles necessary and entered the club unseen from the rear.

There was no one about and Little George quickly found Newcombe in the club's small office, having a coffee and debriefing from Carson.

'Sorry to bovver you, major, sir.' This latter was addressed deferentially to Carson, whom he had never actually met. 'Could I 'ave a word wiv you please, private like?'

Newcombe saw the concern on the little cockney's face and asked Carson to excuse himself for a moment.

'What is it George?' he asked when they were alone.

'Carson's bein' followed, major. Things seemed okay till we got back from Spain when, like I told you, I had a feelin' someone was snoopin' around – picked him up at the airport I reckoned. But I could never pin anyfink down like. Then today, this joker turns up outside Carson's place just as 'e's leavin' and follows 'im straight to the door 'ere. 'e's out there now in the lay-by over the road, standin' out like a sore thumb.'

'Do you think he saw you, George?'

'No way; I knew where we was goin' so I could keep a good distance back. Not a chance 'e saw me.'

'Okay George, you said you wanted some action. Here's what I want you to do. . . .' He explained for some minutes to George then called Carson back in. 'Tony, this is George, I need him to run an errand for me. Can he take your car? It'll only be for about an hour and we've got lots to talk about still.'

'Sure thing,' replied Carson handing the keys over. 'Nice to meet you George.'

'See you later,' said Little George as he strolled purposefully out.

George revved up Carson's car and flew out of Marshall's forecourt. He slowed a little until he was sure the tail was following and then accelerated hard heading for open country. George took increasingly smaller roads and drove towards some woodland he knew well. He pulled off the road, leapt from the car and doubled back to wait for his follower, who appeared just seconds later.

Henshaw had been taken completely by surprise by the sudden departure and had followed with a certain sense of unease. This behaviour was out of character, as far as he knew, but he felt he was on to something and should press ahead.

When he saw Carson's empty car, he was quite alarmed and although at a standstill, kept the engine ticking over. After some minutes, however, he switched it off and seeing no one about, stepped cautiously out of his vehicle and started towards the other.

Henshaw never heard or knew what hit him, for Little George had moved silently from cover and chopped him behind the ear with fearsome power. He was dead instantly, before he even hit the ground.

George quickly went to Henshaw's car and searched it thoroughly. He was constantly alert to danger and wore gloves. He found a file on Carson on the passenger seat and some other odd documents. He took all these back to Carson's car, collecting a wallet and ID papers from the inert body as he passed, and left to report his findings.

Newcombe was not amused. 'I said "distract him or knock him out if you have to". I didn't say fucking kill him.'

'Sorry sir,' said George, but not looking it. 'But I guarantee you no one was about to see it 'appen and I didn't see another motor comin' or goin'. I guess I must 'ave 'it 'im a bit too 'ard, that's all.'

'That is not fucking all,' shouted back Newcombe. 'If MI5 or the police are able to track this back to us, we'll all be up shit creek. Now, not a word to anyone, okay? Not Carson, not Marshall – no one. I'll get Carson to change cars and he won't come here again. Thank God no one knows him here yet, anyway.'

'Yes sir – sorry again sir.'

'Yes, well, it may turn out for the best after all,' said Newcombe calming down. 'Since we've got this file and you've taken the man out, maybe we've stopped the thing in the bud, whatever the "thing" is. Anyway, no use speculating now. Send Carson back in here can you and get lost for a while back in Shoreham.'

George turned to leave but Newcombe stopped him saying, 'And George – when I want someone killed, I'll tell you, okay? Until then, tread lightly mate.'

''s sir!' George snapped rigidly to attention, saluted and left.

Summer 1995

Tel Aviv, Israel

THE MEETING IN THE HEADQUARTERS of Mossad was subdued and intense, as was often the case. The director, Ari Diarra, was a battle-hardened veteran of most of Israel's war-torn, turbulent and insecure history and although now in his seventies, his acute and sharp brain ran what was probably the world's most effective secret intelligence service.

The subject under discussion was the next GCC Summit meeting. All around the table could scarcely believe the news of the intended location. Everyone in the whole region was so paranoiac about security that the idea of them all leaving for any reason seemed so absurd as to be scarcely credible to this cynical group of senior officers and department heads.

Ari Diarra had just summarised all the available known facts and they were now assessing the implications and possible ramifications of the Antiguan summit. These seemed endless but after a while they had concentrated the options down to just three.

The first was that Iraq would mount an operation to eliminate the six leaders in Antigua. This was the least likely option, as the logistics involved and the organisation required would be extremely difficult for Baghdad.

The second was that Iraq might in some way launch an attack on the region, capitalising on the absence of its leaders, and spread as much turmoil and confusion as possible. This, too, seemed logistically stretching for a country whose military resources and capability had been so emasculated by the United Nations since the Gulf War.

A final possibility was that enough dissent could be mustered and supported by Baghdad to arrange a series of coups. This was the old Eastern Bloc strategy of destabilisation which had worked so well for the Soviet Union for many years. If Iraq could place sympathetic leaders into the main GCC member states, it could group together to throw out the Western overseers and then form a pact so strong that a very real threat would then be imposed upon Israel and, indeed, the rest of the world.

This third option was certainly the most worrying. No one really cared if the leaders were all killed. The more confusion and lessened co-operation between states throughout the Middle East the better, as far as Israel was concerned. But if in a void created by their removal, Iraq could unite this diverse bunch of factious tribes, then this could really spell trouble.

So it was decided to concentrate all assets on first, determining Baghdad's specific strategy and, second, preparing appropriate plans for disinformation and confusion to block any such unification process.

Ari Diarra concluded the meeting with his favourite expression: 'Remember, gentlemen, divided they fall, united we're in the shit!'

Porlock Weir, England

Following the killing of henshaw, Newcombe had decided that there should be no further meetings of the group at the club. Instead he felt that they should set up headquarters at Porlock without delay, the more secure for everybody.

Major Bennett was having more fun than he had for years. All of the bustle around the manor was a pure joy and the slick, professional way that Nick Chater and his group were preparing the place was bringing life back into the old soldier.

By mid-June, Porlock was crammed with tourists and the local arts-and-crafts shops were booming. The group therefore melted into the crowds and through walking, swimming, sailing and diving, intimately familiarised themselves with the locality.

Both Gunter and Marshall had visited a couple of times but generally were keeping clear. Gunter was working to his own agenda in any case and Marshall was now fully involved in Antigua helping out Beaumont at the St Peter's Club.

Newcombe had arrived shortly after Chater and taken over control in Porlock where he had been joined by Scott and George. Masterson and Cooper were working in Cowes to make the old Vosper seaworthy. The plan was then to sail round to Porlock and complete fitting out and sea trials there, but much was to be done first.

Carson was not invited down and was, if anything, kept at arm's length. He was puzzled by Newcombe's vehement insistence to sell his car, but had gone along with it nevertheless. He still thought Newcombe a bit over the top on security – after all, nothing had really happened as yet – and the group leaders' elaborate new system of communicating he found somewhat irksome. However, he was the boss and, more importantly, the paymaster, so he did as he was bidden.

Newcombe had decided to tell no one about the Henshaw incident and George followed orders. Nothing would be gained from discussion and it seemed that the local police had drawn a blank. However, he was still very much concerned by the inevitable storm that would be raging over the violent death of the agent and continually pondered over how much MI5 actually knew. Maybe the file George had taken from Henshaw's car was the only record on Carson but equally well it may just be a copy. If that was the case, then the police and security services would all be looking out for the arms dealer and so the less contact the club members had with him the better.

There was little else that could be done except wait and hope for the best and allow another indifferent British summer to take its natural course.

London, England

SARAH RENARD WAS VERY UPSET by Henshaw's death. She had been in MI5 for several years now but this was her first 'combat' fatality. The service was completely mystified by it as there seemed to be no accounting for Henshaw's presence in the Herefordshire region and there was no record of any sensitive cases that he was known to have been working on.

Thorough investigations were made but as the weeks went by, no clues emerged to account for the mysterious affair. Accordingly, Renard made no mention of it at the Joint Intelligence Committee meetings and the incident slowly but inexorably began to cloud over.

The InterContinental Hotel was also a favourite of Kate Lladro and it was here that she had arranged to meet Carson to discuss his purchase.

They met in her suite but on this occasion, Lladro was clipped and business-like. She invited Carson to help himself to a drink and while he fixed it, asked, 'Tell me Tony, who do you know of who may be interested in your activities?'

'God knows – why?' Carson was puzzled for he hoped that many people were interested in him professionally, but this was obviously not the direction of Lladro's question.

'Because you were being followed when you were at the villa in Tamariu,' she replied bluntly. 'Any ideas? Your new-found friends for instance?'

'I can't think why they should. Are you sure about this Kate? I mean, maybe it was a prospective client or some such?'

'Did they contact you?' He shook his head in reply. 'Then why don't you call up your colleagues and see what they know. I don't like snoopers around my back door Tony, so unless we clear this up double quick, the deal's off. Here's the 'phone.' She pulled it over from the desk and dropped it on Carson's lap.

He dialled a number and left a message on an answering machine as he'd been told. Ten minutes later, Newcombe called him from a pay phone.

'Morning Tony, how are things coming along?'

'Well, there's a possibility I may have a problem. It seems I'm being followed.'

'*Were* being followed, Tony. We've taken care of it.'

'For Christ's sake, who by and why the hell didn't you tell me?'

'We figure it was a standard surveillance operation which is often in place with people like you. We used to do quite a bit of that sort of thing when I was in the regiment. It's nothing to worry about and the spook that was on your tail is now off it. You've changed your car and our communications are secure so you've nothing more to worry about. That put your mind at rest?' ·

Carson looked over at Lladro on the extension, who nodded back.

'Yes, okay. But you might have told me. Is there anything else you want to clue me in on?'

'No, nothing at all. Tell me, how's the shopping going? Is everything on schedule there?'

'Yes everything's fine. Look, Mike, I can't stop now – just wanted to check out this shadow. I'll call you again soon.'

'Okay, Tony, take care.'

They hung up and respectively reviewed their positions. Newcombe, although concerned, felt that it had probably been George who had been spotted and that using Henshaw as the scapegoat had been a stroke of luck. Anyway, there was nothing that could be done about it – they'd just have to be more careful. Lladro, too, seemed mollified by the explanation. She was well aware of the considerable scrutiny under which she and others in her profession were kept, but she liked always to be on top of things, never leaving untied loose ends.

She and Carson, therefore, discussed the details of the purchase and the issue of tailing was forgotten.

Antigua, Leeward Islands

Ever since Beaumont had fully taken over at the St Peter's Club in April, the staff had been running at fever pitch.

His first task had been to split the management into two teams. One was to be responsible for the day-to-day operations of the club and looking after the guests. Wilkinson was in charge of this as it required little change from the established routine.

The other group, reporting directly to Beaumont, was the one that would make the summit happen, and this needed the highest levels of skill, expertise and vigour available. It consisted of Elliott, Barton, Schwartz and the club's financial controller, an American from Harvard called Arthur Jenkins, whose accounting ability was inspiring. The team was completed by a local man, Desmond Brown, the purchasing manager, whose skill at procurement on so corrupt an island was second only to his skill as a cricketer, a game at which he had represented his country at international test level many years previously.

After much detailed briefing and subsequent planning, the group had set about their various tasks. There was so much to be purchased, from linen, glass and chinaware, to new furniture and recreation equipment. There were endless maintenance and service requirements for a full refurbishment programme and complete new communications equipment, from telephones and radios, to pagers. There was also a new conference hall to build and equip to lavish standards of quality and opulence.

A need for some highly skilled supervisory staff to augment and help train the existing personnel was also high on the agenda and all these had to be sourced from overseas, visas applied for and approvals sought.

Finally, there was the endless public relations. Everyone who was anyone on the island wanted to be involved somehow and although in most cases they were unneeded, Beaumont knew that if any of them set their mind to it, they could doom the entire summit.

So they all went about their work with a high commitment and unsurpassed enthusiasm. As the hotter, mid-summer season approached, obvious progress was notable and, to Beaumont's relief and amazement, he found that they were on schedule.

Now he had to prepare for the first field visit from the GCC security chiefs and he wondered what surprises this would bring.

Much as their masters would inevitably do in five months time, they arrived separately and awkwardly, collectively causing the maximum amount of inconvenience and difficulty possible.

The idea of travelling out together was inconceivable and so six different large airplanes made six significant interruptions to the normal summer schedules and Antigua received its first taste of things to come.

The reception committee this time was of a slightly lower key than before. It was nonetheless attention grabbing for all that and its very repetitiveness caused much interest on the island's decrepit old roads. One by one the parties arrived, each consisting of the senior security personnel, political officials and protocol officers from the respective royal courts. There were also the captains and senior officers of each of the royal yachts and an assortment of secretaries, advisors and others.

July and August tend not to be too busy in Antigua for tourism, as it is unquestionably the hottest time on the islands and the least comfortable. The trade winds peter out and the place becomes clammy and overbearing. It is also the time of year when hurricanes are spawned. This, however, did not deter Awaida from insisting upon a huge barbecue party around the poolside that first night, with all the usual steel bands, fire-eaters and limbo dancers to set the mood. There was dancing and merriment and company for those who sought it, which were many. Elliott had been working overtime for Awaida on this assignment, for the club's master was determined to make this a memorable affair. And indeed it was long after midnight when the last of the revellers meandered slowly off to bed leaving the steel drummers to smoke the last of their ganja, pack up and go home. Then only the tiny tree frogs were left, chirruping to the full moon and the stars.

General Ashman had scheduled the first meeting for the following day at ten o'clock but it was nearer eleven when everyone had finally turned up. He was seated at the top of a U-shaped table to Awaida's left, with Beaumont on the right. Delegates sat in their national groupings along the sides with assistants at support desks behind them.

When everyone had eventually settled down, Awaida opened the proceedings by welcoming everyone and for those who didn't already know them, introducing Beaumont and the general. He liked public speaking even less without Cognac so he handed rapidly over to Ashman and lit a large cigar on which he munched happily as the meeting unfurled.

The general began by outlining the agenda for the next few days. Although there would be some group activity, for the most part the delegates would be splitting up into functional groups. For example, Schwartz would be taking all the royal yachts' personnel on detailed reconnaissance and familiarisation inspections of the deep-water anchorages, harbour facilities, related local communications procedures and so forth. The protocol and royal court personnel would be determining the order of the summit's meetings, the tours, shows and dining schedules, principally with Elliott. The security scheduling and control linked with the island's local defence forces was a major issue and this was being co-ordinated with Barton.

Having outlined the agenda, he presented a résumé of progress to date and the current schedule of activity. They finally broke for a light buffet lunch and then went their respective ways, some in fleets of taxis and boats and others back to meeting rooms and planning. It had been decided for everyone to make their own arrangements for dining that evening, so the next formal get-together was set for ten o'clock the next day.

There was an air of enthusiasm and excitement amongst them all in the morning. After years of organising these summits in the Middle East, they were all distinctly bored with them. This conference in Antigua thrilled and inspired even the most complacent and, for the first time in ages, they were really looking forward to it.

Beaumont, however, had a dampener to put on the proceedings. He had discussed it with the general first and they had decided that all should be briefed straight away.

'Gentlemen,' began Beaumont in a sombre mood. 'I am afraid we may shortly have a problem.'

The clink of coffee cups and rustle of papers stopped and everyone now gave him their fullest attention.

'You may have noticed this morning that the sky has become overcast and a strong wind has picked up. The early-warning storm watchers indicate the formation of a hurricane in the mid-Atlantic. At this stage it's unpredictable and has not developed any specific characteristics. However, we're watching it closely, because if it does flare up and comes in our direction, it could be with us in as little as forty-eight hours.'

'What exactly are the implications for us should this happen?' Brigadier Ayyad spoke for them all. Most were familiar with the occasional downpour but had only ever heard about serious tropical storms and hurricanes.

'If it does form up, we'll be isolated here for maybe several days, maybe a week, and it will be very unpleasant. There'll be much damage and real life-threatening danger will exist.' They didn't like that last bit, thought Beaumont. 'So if you are in any doubt, we suggest . . .' he looked over to the general, '. . . you leave the island this morning and head for mainland USA, well north of Florida and the southern states. You would be able to come back when it's all blown over.'

Everyone started talking at once and, except for the seamen, seemed to be in a state of high anxiety. They could not grasp the concept of being in the way of a hurricane and most felt that Beaumont must be exaggerating. Some even said as much but Beaumont calmly replied, 'Gentlemen, this is not a debate. I am not going to argue with you. I have advised you what could happen in the worst scenario. It's entirely up to you what you elect to do. Meanwhile, if you'll excuse me, I have preparations to make.'

He left the room and closed the door on the babble of excited voices beyond.

Like most organisations in the islands, particularly those orientated towards tourism, the club had a well-planned and -rehearsed hurricane procedure, arrived at after bitter experiences over the years.

The first issue was to ensure that all guests had the option of leaving while flights were still going. They normally did not take much persuasion and by midday, all but a few long-staying and adventurous types had departed. The GCC contingent had elected to stay, however, the Saudis setting the example with Ashman and everyone else inevitably following suit to save face.

By lunchtime, the big C-130 based on Antigua and used for storm reconnaissance, had returned with the news that a full-blown stinker had developed. In co-operation with the US Meteorological Office, the storm was then christened 'Hurricane Salome'. People who knew their scriptures remembered what an unpredictable and nasty piece of work she had been.

Alerts were broadcast the length and breadth of the Caribbean and mainland America's southern and eastern seaboards. Everywhere people reacted, battening down their homes and possessions, and prepared themselves to cower impotently in the face of one of nature's most malevolent forces.

At the St Peter's Club, a skeleton staff was left to look after the remaining guests while the rest went about their prescribed tasks. The beach and pool attendants gathered up all the loose furniture and, to the amazement of those few guests still around, sunk it all in the club's swimming pools.

The boats were towed round the promontory to Indian Creek and the mangroves at the far end. Here they were tethered in the shelter of the creek where they could ride out the storm and sustain relatively little damage against the flexible, giving swamp bushes and trees. The smaller dinghies were taken to the same place but sunk between the thick and secure mangrove stumps. They would be as safe there as anywhere and could be easily refloated later.

Back on the grounds of the club, Colonel Wilmot was making his way to his villa when he saw a group of groundsmen pruning coconuts from a tree. He thought this strange against all of the bustle going on elsewhere and stopped and said so. 'Shouldn't you lot be getting on with some work? Don't you lazy loafers know there's a storm coming?'

The group of friendly Antiguans just laughed at him and carried on with their business. This infuriated the colonel who was not accustomed to being ignored and laughed at.

'Did you hear what I said?' he bellowed and was about to become even more embroiled when Trevor Barton came up and guided him away.

'Can you imagine, colonel,' he asked softly, 'what happens to a building or a body when coconuts start hitting it at 150 miles an hour? Well, that's what happens in a hurricane, so we collect them all in out of harm's way, do you see?'

'My God, it hadn't occurred to me. Maybe we should get out of here after all. I better round up the rest of my group.'

'You've left it a bit too late, I'm afraid colonel. They've just closed the airport. This one's really moving in fast. Now if you'll excuse me, I must be getting on.'

'Yes, of course,' replied Wilmot, feeling particularly helpless and vulnerable. He was not used to being anything other than totally in control of his surroundings and the people about him and he was not enjoying the experience.

Meanwhile, other staff were securing rooms while yet others were preparing the emergency shelter, a place they might very well have to spend several days in. It had access to the main food supplies and larders but everything would have to be cold as all cooking equipment would be shut down for safety.

Toilets were already accessible, so the provision of orderly sleeping arrangements and entertainment in the form of videos, board games, cards and books were the priority.

Fresh water might become a problem, so a tank was erected and appropriate plumbing installed. Other emergency equipment for fighting fires, digging out of collapsed buildings, first aid and so forth were also prepared and finally equipment for communication with the outside world was established.

By early that evening, the wind had picked up and was gusting at gale force 8. Sheets of rain were falling and the sky was dark and brooding.

After dinner Beaumont had called everyone together in the emergency shelter, both guests and volunteer staff who had elected to stay and help. The shelter had been a nightclub and adjoining casino, but now it bore no resemblance to either such activity.

As the storm seemed to be approaching so rapidly and, according to the weather reports, heading more or less straight for them, he had decided to move everyone into the shelter that night. The club would then be shut down completely and they would just have to sweat it out and hope for the best.

The guests were incredulous. Ayyad particularly was being somewhat scathing about the preparations and generally was stirring up trouble.

'I can't believe what you're doing here,' he said. 'Anyone would think it was the end of the world. For the love of Allah, it's only a storm.' Some of his colleagues grimaced at Ayyad's blasphemy but kept their own counsel. 'Besides, if you think I'm going to share a dormitory with anyone, you've got another think coming. I'm off to my own room and that's an end to it.'

A chorus of assent met this action and several people around the room made to get up and moved off towards the door after Ayyad.

'You are all free to do whatever you please, of course,' said Beaumont. 'However, it is my duty to advise you, for the last time, that there exists very real danger for you out there. If you go outside, there is a distinct possibility that you will die.'

'I really think you'd be best to follow Mr Beaumont's advice.' This from General Ashman. 'He and his people do know the islands and the impact these storms can have. Why not do as they suggest?'

'When I want advice from a hotel manager,' replied Ayyad nastily, 'I'll ask for it.' With that, he opened the inner door to their sanctum and strode out. The roar of the storm was horrible and unlike anything most of them had ever heard. Those that had been emboldened by Ayyad's belligerence now backed away from the door. Barton jumped up to secure the outer door after Ayyad and then shut the inner one securely. No one else now seemed to feel like following the truculent Bahraini.

They heard the storm rising in ferocity throughout the night and few of them had much sleep. The pressure on the ears alone was of such discomfort as to banish any possibility of rest and even the small slits of windows that were left open throughout the club to prevent vacuum damage helped little. The cacophony of the wind and the rain throughout the club and grounds was almost deafening and certainly very alarming. Every now and again, a mighty crash would signify the destruction of some piece of the club – a slab of roof maybe or a sheet of glass smashed by flying debris.

The roar of the sea could also be heard, pounding against the rocks around the club's little peninsula and doubtlessly removing the jetties and walk-ways in great ripping and tearing chunks.

As a storm, Salome was as heartless and uncaring as her namesake. She bombarded the coral reefs and obliterated in seconds that which it had taken nature centuries to build. She pulverised beaches and low shorefront with waves of crushing dimensions and shredded the rickety houses of the people who made these usually idyllic shores their homes. And this cruel force took many lives to satisfy her hunger and quench her vengeful appetite.

And then, for a while, she rested.

People who still had them came cautiously out of their homes and surveyed in a state of shock the carnage all around then. Everything was flattened, broken, smashed and this was made all the more strange by the eerie stillness that followed the tumult. The wise ones quickly made good what damage they could and once again took shelter. For they knew that the calm and peaceful eye of the hurricane was just another of her evil tricks to lure the unwary out from cover, only to be sent to oblivion as the full might of the storm returned.

When she attacked again, it was if anything worse than before. The din and commotion numbed the senses, as salvo upon salvo of fury was unleashed upon the defenceless islands and their insignificant custodians.

By mid-afternoon the following day, Hurricane Salome had satisfied herself with the Leeward Islands and gone in search of other prey to dance with in the Gulf of Mexico. Finding none, she turned north, but before reaching the southern shores of the United States, lost interest in her satanic quest, and petered out into a localised tropical storm. She was still violent for all that, but now lacked the single-minded sense of purpose that had originally possessed her.

Millions of people breathed a sigh of relief and then tuned to CNN and the news of a shattered Caribbean.

They found Ayyad not far from the shelter. He was barely recognisable and lay utterly crushed beneath an electric gardener's truck that had broken its securing chains and been tossed like a feather through the air. He seemed as aggressive in death as he had been in life and although no one wept for him, the very violence of his passing had the fainter-hearted retching uncontrollably.

And everywhere else they looked, destruction and desolation confronted them. There were many varieties of seabird, twisted and mangled amongst the smashed palms. Fish of all descriptions were lying around the grounds, their glorious colours fading in putrefaction while others flopped spasmodically in their final death throes. There was even a large dolphin in the middle of one of the tennis courts. Gashed, bleeding and confused, it was a pitiful creature, once champion of its natural environment but now a helpless wreck awaiting a kindly bullet from Barton who, to some people's surprise, had emerged from the shelter carrying a rifle and an automatic pistol.

Everyone, guests and staff, were organised into search and clear-up gangs by Barton and, to Ashman's amazement, followed their orders and appointed tasks almost with relish. Their minds and senses had been numbed by nature's awesome show of strength and everyone had been greatly humbled by the experience.

The damage was extensive but mostly repairable and after a while a semblance of order had returned to the community. Huge amounts of foreign aid poured in, particularly from unusual sources in the Middle East and, slowly but surely, life returned to normal. The mental scars of the disaster, however, would remain for many years as the battered and shaken people of the islands buried their dead, rebuilt their shattered homes and lives and addressed themselves to their future.

Basra, Iraq

IN THE MARSHES AND SWAMPS to the northwest of Basra, in southern Iraq, lies the confluence of two of the world's most famous rivers, the Tigris and Euphrates. Sweeping through history from the mountains of Turkey, they have formed the great river basin of Mesopotamia. Here it was that one of the great wonders of the ancient world, the hanging gardens of Babylon, were created and this once rich and prosperous region attracted archaeologists from the world over, religious scholars and historians, the itinerant and curious alike.

But not so today. Visitors are discouraged and travellers to the country do so very much at their own risk. For this is now Iraq, led by the tyrannical Saddam Hussein.

The man in question was at that moment peering through a pair of high-powered night binoculars and grinning with satisfaction. He was watching a military exercise which was the culmination of many weeks' preparation and training and he was grimly pleased with the result.

A small band of highly skilled and experienced Republican Guard soldiers had just completed a simulated attack on a structure that looked rather like an oil refinery. The defenders had been subdued quietly and quickly and within a matter of minutes the attackers were retreating, leaving behind them a stygian roaring and flaming torment of metal and burning buildings against the backdrop of the night. The entire operation had lasted less than fifteen minutes from landing to departure in their small, fast inflatables.

'Are all the teams this good, colonel?' Saddam Hussein asked Colonel Rousan who, along with a small group of trusted, inner-circle commanders, was breathing a sigh of relief at his master's pleasure.

'All of them, sir,' replied the colonel crisply. 'Those that were not up to scratch are no longer with the Guard.'

Failure was not tolerated, much less forgiven, by Saddam Hussein.

So it was out of self preservation that Rousan considered it unnecessary to mention that one of the 'failed' officers had deserted from his barracks to avoid punishment. Full searches had so far proven futile but he wouldn't get far; it was just a matter of time before his inevitable capture and execution.

'In that case, how can we possibly fail?' With that, Saddam turned on his heel and walked off to a waiting car, shepherded as always by his ever faithful and gigantic bodyguards, Taher and Fuad.

'How indeed?' mused Rousan, knowing that if they did, his head would be the first to roll and very horrible too would be its falling.

He decided that he needed some insurance. He had never really trusted the military to do the job properly and so the more confusion and disinformation he could spread and the more information he could collect on the intentions of the allies the better.

He was going to have to start getting rough again. The thought did not displease him.

Porlock Weir, England

THE NEW RESIDENTS AT THE MANOR had been following the progress of Hurricane Salome with obsessive interest. They had all experienced dirty weather during their careers, mainly in the form of Far Eastern typhoons, so they knew just what could be happening on the island. Their big concern now was the possibility of the summit being relocated back to Saudi Arabia and so they waited anxiously for news from the island.

Over a week had elapsed since Salome's passing and it was now early August when Marshall first called up. Communications with the islands were not great at the best of times but after a full-frontal assault by a determined hurricane they were a shambles.

Damage however, seemed to be largely superficial and the main infrastructure seemed to be intact. This was certainly the case for the southern part of the island, which had been shielded by mountains.

Marshall reported that a full damage assessment was now in place at the club and a decision was to be made in a few days as to whether the summit would go ahead. Most, it seemed, were optimistic but the decision would ultimately be made back in the blinding heat of the Middle East. Following this, assuming it went in their favour, another recce would be needed as soon as possible. The surrounding seas particularly would need rechecking, as reefs had moved and debris and flotsam on a huge scale, including many boats and houses, had accumulated around the shores.

So everyone waited tensely and anxiously for word from Marshall and went about their tasks without enthusiasm or vigour. At this stage, it would be too devastating to abort their plans, the prospect of which filled everyone with dread.

Taif, Saudi Arabia

INDEED, A SENSE OF DREAD was being experienced by many that hot and sweltering summer in the wake of Hurricane Salome. Many felt that the GCC representatives should not have been exposed to such risk. The very idea, therefore, of sending their leaders to the same place was unthinkable and they strenuously argued for the summit to be rescheduled to more familiar, less exciting, surroundings.

Ayyad's death had been unfortunate, even though it had been his own fault, and was yet more ammunition for the opposition.

Finally, the various security reports from the visit had not been encouraging. For people who were accustomed to having complete control of their surroundings, the St Peter's Club was a nightmare and they were all privately delighted to have the hurricane as an excuse to cover their own, so far well hidden, inadequacies.

The only two exceptions to this disquiet were Ashman and Kenwright. They were the last to leave Antigua and had flown back together, taking full advantage of their extended privacy to agree on a common approach to take to their respective leaders.

Kenwright flew down to Salalah in southern Oman where Sultan Qaboos was at his summer residence, while Ashman sought an audience with King Abdullah at his summer palace in the cool mountains of western Saudi Arabia in Taif.

Almost a further week passed before he was able to see the king and he was shown in to his private majlis. Here a table was groaning with the weight of sticky pastries, sweet meats, fruits and all manner of other foods, to be washed down with juices and cinnamon flavoured Arabic coffee. The air was heavily scented with burning frankincense and there were just the two of them plus a secretary, servant and body-guard.

As custom dictated, they talked of a myriad inanities before finally coming to the business in question.

'So, John, I gather you've been upsetting my fraternal rulers,' started the king with a huge smile. 'Whatever have you been up to?'

His English was immaculate, which disguised the ruthless pirate that lurked behind the urbane exterior. This was not the way the general had envisaged the interview starting and he was now both concerned and apprehensive with his unpredictable boss.

'Your Majesty is aware of the reconnaissance trip we recently made to Antigua for the GCC Summit Conference,' he began stiffly. 'Unfortunately, a hurricane interrupted our visit and some of the, er, guests, did not exactly radiate examples of bravery and leadership. I imagine, Your Majesty, that it will be from these quarters from which you have received any such negative feedback.'

The King was rocking with laughter at this stage. He liked the general, with his quiet and thorough professionalism and particularly his classical stiff upper lip; he was so very British, he thought. The masterful understatement concerning the bravery of his neighbours was too much for him, however, and tears of mirth coursed down his cheeks. Eventually, he was able to continue.

'Do you know, John, I have received several messages from the highest levels urging me to discontinue this venture. People from within our own country, even, have got the knives out and are after my blood, Awaida's and yours in that order. They'd love an excuse like a really bad summit to give me the old heave-ho!' He paused and took some more coffee. 'What do you think we should do, John?'

'Nothing has changed, Your Majesty. The original criteria for holding the summit in the Caribbean is still good and by December, no one will even know there had ever been a storm there.' Maybe not quite true, he thought, but what the hell! 'I still believe it would make a good and much-needed change for everyone, and it will position you as a strong and forceful leader, willing to break with tradition and historical group pressures. . . .'

'Providing it works,' interrupted the King. 'What about security? We're not going to be fully in control of the people and environment. That's what is really worrying everyone, you know.'

'I quite understand that, Your Majesty, but in fact the security will be much tighter and more controllable than it might appear. For a start, all dignitaries will be living aboard their yachts, fully guarded and patrolled by their own people – more so, in fact, than at the usual summits.'

'That's a good point – I'll remember that one. Do go on.'

'Well, Your Majesty will recall that the club sits on a peninsula with narrow and well defendable approaches. The local people and security forces will not be allowed near and we will be fully in control of the area. Access will be restricted and managed in much the same way as we usually handle it.'

The King was nodding approvingly.

'The only times where there could be a slightly enhanced level of risk are on the journeys to and from the airport and for the days when boat racing and partying on the clifftop are proposed. But even this will be a very limited risk and our security forces will be fully in control. Frankly, Your Majesty, I really don't see a problem.'

'You mentioned the journeys to and from the airport. Tell me more about that.'

'For a start the roads themselves are appalling – full of potholes, narrow and bumpy. Thick vegetation and ramshackle housing comes right to the road's edges for most of the way and animals and people stroll mindlessly around them without a care. The possibility therefore exists of ambushing, with or without mines, or just genuinely having an accident. This would be easily overcome, of course, if transfer to and from the club were made by each ship's own helicopters and a formal reception either could take place at the airport before the chopper flight or after, say on Your Majesty's yacht.'

'I like that idea – receiving them all aboard the yacht – yes, that would be very different too. So you feel we should go ahead with it?'

'Absolutely, Your Majesty.' By now the general had restored some of his self-confidence and was feeling more relaxed. His comfort was short-lived.

'So what about coups and so forth that will threaten us all in our absence?'

'Your Majesty, every summit conference exposes five of you to that risk. All of you going together to a different venue is really very little different to what you have all been doing for years. Besides, if there's anyone you're not sure about, take them along with you.'

'All right, all right, your point is made. We will continue as planned.' The King broke off and looked around conspiratorially, then with a grin and a wink, continued. 'If only, though, to upset my brothers. They can't possibly refuse without losing face. Yes, I think the whole thing might be rather fun.'

'Very good, Your Majesty, I will proceed with finalising the appropriate arrangements.' He stood to leave. 'I have taken up much of your valued time – is there anything else I can do for you?'

'Well, yes, as a matter of fact there is, John. One of the calls I had was from our friends in Bahrain. They insist on a certain condition for attendance.'

The King briefly explained to Ashman, who looked not at all amused. 'Never mind, John, I expect your man Beaumont will understand. He went through some such problem once in Oman, I believe, when the Kuwaitis had a similar issue. Anyway, there it is, so please attend to it. Keep me informed John.'

And with that, the audience was over. The general bowed himself out and made straight for the rooms he used when in Taif for residence and offices. Beaumont would climb the wall, he thought, but that was his problem.

As he started making telephone calls, he remembered absently that it had been Saudi Arabia that had caused the 'similar problem' before, and not Kuwait. Marvellous things, selective memories, he thought.

Antigua, Leeward Islands

The first priority at the st peter's club had been to determine if in fact it could now be made ready for the summit. Once the debris had been cleared, however, it was apparent that little significant and structural damage had been caused and that the deadline could indeed be met. A detailed action plan had been drawn up and everyone was bent to their respective tasks with renewed and refocused vigour.

It was therefore rather surprising to everyone within earshot of the executive offices to hear the explosion that suddenly erupted from Beaumont's office. In the old days, his temper had always been on rather a short fuse but since his arrival this time he had been of a far more even disposition. Now, however, he seemed to be having a complete meltdown.

Most people made themselves scarce except Joyce, who had never really been bothered by these behavioural excesses. However, when the telephone was ripped out of its wall socket and flew through the air to crash into the wall opposite, even she realised that the call just received from Ashman could not have brought good news. She kept her counsel as her deranged boss stormed out of the office towards his car in a flood of curses, hissing and spitting and generally damning everything and everyone. She didn't actually notice that the barrage of invective was principally aimed at the occupants of the Middle East.

Beaumont hurled his car around the decrepit island roads and it was only a matter of luck rather than good judgement that no one was killed on the relatively short drive to the Copper & Lumber

Store. He wanted to get seriously drunk, even though it was only mid-morning.

Marshall had had his share of problems to sort out after the hurricane and he was just now on his way into the capital to purchase some ironmongery, when Beaumont stormed in looking like he wanted to kill someone, which in fact he did.

'What's up with you, mate?' he asked innocently. 'Looks like you need a drink.'

'Fucking Bahrainis!' was the only answer he received as they went over to the bar and Marshall poured out a massive Black Label with ice and soda for his early guest. He himself took a Red Stripe.

Beaumont downed half of his before continuing his litany. 'Just because that arsehole Ayyad thought he was stronger than a bloody hurricane, this is their cretinous way of showing how fucking clever they think they are. Christ, when it comes to monumental imbecility they take the biscuit. Hypocritical bunch of. . . .'

The invective continued almost uninterrupted for another scotch, while Marshall nurtured his beer, amused by his friend's unusual behaviour and intrigued to know its cause.

Eventually the hotelier slowed down, finished off his drink and started a third. Then to Marshall, he said, 'Do you know, Bill, what those pricks want?'

'Can't imagine, mate, but judging by your reaction, it can't be anything too serious!' He grinned and slapped him on the back. Beaumont just managed a smile before continuing.

'They've said the use of the word "Saint" in the club's name is "offensive to their Islamic values" and it must be totally removed from everything – china, cutlery, stationery, brochures, uniforms – fucking everything, or they won't come. The Saudis said "Of course Emir, no problem Emir, probably would have done it ourselves anyway Emir," and then phoned me this morning to bloody fix it.'

'Christ, that is worth a tantrum,' said Marshall appalled by the idea and just beginning to understand a little of the perversity in the minds of rich Arabs. 'I think I'll join you in that scotch.'

They drank and brooded in silence for a while then Marshall spoke his thoughts aloud. 'Seeing the way they all behaved with their boozing and whoring, I wouldn't have thought they had many values, Islamic or otherwise. Anyway, I guess this means that the summit's still on, huh?'

'Yes, it's still on,' replied Beaumont somewhat disinterestedly. 'I don't know why I should be so surprised really. In Oman we had a logo at the Al Bustan – a red cross shape – and some Saudi cleric said that was offensive and we had to change that. Bloody thing was sown into carpets, laid into marble, everything. But at least we had more time then. Still, I suppose it'll provide the club with spares of everything for a few years.'

The two continued their morose party while the bush telegraph went to work. Russell had overheard most of the story and a couple of phone and radio calls later, the whole island knew that the St Peter's Club had just been renamed 'Peter's Club'.

Amman, Jordan

THE LAST THREE MONTHS HAD PASSED frustratingly slowly for Prendergast. He had introduced new elements to his already extensive network of agents and general informants but had so far come up with nothing new on Saddam Hussein's plans. Rousan had not been seen or heard of since Ali Said had taken his last flight of fancy and his extensive bugging operations in the various hotels in which prominent Iraqis stayed when transiting to and from their home country had revealed nothing of relevance.

Prendergast had reluctantly concluded that he was going to have to go into Iraq personally to pursue his inquiries. He had done this before on several occasions and his disguise and cover had always been impeccable. However, the stakes were higher now and he did not relish the forthcoming mission.

A chance telephone call from one of his hotel informants interrupted his thoughts. It was not a place he often heard from, being a hotel of a somewhat lower profile than the preferred five-star favourites of his usual targets. The Palestinian who ran the reception, however, was a good chap and although not a frequent caller, had proven himself to be reliable and useful in the past.

'Mr Oswald,' he began, as usual, somewhat nervously. 'It's Yacoub from the Hishan Hotel. We've someone here you may be interested in.'

'Good to hear from you again, Yacoub, how are you?' asked Prendergast soothingly.

'Fine, fine, thanks. Look, I can't stay long.'

'Okay Yacoub, what do you have for me?'

'Well Mr Oswald, last night an Iraqi guy checked in. He didn't have a booking and he was very, very nervous, Mr Oswald.'

'What's his name, Yacoub?' asked Prendergast encouragingly.

'His passport says Firas Al Rahman, age thirty-one, single and profession given as businessman. But for sure, Mr Oswald, he's a soldier. Very fit, short hair, tall and strong.'

'I see. Tell me, Yacoub, you say he was nervous. Why did you think that?'

'Mr Oswald, he was sweating a lot and always looking round. He was very restless and kept his left hand in his pocket – I think he had a gun there Mr Oswald.'

'Good, good – well observed, Yacoub. How long is he staying?'

'He said a few days, wasn't sure – paid cash for a week's deposit though and said he wasn't to be disturbed. I – er – put him in one of your – er – special rooms, Mr Oswald. Was that okay?'

'Sounds fine, jolly good Yacoub, you've done well – many thanks. Can you keep me posted on his movements and maybe we'll pay a little visit shortly – okay?'

'Yes sir, Mr Oswald sir, thank you very much sir.'

'Bye Yacoub,' concluded Prendergast and hung up. He then turned to his computer and started checking names. Some minutes later, as the green letters stared back at him from the old monitor, his pulse quickened, for now he possibly had a lead.

Al, Rahman – Firas – Captain, Republican Guard
Born 06 JUN 1969.
Single – no dependants – parents deceased.
Joined army 01 JUN 1985 – Undistinguished record then applied for and joined Republican Guard on 15 NOV 89.
Involved with initial assault troops on Kuwait City in Gulf War, 02 AUG 1990, holding rank of sergeant.
Decorated with Medal of Valour by Saddam Hussein 12 JAN 91 and promoted to captain.
No further action in Gulf War.
Joined Special Services unit 20 MAR 1993 for special duties.

'Well, well, well!' mused Prendergast aloud. 'This seems like a chappy who needs talking to.' He called his deputy to discuss the situation and plan a meet. This needed action, and fast.

The problem with communities in which high-level intelligence activities are taking place, is that there are always other interested parties listening and observing.

Accordingly, Yacoub's call had been noted by the evening porter at the Hishan, whose reporting line went east instead of northwest. The chief of intelligence at the Iraqi embassy, who ran similar and possibly more extensive networks even than Prendergast throughout Jordan, received the news of Captain Al Rahman's arrival at about the same time as his MI6 counterpart. He did not, however, discuss it with his deputy but rather sent a brief coded message by radio to his boss in Baghdad, Colonel Rousan.

His reply came back rapidly and succinctly. He was thanked for his information and invited to forget it. 'I sometimes wonder why I bother,' thought the frustrated officer, and turned his attention to other matters.

However, in another part of town, a muscular young man received his instructions by telephone, and straight away set off for the Hishan Hotel.

When Prendergast's deputy arrived at the Hishan a couple of hours later, he asked the clerk at reception for Mr Al Rahman's room and was immediately given the number. He arrived outside the door which he found to be slightly ajar, knocked and then cautiously pushed it open.

The deputy was not a very experienced operative and the sight that greeted him made him instantly throw up. When the retching stopped, he was still shaking and sweating but was able now to look at the grotesque sight before him. The body of what had once been a strong and athletic man was now laying chest down on the floor. His head was almost totally severed from his torso and his life blood surrounded him in a huge pool, only partly absorbed by the threadbare and grubby carpet. Pulling himself together, the deputy called his boss which led to a succession of sensitive telephone calls throughout Jordan's General Intelligence Department.

Later that day, Major Ibrahim of the GID called Prendergast to confirm that the affair had been wrapped up. However, would Prendergast mind explaining why the British were interested in the corpse of a Jordanian national who, until his unfortunate demise in a strange hotel room, had been a bulldozer driver on the country's never-ending road developments?

The race was now on to find a resourceful and frightened Iraqi captain.

Autumn 1995
Porlock, England

A DULL AND DREARY SUMMER had come to an end. All the schools were back and tourists were rare, except for the elderly who had few cares for the weather and even fewer responsibilities. They pottered into Porlock Weir, looked around the drab, boulder-strewn beach, surveyed the grey and inhospitable sea and the overcast and still greyer sky and mostly drove straight back out again. Depression they could get for free at their age – they didn't need to come to gloomy, remote North Devonshire villages for it.

The group staying at Tytherleigh had blended in well over the previous weeks and were by now well acquainted with both their environment and neighbours. They had cultivated an air of eccentricity and were now known locally as 'Bennett's barmy boys'.

This suited their purpose well as they advanced their cover of setting up an adventure training centre. Newcombe had been in touch with some of his previous contacts from Wales and had several school expeditions booked for the autumn. They rightly reasoned that this would reinforce their alibi and, equally importantly, provide everyone with something to do. They had all become very fit, were fully familiar with their plans and now were restlessly biding their time.

It was high tide and pouring with rain on the morning that Masterson and Cooper nursed the Vosper over the shallows into the tiny harbour. The deep, throaty rumble of the engines invited some curious inspection from a few locals, but mostly they had the place to themselves.

Bailey, however, had come out from his pub to see the harbour's new arrival and cat-whistled at her appreciatively.

'What are you going to do with that little beauty then?' he called over to Newcombe who was just going round to the old lock gate at the inner entrance of the harbour, in which a few yachts floated idly. 'Didn't you lot know they've got things called helicopters now to pick people out of the drink?' and consumed by his own wit, stuck his hands on his huge hips and roared with laughter.

Newcombe rolled his eyes and ignored him, while Chater, who was running up to join his boss, provided the explanation.

'New bit of gear for the AT centre. Not bad, eh?'

'Take me for a ride, Mr Chater?' called Jill from an upstairs window. He looked up, waved a hand dismissively, muttering under his breath, 'Get out of it.'

'Blimey,' said Bailey, wiping a tear from his cheek, seemingly not to have noticed his daughter's flirtation. 'I thought for a moment you'd declared war on the Taff's.' And pointing to the southern coast of Wales across the estuary, he again collapsed with laughter before retiring back into the warmth of his hostelry.

'He's a bleedin' nutter, that one,' said Little George who'd only recently arrived in Porlock and joined up with the group.

'Yeh, so is his nympho daughter. Right little hussy, she is. She'll get herself into trouble one day,' predicted Chater lugubriously. They had now all assembled in the dock and were critically eyeing up the Vosper. Masterson and Cooper had done a magnificent job on her and she rested at her mooring with the pride and understated strength that was her hallmark. She was the same sea-grey colour as when she had first been commissioned but now lacked the RAF insignia. Instead, painted on her stern was her new name, *Al Batross,* which everyone thought very funny, and her new port of registration, Cowes.

When everyone had inspected her thoroughly, she was battened down and the two sailors taken over to the Anchor for a much deserved toast.

'*Al Batross*' they all roared in unison and then laughed happily. Bailey, who didn't understand what on earth they were talking about, laughed with them anyway.

The next few days were spent familiarising themselves with the boat and conducting essential sea trials. Time was marching on and it was imperative that the team were fully acquainted with the vessel's capabilities and workings.

Then came the day for which they had all been longing – the collection of their arsenal. Kate Lladro had a much larger consignment of weapons heading north into the Irish Sea and so the relatively small order of Carson's was easy to piggyback on to it. Most of the team were galled at the idea of arms being supplied to the Irish. However, they soon realised that their mission was also distinctly lacking in moral virtue, so they buckled down to the job in hand and kept a lid on their thoughts and reservations.

The rendezvous with the large fishing boat was scheduled for dusk, 200 nautical miles due west of the Bishop Rock lighthouse on the Scilly Islands. Masterson was somewhat anxious about this as the seas in this area were turbulent and unreliable at best. The idea of ship-to-ship transfers did not amuse him but he reasoned that they would soon enough be up against even more demanding challenges, so he kept his own counsel.

The group set out from Porlock an hour before dawn of the day prior to the rendezvous. It consisted of Newcombe, Chater, Little George, Carson, Masterson and Cooper. They wanted to recce the pick-up area thoroughly before they met the fishing boat. They certainly did not want to get picked up by the authorities for gun running for the IRA.

Scott was staying back at Tytherleigh to co-ordinate with the Vosper in case of emergency and to establish radio communications that could not be traced immediately it was used. The idea was that they could radio from or to their base at Porlock using a scrambler. There they would have a receiver linked into a telephone network that would eventually be routed to wherever they wished. The network accessed a system once set up by the SAS for their secure use to make untraceable calls when on clandestine missions in other countries. Newcombe had been relieved to find that it was still operational.

The trip was relatively smooth. A slight Atlantic swell was running but it was clear and dry. Once the dawn came, the night chill dissipated and the trip was enjoyed by all, punctuated with the occasional sightings of tankers and cargo vessels being spewed out of the English Channel to all the points of the globe. They kept their distance as much as possible from these busy sea lanes. They were, after all, a bit of a novelty on the high seas and needed to keep a low profile.

They reached the rendezvous at noon the next day and began to quarter the area with radar and binoculars. As the day wore on the tension slowly mounted. By late afternoon the group was becoming anxious as there was still no sight of their contact and it was almost dark when the first blip showed up on the radar. The arranged codes were exchanged by radio between the two vessels and they slowly moved together. They were in hailing distance when Newcombe suddenly felt an overwhelming sense of vulnerability and unease. They were totally unarmed, coming up against a bunch of ex-perienced and doubtlessly cutthroat buccaneers. Their only advantage was a superior craft and, hopefully, the fact that the rogues probably did not even consider that they might not have a weapon.

'Ahoy there, *Al Batross*,' called a guttural Spanish voice from the fishing vessel's bridge, 'we have a small package for you. Send your tender over and we can both be on our way.'

Although dark now, Newcombe could just make out the name of the ship, *Pila,* registered in the eastern Spanish fishing port of Palamós. This accounted for the now almost overwhelming smell of dead fish wafting over the water. He hoped the weapons were well sealed.

'Ahoy *Pila,*' he called, 'our tender's a bit small – can you dispatch yours?'

'Negative *Al Batross,* and you better hurry up since the fishing here's real bad and we don't want to hang around.'

'Where's Suarez?' called Carson. 'He usually manages this run for the Señora.'

'He couldn't make it, all right?' came the blunt reply. 'Anyway what's it to you? You want your gear or not?'

'Okay, okay,' called Newcombe, 'we're on our way.' Then to his men, 'Jim, Nick and Tony – you take the Zodiac over but for God's sake watch out. I don't trust this bunch. Brian, get our boat as close as possible. Let's move it fast, we may have to make a couple of trips.'

'Or a quick getaway,' murmured Jim.

Just then the tell-tale sound of a bullet being loaded into the breech of an automatic pistol was heard and they looked round to see Little George arming a .32 calibre Beretta. He handed it over to Chater and said, ''ere you are, me ol' son. Never know when it may come in 'andy. Mind you, bloke your size is more frightenin' wivout a gun than wiv it. There's five more roun's in the magazine and 'ere's a couple o' spare clips for good measure.'

'Thanks, George,' replied Chater, making the automatic disappear into a huge hand.

Then to Newcombe's relief, Carson also produced a handgun, but it was too dark to see which model. 'Cagey bunch!' he thought. Cooper then added, 'Apart from various knives which we all seem to have, there's also a twelve-bore shotgun in the wheel house and a flare gun. Don't worry, we'll manage this bunch okay, and if we can't we shouldn't be trying the main mission anyway.'

'That's true enough,' answered Newcombe. 'Right lads, let's move it and get this over with ASAP. Good luck.' The large inflatable was now in the water, engine running and Masterson at the controls. Chater and Carson jumped in and they set off on the short distance to the *Pila*.

Although anxious, this was the first bit of real action and danger most had had in many months and they were all quietly and professionally enjoying it. They came alongside the *Pila* and a line was thrown over to them to tie up. A couple of burly sailors dropped a rope ladder over the ship's side, as although the gunnels were not too high above the water, in the swell it was too much to jump or clamber over safely. Masterson stayed in the Zodiac while Chater and Carson went aboard.

They were greeted by a thick-set, swarthy Spaniard with a cap set at a jaunty angle on greasy, unkempt hair and a foul-smelling cheroot wedged in a mouth displaying more gum than teeth. A tatty old oilskin jacket hung open to reveal a revolver stuck into his belt and a large fish-gutting knife in a sheath at his side. There were two other crew members visible and each seemed more piratical than the first, who now introduced himself.

'I'm Alvarro.' He did not offer a hand in greeting. 'There's your gear, so get it off quick and we can all get out of here.'

'We'll go as soon as we've checked it, Alvarro.' This from Carson, who to Chater's surprise, had just become unusually more authoritative and forceful.

'Okay, but hurry it up.' He gestured to two of his henchmen to give them a hand to open up the boxes. The four started opening up the crates, but as the top-of-the-range hardware inside showed itself under the vessel's stern lights, a greedy gleam came into Alvarro's eye. He whispered instructions to his two other crewmen, José and Carlos, and they quietly raised their weapons to cover the group.

'That's some pretty fancy gear you've got there Carson, isn't it? Suarez had told us it was just a bunch of old AK47s but this stuff must be worth a fortune.'

Carson felt the extra danger immediately and turned round to see a large old Colt revolver pointed at his chest.

'Not a sound from either of you' he said as he pulled back the hammer. Chater spun around but stopped still as he, too, saw himself neatly covered by another crewman. The other two pulled away and joined their leader.

Alvarro told José to get Masterson in from the tender then instructed the two Englishmen, 'You, lie face-down on the deck, hands on your head – quick.' He reinforced his order with a flick of his gun and they obeyed.

Alvarro was about to issue further orders when he was interrupted by José, talking fast in Spanish and seemingly very distracted. Cursing, he stomped over to the side looking around. The boat seemed to have disappeared into the darkness and the inflatable was now empty. 'Where the fuck they all gone? Your friends all got cold feet, huh? Well, they don't got any guns and they just lost two compradors. He raised his revolver, but to his astonishment heard not the single shot from his Colt but the loud clatter of a small machine gun. It was his last thought as he fell back lifeless to the deck. José went the same way and Carlos, who was twisting round to return fire, found his ankles grabbed in a vice-like grip, and had hardly hit the deck when two massive hands grabbed his neck and snapped it like a dry twig. The remaining two crewmen had taken cover and were shooting with an automatic into the darkness by the wheelhouse from where the machine gun had sounded.

At that moment an arc light pierced the darkness and the throaty roar of the Vosper rumbled by just feet from the fishing boat. The light picked out one of the crewmen, who was completely exposed from the seaside, and the blast of the twelve-bore from Newcombe lifted him off his feet and hurled him through the glass window of the wheelhouse.

There was a cry from the darkness as *Pila*'s sole survivor decided that enough was enough. 'Please señors, please, I surrender, I. . . .'

There was an ugly sounding gurgle followed by the thud of a body landing heavily on the steel deck.

Masterson emerged from the shadows, dripping wet, with a small Uzi submachine gun in one hand and a large hunting knife in the other. He called out loudly and clearly. 'Ship under control, major. About to conduct search of vessel and secure. Tony, let's check out below. Nick, make sure these jokers are all has-beens.'

'You all okay?' called Newcombe.

'Affirmative, major,' replied Masterson and disappeared down a hatch, followed by Carson. There was not much to check and they were back on deck in minutes. Chater had completed his inspection and found that indeed, the Spanish crew were all history. He looked up at Masterson with a grin.

'You SBS guys don't hang about do you? Bloody heck, that was some nifty work.'

'Yeh, well . . . major,' he called over to the Vosper. '*Pila* secured and under our control. All crew dead and accounted for.'

'Shit!' muttered Newcombe under his breath, then louder, 'Good work. We're going to try and get alongside you and tie up. Can you put down some fenders and be ready to take lines?'

'Will do.' The party aboard *Pila* put down their various weapons and prepared to receive *Al Batross*. Although the swell made it difficult, Cooper's superb seamanship soon had the old launch in position and firmly tied up to the fishing vessel. He stayed aboard with the engines ticking over while Newcombe and George clambered up to the Spanish boat. George was grinning hugely and really seemed to be enjoying himself. The others, however, all seemed more serious. They were efficient at what they did and had been highly trained for it to varying degrees. They did not actually relish taking life, though, and now was a time to consider their position and circumstances carefully.

Carson by this time had fully checked the cargo. Their own consignment was complete to specification while the main bulk seemed to consist of old AK47 assault rifles and ammunition, explosives, mainly old-fashioned sticks of dynamite and attendant detonators and wiring.

'So, what shall we do about this little lot?' asked Chater.

'Nick, George and Tony, you get our gear transferred to *Al Batross*,' commanded Newcombe. 'Then cast off and one of you bring the Zodiac round and get her aboard and stored also. Jim and I will fix this boat to scuttle her, then Brian can come by and pick us up.'

'What about all them guns?' asked George. 'Reckon they could come in 'andy, major?'

'No. They're not ours and we don't need them. Come on, we've been here long enough. Let's get moving.'

They went about their respective tasks and Masterson and New-combe rigged the whole vessel with the explosives to blow her out of the water, along with the grisly remains of her crew. The task took longer than expected but after half an hour they were ready with fuses set for detonation in ten minutes.

The others had completed their orders and were now waiting astern of the doomed fishing boat. Cooper brought the Vosper in close and the two jumped aboard as she passed, eager hands catching them as they landed.

'Right Brian, get us the hell out of here.' Cooper did not need a second bid and in seconds had the powerful launch travelling at full speed away from their fateful rendezvous.

The fireball that preceded the roar actually erupted several minutes early, but they were safely out of danger by then. What was left of the *Pila* sank immediately along with the evidence of her last hours.

'Well, that was a dandy evening's caper,' said Chater pulling on a large gin and tonic. The victualling of *Al Batross* had included a well-provisioned bar in the main cabin, among less indulgent commodities. 'What else have you got planned for us this evening, Mike?' Out of the combat situation, the use of rank was again replaced by the informal camaraderie of first names for their leader. This had not been discussed but just seemed to come naturally.

Newcombe replied, 'Let's get back home and talk it through with Ian after a decent meal and rest. It's been a while since any of us had this sort of action and we need to get right out of the combat zone to discuss tactics and implications.' He swallowed hard on a beer.

'I agree,' said Masterson. 'If you gentlemen will excuse me, I need to get out of these clothes and warm up. Right now I'm freezing my bollocks off.'

'Yeah, go ahead Jim,' said Chater. 'Incidentally, that was a nice job you did back there – thanks pal.'

'Forget it.' And with that he retired to the bunks up forward.

As Cooper took the Vosper home, the others relaxed and slept. Only Carson remained awake and kept Cooper company in the wheelhouse. He was quite shaken after the ordeal and they spoke little. He could not help wandering what Kate would think of all this when she eventually found out. The lady would definitely not be amused!

Tel Aviv, Israel

IT WAS WITH CONSIDERABLE CHAGRIN that the intelligence officers gathered with Ari Diarra admitted that they were still no closer to determining Saddam's plan for the GCC Summit Conference. All their usual information sources had drawn blanks and one had ended up in Baghdad's dreaded Abu Ghraib jail for asking suspicious questions – he would never be heard from again.

The only information of interest was the news from Amman regarding the Iraqi captain who was on the run. Whether there was any connection could not yet be determined, so all resources were set in motion to find Captain Al Rahman.

Ari Diarra also decided it was time to talk with Oswald Prendergast and find out just what the Brits were up to. They always seemed so vague and hopeless but he knew this to be a cover for a keen and efficient intelligence service. He was sure Prendergast would be after the same information as Mossad and felt that this was perhaps one occasion when the pooling of resources would be advantageous. When the short meeting was over, he made his call.

Antigua, Leeward Islands

THE NEWS OF THE CLUB'S NAME CHANGE had met with mixed reactions. Mainly, however, most of the staff thought the whole thing highly amusing.

Meanwhile, the preparations for the big event were continuing at a pace rarely, if ever, seen on the islands. Grandstands were being constructed on the far side of Mamora Bay and at Shirley Heights. Conference and dining facilities were being built to a quality and standard unimagined by most involved, except for the gangs of Asian workers who had been flown in to create the sumptuous arrangements.

Marshall, along with the Nicholsons, had managed to arrange a series of world-class boating events for the summit. The yachties, however, had commitments the other side of the world and so it had been agreed to just stick with the powerboats. Anyway, everyone figured that this would be more fun for the principals in the audience, especially now that the Bahrainis were fielding a team to challenge the long-running winning streak of their rivals from Dubai. They had for years been dominating international powerboat racing and it would be fun to see new faces on the winners' podium.

Beaumont, Marshall and Schwartz were having a beer at the pool deck, when a familiar figure came up and joined them.

'Well, well, well, just the very gentleman I'm looking for. Fancy buying an old seadog a Red Stripe?'

'Sure Mike, sure. Have a seat,' offered Beaumont and Mike Church, ex-chief petty officer, Royal Navy, needed no second bidding.

Although he was now a smuggler and a drunkard, Mike Church considered himself primarily the skipper of the fifteen-metre charter yacht *Paladin*. On this fine vessel, wealthy tourists would see the Caribbean islands in their fullest glory and be entertained by the endless tales of one of the world's last great seafarers. The fact of the matter, though, was that Church rarely ever had charters at all and his agent, the wheeler-dealer and piratical John Gavat in Antigua, usually only ever came up with smuggling ventures. Still, as long as he was able to keep *Paladin* afloat and his belly and brain full of Pusser's Rum, he was happy enough.

However, Church now had a five-day charter out of English Harbour in Antigua. Titi, the ever smiling local owner of Colombo's Bar and Restaurant, had arranged it for him (probably because he was owed so much money from Mike) and he had duly collected the 'couple' as scheduled. Church, meanwhile, hitched a lift round from English Harbour to scrounge some liquor and food supplies from his sometime benefactors at the club. He left behind his mate, the big, burly and friendly South African, Steve Hellerman, who was now preparing the yacht for departure, and Ann Fraser, who Church used as a cook and hostess on the few occasions he had important charters.

After a couple of drinks, Church asked of his host, 'I don't suppose you could lend me supplies for the charter? I'll be able to pay you back at the end, I mean, it's good money.'

'Mike, it never occurred to us for a moment you'd come round for the love of our company,' sighed Beaumont. 'You still owe us a couple of hundred EC dollars from the last trip.'

'I know, I know, but I'll make it up to you, honestly.'

'Okay, I'll have them make up a box, but this is the last one.' He ordered the necessary victuals and told Church to wait for them in the lobby.

It was early evening when Church returned to English Harbour, several more bottles of Red Stripe the worse, boarded *Paladin* and told his crew to prepare for departure. He was not going to let on to the charterers that the engine had not been working for months, so off they sailed into a glorious Caribbean sunset.

Tortola, British Virgin Islands

W HAT TITI HADN'T TOLD CHURCH was that the 'couple' were two gays from New York whose main interests were centred on the bedroom. Accordingly, the scenic trip that Church had planned and the gastronomic delights of Ann were all in vain. After a couple of days, the boys were craving dry land and took their leave in Tortola where Church and Hellerman diligently set about drinking their earnings. Ann, who had seen similar displays before, remained on board, tidied up and took an early night.

At around midnight, in a state of total inebriation, Church and Hellerman staggered back to *Paladin*. Rather than sleep, however, Church decided to set sail then and there for Antigua. Hellerman was too dazed to argue and so they set off.

When sober, Church's skill as a navigator was excellent. Indeed he was one of the few skippers in the region who actually possessed and knew how to use a sextant. However, on this particular starry night he didn't even look at his compass and, even if he had, it was not long before he fell asleep at the wheel.

One of the delights of the Caribbean waters are the endless succession of beautiful coral reefs, home to myriads of exotic fishes.

But to unlucky or unwary sailors, they have spelt disaster for centuries, and that night Mike Church and his hapless crew joined their ranks.

Paladin hit the reef with such force that both Ann and Hellerman were thrown from their bunks and woke up sprawled on the cabin floor. Church woke with a start, leapt to his feet but before comprehension fully dawned, was struck violently on the head by the wildly swinging boom and passed out.

Hellerman, although sobering up fast, was still somewhat dazed, so Ann took charge. They took account of their position and by putting up more sail, pushing and shoving with boat hooks, floated themselves off the reef. A quick inspection revealed that *Paladin* was holed in three places and was taking water slowly. She did not appear to be too badly damaged, so with the lights of Tortola still visible, they limped back to harbour.

The next day Ann flew home to Antigua, without having been paid, while Church and Hellerman nursed their hangovers and contemplated their gloomy position. They had a damaged boat in need of repair, no work and no money. Hellerman could skip off but unless a miracle came in for Church, he was about as completely bankrupt as could be. He searched for his miracle in the last of the Pusser's Rum.

London, England

T HE PRIME MINISTER ENTERED the room and everyone stood.

The OPD committee were meeting at the ungodly hour of six AM and, although prepared for it, most did not feel at their freshest. Sir James Parsons, who over a lifetime of government service had become used to the unexpected with politicians, asked himself grumpily for the umpteenth time why it was that prime ministers always seemed to have so much energy – or most of them anyway, he corrected himself. Before all were fully again seated, the prime minister asked: 'Well, Sir William, full update please.'

'Certainly, prime minister,' and for the next ten minutes the director general of MI6 proceeded uninterrupted.

'So what you're saying, Sir William,' he finally interjected, 'is that we know nothing except that our turbulent friend in Iraq is up to something! Wonderful!' Some of the committee members shuffled uncomfortably in their seats, hoping to distance themselves from the hapless intelligence chief. This was an awkward situation for all of them and they were glad for MI6 to be in the hot seat, however temporarily, before their turn came.

'Well, prime minister, we are certain he's planning some kind of destabilisation in the region.' Replied the SIS chief defensively. 'All the signs point to it and the opportunity is perfect. As soon as Prendergast finds this Captain Al Rahman, we'll know more and be able to take things from there.'

'That's all very well but we're getting short of time and suppose he doesn't find this chap? What then, hum?'

'I have every confidence we'll get him, prime minister and. . . .'

'Well I don't share it,' interrupted the PM uncharacteristically. 'I want every resource put on to this and I also think it's high time we talked to our allies on the subject. Should have done so ages ago. Please see to it. Now, how are the GCC Summit plans going for the Caribbean? I suppose there's no chance they've changed their minds, is there?'

The foreign secretary drew the spotlight from Sir William and advised the committee on the situation. He even brought a refreshing chuckle from the group when describing the St Peter's Club name change at the insistence of the Bahrainis.

'Should we tell them of our concerns, do you think?' asked the PM of his eldest, most trusted and experienced statesman.

'I don't think so yet, prime minister. Frankly, we really don't have much to tell them and we'd end up looking rather silly. No, I feel the best thing is to get something concrete in our hands before we start worrying them.'

'All right, I agree. Does anyone else have anything to contribute? No? Then perhaps Sir James, you'll be good enough to bring us back together again when we have something to talk about.' And with that frosty remark, the prime minister made his exit.

Sir William took himself off to his private office and on his secure line tried contacting Oswald Prendergast in Amman. He was out and so an appropriately cryptic message was left for him to call back. He then lifted the phone and placed a call through to his long-time colleague in Tel Aviv, Ari Diarra.

'Well William, I wondered how long it would be before you called.' Diarra laughed to take the sting out of his words. 'Actually, I was going to call you. I've just recently spoken to your man Prendergast. Naturally he's being a bit cagey – maybe he needs a nudge from you to lighten up – but I think this is one we should work on together. What do you think?'

'Quite agree, old boy, quite agree. If that bastard's up to mischief again, we've got to get him. How are your enquiries going then?' Sir William tried not to sound too hopeful.

'Frankly, William, we've got nothing that you guys don't know. Anyway, I proposed to Prendergast that we meet up in Istanbul and discuss a joint plan of action right away.'

'Fine, I'll give him full authorisation to pool resources and liaise with you chaps. Anything else?'

'Well yes, there is one thing you may wish to sniff around a bit. Not so much your territory really, so you may be in the dark. We had an agent over on your patch a while back, I won't give you his name,' they both chuckled at this, 'who was keeping an eye on an arms dealer who'd had a bit of a run-in with the powers that be in the Emirates. Nothing very exciting really, more routine than anything else.'

'What of it,' asked Sir William, interested? 'What's the dealer's name?'

'Man called Carson, Tony Carson.'

'Oh, I know the one. Worked for Short Brothers, pretty legit', though, isn't he? "5" was keeping an eye on him.'

'Yes, well that's the point. It seems that Carson has dropped completely out of sight and the shadow from MI5 ended up dead in a wood.'

'Good God, when was this? Renard's said nothing about it.'

'Well actually, it was early summer, when we first all started getting a whiff of things. We didn't connect it up then with Iraq and it still may be irrelevant, but since none of us have much to go on, and Carson is a well-connected international dealer, maybe we should follow it up, one way or the other.'

'Too bloody right,' seethed Sir William. 'This is exactly the sort of nonsense we get into with amateurs running the services. I owe you one for this Ari – thanks.'

'No problem – Let's get things rolling and we'll keep in touch. You take care of yourself now, William.'

'You too Ari, 'bye.'

The ripples from a bad-tempered prime minister in England first thing in the morning were spreading. By the time Prendergast returned Sir William's call, his boss was in a rare and foul rage. He was apprised of the information from Mossad and told to get some results or not bother coming home. Not being used to having his head so summarily bitten off, his usual calm and poised façade evaporated and he too hissed and spat all the way to Istanbul that evening on a Royal Jordanian flight. By the time it landed, the entire crew wished they had not had the particularly unpleasant passenger in seat A2.

Sarah Renard, too, was surprised by Sir William's sharpness, but attributed this to the roasting he had received early that morning. Usually they got on fine. Anyway, she agreed to his demand for an urgent meeting, which normally would have been over lunch, and they met in his office later that morning.

Sir William was barely able to be the courteous gentleman for which he was renowned. After offering his guest coffee, he said, 'I'll come straight to the point. I understand a few months ago you lost an agent involved in a surveillance operation on an international arms dealer who has since disappeared. In view of the issues currently facing us, I was wondering if there was something you'd like to tell me?'

The director general of MI5 had not been a hardened intelligence specialist but rather a professional businesswoman. She had been very upset by Henshaw's death but, until now, had hoped the case to have been forgotten. Before she even replied, her face had spoken volumes to her inquisitor.

'We didn't know it was a dealer he was on to. We'd followed up on all his current files but there was nothing like you've described.' She was trying to put a brave face on the situation. 'Anyway, who was the man and, now I think of it, how do you know so much about it all of a sudden?'

'Never mind how I know,' replied Hood in a rather superior manner. The dealer's name is Carson. Here's a file on him. Perhaps you would be kind enough to activate a full-scale investigation and hunt for him and let's see if we can find any connection with this Iraqi business. Frankly, whether we do or not, I'm sure you will now want to have words with him in any case.'

There was little more to be said and as Renard rose to leave, Hood stopped her and said, more gently than before, 'We're on the same side, you know Sarah. It's imperative we talk more, at least if only to each other. Keep me posted, all right?'

She nodded and left.

Amman, Jordan

Captain al Rahman was frightened. It was not so much the idea of dying that worried him. He was, after all, a professional soldier and violent death was always possible. No, it was more the way in which he might die and the time it would take that upset him which, if he fell into the wrong hands, would assuredly be excruciating and long.

After his unexpected visitor at the Hishan Hotel, he realised he could not go anywhere in public and so determined to risk contact with an old acquaintance from his early army days.

Brigadier Samir Raslam was a bluff old warrior who claimed to have survived more campaigns in the region than historians had documented. Whether or not he had ever been a brigadier was similarly ill-documented. He sported an enormous handlebar moustache and had a perpetual air of apparent good will about him, an impression rapidly dispelled when one saw his eyes which were black and humourless.

He was currently the chief security officer at the InterContinental Hotel in Amman where he was feared and despised by the management and staff alike, including the general manager. He led a soft and easy-going life there, fabricating evidence and arranging the occasional arrest of certain staff to secure his position.

Al Rahman had met Raslam whilst he had been on a training secondment to Iraq in the late 'eighties, when still a serving officer in the Jordanian army. Al Rahman had been a good student and it was largely thanks to his mentor that he had later secured his post in the Republican Guard. It was thus to his former teacher that he now turned.

When his office phone rang, the security chief could not remember his caller, but pretended he did. The young Iraqi officer asked for a meeting outside the hotel, but the brigadier insisted that he come in and see him in his office.

'After the meeting, then we will have some lunch.'

He was not going to miss a chance to show off his nice desk and office and sign the bill in the restaurant to this lad. One never knew how important chance contacts like this could turn out and it so was necessary to impress – pleasant also.

When the captain arrived in the hotel there was no sign of Raslam in the lobby as he had promised. Al Rahman prowled restlessly around, his anxiety mounting and eventually went to the porter's desk to have him paged.

If there were networks covering small hotels such as the Hishan, Amman's larger hotels were riddled with them. Several people had noticed the man who seemed uncomfortable in the rarified atmosphere of an international hotel lobby. However, it was the head porter who paged the security chief, then made a more discreet call, this time not through the hotel operator.

The call was answered in old downtown Amman in a small and shabby, yet completely legitimate gun dealer's shop run by Rashid Masri. He was an old and wizened man, seemingly with a perpetual running nose and rheumy eyes, who appeared on the face of it to be as decrepit as his squalid little shop. Of Palestinian origin, he was also a deep-cover agent who ran Mossad's operations in Jordan.

He received the news of the visitor to the hotel dispassionately, thanked his caller, whom he had never actually met but sent regular and generous payments to, and dialled the British embassy. He politely asked for the second secretary, Commercial Department, a Mr Prendergast, proposed a potentially lucrative business opportunity for the United Kingdom and could perhaps the second secretary meet him at his head office forthwith?

Prendergast was well aware of Masri and held him in high esteem. Especially following his recent meeting in Istanbul, if Masri was asking for a meet now, it must be of the highest priority, so he left the embassy and soon entered the seedy shop downtown.

Mr Masri was at that moment praying. Prendergast was therefore obliged to contain his curiosity for a further five minutes, wondering as he did so with which God and religion his host was actually communing. He surveyed the old guns, some rusted and useless, some weather-beaten and worn, all second-hand with highly questionable mechanisms; dust-covered cartridge cases piled up haphazardly, old shotguns and the occasional ancient rifle. There was even an old bolt action, Lee Enfield .303 which quite took him back to his school cadet corps days.

His reverie was interrupted by a croaking old voice. 'Nice to see you again, Mr Prendergast, tea or coffee?'

'Hello, Mr Masri, er, tea please, thank you. How are you?'

'I'm well, thank you, well.' He broke into a bronchitic coughing fit. He then poured some tea from a dirty old pot, which seemed to be constantly simmering, into two chipped glasses and passed one to his guest.

'Thanks awfully, Mr Masri,' said Prendergast anxious to find out the reason for his summons. 'So what is it you wish to discuss?'

Masri relayed the message from the porter. 'Could be the one we're all looking for. Maybe an idea to check it out before the others do. If we know, others will too.'

'Quite, quite – I'll get onto it straight away. Can I, er, use your phone a moment?'

'Help yourself.'

Prendergast discreetly arranged to meet his deputy at the Inter-Continental's lobby in fifteen minutes. Just then, another customer entered the shop and, without pausing for thought, old Masri passed a box of fifty 9mm cartridges over to Prendergast and said, 'Thirty dinars please.'

'Old crook!' thought Prendergast, but duly paid and left. At least they were the right shells for his own gun so they would not be wasted.

Prendergast arrived a little later than his deputy who had already marked their target. Sitting in the coffee shop, the old warhorse with the enormous moustaches stood out a mile and his nervous and twitchy guest even more so. Raslam had not so much as asked after his visitor's health or circumstances, preferring infinitely more the sound of his own voice.

Prendergast and his deputy took a table nearby and ostensibly began considering the menu. 'Tell you what, go back to the lobby and think up some ruse to get Raslam out of here. I'll then make the approach on chummy.'

'You sure that's wise, chief?' asked the junior officer. 'He's already killed one person and he looks about ready to do it again. Better if I stayed, don't you think?'

'We haven't got time – just get back as soon as you can. Now go.'

The younger man left but instead of going to the lobby, went through a service door from which a staff member had just emerged. He briskly walked a short way down a rather dirty corridor and soon found what he was looking for. A couple of employees passed him but did not so much as look at him. As soon as the passage was empty, he elbowed the glass of a fire alarm. He then quickly retraced his steps to the coffee shop.

Raslam was reacting slowly to the ringing alarm which, although not loud in the public areas, was still quite audible. He shovelled another mouthful of food into his mouth, and as he rose to leave, said to his visitor, 'Don't worry, it's just another false alarm. I'll be back soon.'

Al Rahman seemed unconvinced and decided to leave. Things were not going as he had hoped. He was about to rise when two Westerners sat down at his table and with huge smiles and flawless Arabic, extended to him a warm and friendly greeting.

'Hello, Captain Al Rahman, I'm John Smith from the British embassy,' lied Prendergast smoothly, showing the surprised captain one of his embassy identification cards. 'This is my assistant Mike

Jones. We know you've been having a little trouble and would like to offer our help.'

Everything had happened so quickly that Al Rahman could barely muster his thoughts. The stress of the last few days finally overcame him and he sank back in his chair with a deep sense of relief.

Seeing the tension go out of the man, Prendergast too relaxed somewhat. Nervous and unpredictable targets could be very dangerous, and they were glad to see the fight go out of their man.

'Tell you what, captain. It's a bit public here and one never knows who else is around. Why don't we go off to our embassy? You'll be completely safe there and we can have a little chat in peace.'

Al Rahman looked at the two agents and merely nodded. The idea of moving was making him feel uncomfortable again but he realised he could not stay where he was much longer.

'Good show,' continued Prendergast. 'Mike, why don't you get the car round and see that the coast is clear. I'll be out with the captain in a jiffy.'

The younger agent left and was followed a few minutes later by his chief and Al Rahman. Shortly afterwards, a rather cross and mystified security chief returned to his table to be advised by a waiter of his guest's departure. 'What the hell,' he thought, 'the fool didn't have anything to say anyway.' He continued his lunch wondering who he would invite to confess to the vandalising of the fire alarm.

Part II
The Mother of All Summits

Winter 1995

Porlock Weir, England

NOVEMBER HAD BEEN A STORMY MONTH and it was not until early December that *Al Batross* finally set to sea with her deadly cargo and crew.

'Going down to the Med, for some Christmas warmth,' they'd explained in the bar of the Anchor the night before they left. 'It's too bloody cold and wet here and all the girls seem to do is ride around on bloody horses,' bemoaned Chater.

'Rubbish,' replied Little George. 'You just 'aven't met up with the right ones yet.' He nodded over to where Jill was grinning at him, drying up some glasses behind the bar.

'Humph!' was Chater's only reply.

They made for the Canaries to pick up the warm trade winds. Here were many boats making the Atlantic crossing and they wanted to establish some early cover and blend in with the boating community.

The journey was unadventurous and after overnighting in Las Palmas, where they ate and drank heartily and revictualled *Al Batross*, they then set course for Antigua. Although not pushing it too hard, they overhauled many sailing ships with their superior speed and finally sighted land around midday just two weeks after leaving Porlock. Their return journey would be very different and certainly much quicker.

Baghdad, Iraq

THE ROOM WAS FULL OF SOME of the toughest and most capable looking fighting men that Saddam Hussein had ever seen. During his long and bloody reign, he had met and faced challenges from many quarters and seen some of the world's fiercest warriors pitched against him; but these men were different. The very cream of his Republican Guard, they were the Special Forces elite who would now go forth and truly establish his immortality.

Their final briefing had just ended and the many weeks of severe training were now to be put to the test. The tension in the air was almost tangible, although Colonel Rousan wondered if this came from the forthcoming mission or the unexpected sight of their president. From his point of view, it was also aggravated by the total disappearance in Amman of Captain Al Rahman and the death of his trusted assassin. If the president found out about this, he dreaded to think what would happen. He just hoped that he could keep it quiet long enough for the mission to go ahead successfully, after which it would not really matter.

The president said not a word, just moved amongst the men and shook each by the hand, a tough and stretched smile on his mouth yet no warmth from his deep, black eyes.

He at last made for the door, where Taher and Fuad stood alert and watchful as ever, then turned to face Rousan and saluted him. Only those closest heard his whispered, 'May God be with you all.'

Antigua, Leeward Islands

Entering english harbour was like being in a time warp. Old fortresses guarded the harbour approaches just as they had for Admiral Nelson and huge cannons challenged from their ramparts. The harbour was a mass of activity, with yachts and vessels of all shapes and sizes bustling busily about. On the land, buildings that had changed little in 300 years provided the bars, havens, stores and hostelries required by sailors the world over.

They brought *Al Batross* in stern-to at the Copper & Lumber Store waterfront, where Marshall had been keeping a berth for them. He welcomed them effusively and they all repaired to the bar for drinks and a late lunch.

'I was beginning to think you'd got lost,' teased Marshall.

'It was the old seadog here,' said Scott pointing at Cooper. 'Something about conserving fuel and wanting to relax and enjoy the trip.' They all laughed except Little George who had been sick regularly for the first five days before finding his sea legs.

After lunch, Marshall brought them up to date on the progress at the club.

'The place is like a prison and unless you've got official passes, you can't get in or out. And they've changed the date of the summit for the fourth time. Apparently they'll all be arriving next Tuesday the 20th, so you've got five days to be ready.'

They discussed the programme until late evening and then relaxed back to enjoy Jackson's bounteous hospitality.

London, England

THE NEWS FROM AMMAN HAD SHAKEN EVERYONE and the emergency meeting of the OPD committee was highly charged. With just three days to go before the GCC Summit, most had decided that probably Iraq was not planning anything after all, which accounted for the total lack of information. The bombshell that Sir William Hood had just dropped on them was therefore all the more staggering.

'Do you mean to tell me,' asked the prime minister incredulously, 'that he is actually planning to attack all six GCC countries?'

There were some scarcely concealed smiles around the room. The defence secretary continued on from the prime minister.

'Sir William, just suppose Saddam really is planning an attack, whatever is he going to attack with? We know for sure that his military capability is obsolete and he just doesn't have the resources to do what you are proposing. I should have thought that this Iraqi captain is a plant to spread disinformation.'

'I agree,' joined in the foreign secretary, 'and we certainly are not going to start panicking everyone into reacting to a threat that can't possibly exist. Really, Sir William, I'm rather surprised by your service's performance over this affair.'

'So am I,' said the prime minister. 'This meeting is adjourned and unless any concrete developments occur, I suggest we consider this particular affair closed. Foreign secretary, a word please.' He waited until everyone had left the room then continued. 'I rather feel Sir William Hood needs putting out to grass. He's had a good innings, but this entire affair has been handled most ineptly. What do you think?'

'I'm rather inclined to agree, prime minister. As for timing though, I suggest we wait until the New Year. Let's see the next week quietly through, all the GCC heads back home and no fresh incidents from Iraq. I feel this would be the most prudent approach and then we can let him go.'

'Yes, you're absolutely right. We don't want any "I told you so" coming back in our faces. Very well, please see to it.' So deciding, they too left the meeting room.

Tel Aviv, Israel

'THEY DON'T BELIEVE HIM?' asked Shimon Peres incredulously. Israel's prime minister, who along with his popular predecessor Ishaaq Rabin before his recent assassination, had brokered a rather confusing peace accord throughout the region in 1993 and 1994, almost entirely to Israel's advantage. He had gained significant political stature and consolidated his power base immeasurably. He was there to stay.

'So it seems, Shimon.' Ari Diarra and Peres had long been campaigners together, both militarily and politically, and were also friends. When alone, they used first names. 'I've just been speaking to Hood and he says they rejected him out of hand and closed the meeting. He figures he'll probably get the chop for stirring the problem up at all.'

'Well, those idiot Brits can do, or rather not do, what they bloody well like. I want to put the military onto a state of amber alert, cancel leave and get ready fast for something nasty, whatever it might be.'

'I'm with you. We can always say it's a drill, even though it is Christmas.' With no family left of his own, Ari Diarra actually preferred the idea of an amber alert at this time of year. He was smiling wolfishly at the thought of another battle. The idea quite excited him.

'Right, I'll call a cabinet meeting immediately and get things rolling,' said Peres. 'Incidentally, if Hood and Prendergast do get the bullet, d'you think they'd like to work for us?'

Antigua, Leeward Islands

CARNIVAL! A TIME OF JUMPIN' AND JAMMIN'! A time to lavishly decorate and colour gleaming black bodies! A time for steel drums playing symphonies and sweat covered torsos writhing and twisting, leaping and turning. The splendour and exuberance of the people paled even the most exotic flowers and wildlife into drab bystanders, for they had indeed become birds of paradise themselves. These masses moved to a single rhythm like shoals of coral fish disturbed by an alien body in their midst. It was mysterious and, for an outsider, impenetrable – it was a force to be seen and marvelled at but not understood – it was simply, Carnival.

Hurricane Salome had destroyed Antigua's most popular and important annual event, which traditionally took place in August. The summit conference just before Christmas, therefore, was a great excuse to celebrate and, at the same time, bid the island's illustrious guests a very special welcome. It would also do no harm to old Lester Fish's popularity ratings, for there was nothing an Antiguan loved more than a week off work, not that an excuse was usually needed.

Each of the succession of aircraft that arrived throughout the day received a glorious welcome, whether it contained a head of state or clerks and typists. They all looked the same to the battery of friendly islanders on the tarmac to greet them, and they didn't want to risk upsetting anyone.

The cabinet, however, tipped off for each monarch's arrival, were always present on the tarmac to greet them and, after brief exchanges of pleasantries, see them on to their helicopters for the short flight to Mamora Bay. The kings were amazed by the bizarre greetings with so many apparently uncontrolled natives cavorting and gyrating behind the huge frame of Lester Fish. But they smiled and waved politely, for the most part, and scuttled for the sanctuary of familiar machinery.

Their security staff, however, and particularly General Ashman, were suffering from mounting tension as the day wore on. None of the Carnival capers had been planned at all and his efforts to persuade the authorities to curb the locals' enthusiasm met with mystified negation.

'Dis am de Caribbean, mun. Jus you relax now.'

Exasperated, Ashman checked back and forth with Beaumont at the club, where things seemed to be more or less under control. The pandemonium of the previous few days' arrivals of aides, helpers and hangers-on had been a nightmare. Everyone had squabbled over their room assignments, dining schedules and anything else they could think of, but this was for the most part over now. Ministers and senior military and security personnel, so it seemed, were able to check in to a hotel with slightly more decorum.

In point of fact, the only thing that had gone wrong so far was a shuttle bus hitting a cow while taking a group of Omani press corps to the club. It transpired that the senior delegate on the bus had charmed the pants off the initially irate owner of the animal and after handing over some us dollars, which the cowman understood, and a gift of frankincense, which he did not, the party went on their way unscathed, laughing and giggling and seemingly having thoroughly enjoyed the experience. Ashman put it down to shared African roots.

The helicopters clattered one by one over the club and straight out to sea to their respective host yachts. All had eventually decided to anchor in Willoughby Bay or just off the coast in front of the club

– a sort of herd instinct prevailing in such an alien environment, giving them a sense of security.

They certainly made a spectacular sight, glittering and tantalising the many islanders on the hilltops nearby who had come to view the events. As dusk fell, the ships lit up like Christmas trees with a myriad of coloured lights, quite overwhelming the best efforts of a bright young moon and the glory of the Eastern Caribbean night sky.

Across the water, His Majesty King Abdullah of Saudi Arabia prepared to receive his guests aboard his floating palace for the first of the 1995 Gulf Co-operation Council Summit events. This was his great moment, a time when his kudos would be unparalleled and his embarrassing bloody family antics forgotten once and for all.

On land, thousands of people watched patiently and expectantly, mesmerised by the scene below them. Some were laughing and chatting, others singing and dancing, all drinking or smoking and one small group, standing alone, looking on calculatingly and pensively.

And from over the hills, a never-ending pulsating chant and beat spread over and pervaded every part of the island, luring and lulling its listeners into an almost hypnotic trance which would endure for many days. Such was the magic of Carnival.

Arabian Peninsula

PROBABLY THE HARDEST PART of Operation Necklace was the deployment of the Iraqi commandos in such a way as for them to be unnoticed and yet be in position at precisely the same time. For like all commando raids, success depended on stealth, speed and surprise.

To accomplish this, Colonel Rousan had assembled a fleet of vessels, of varying speed, dimensions and purpose to transport the soldiers. All the weapons and equipment that would be needed were stowed aboard the vessels well in advance. Most of the boat owners were naturally sympathetic to the Iraqi cause but some had needed a little persuasion. For whatever the reason and motivation, all were now fully committed to the enterprise.

The first group out had gone by road over the Jordanian border directly to Queen Alia International Airport outside Amman. There they had caught a flight to Aden in Yemen and transferred by taxis quickly down to the old port where they had split into two smaller teams. The first had left almost immediately in an ocean-going fishing boat bearing Korean markings and headed up the coast towards Oman. The second stayed over a couple of nights in a seedy, flea-ridden, waterfront hotel and then they too had boarded a fishing boat, more demure than that of their colleagues, and headed in the opposite direction and then up into the Red Sea.

The second troop to have left had also journeyed from Baghdad over the border into Jordan and thence down the Desert Highway to Aqaba. Here they had split into three units and over a period of forty-eight hours had slipped quietly out of that somewhat seedy town, a distinctly poor relation to Israel's easily accessible Eilat, a short walk around the bay. The first, with farthest to go, had left in a deep-sea sports fishing boat, and another in a fine forty-foot sail and motor yacht, more generally used for the tourists that visited the region. The third group had left in an old fishing boat, which although looking as decrepit as the town, from which it came, in fact had an extremely powerful engine and was most seaworthy.

The last party out were the most exposed and vulnerable. Rousan had considered a land approach and even an air drop, but finally had settled on the sea option. Although harder, the risk was minimised and the combined effect would be greater on their enemies. So over the next three days and nights, ten innocent-looking fishing boats left Basra and headed out into the Persian Gulf.

By the evening of the 22nd of December, all fifteen craft were in the vicinity of their targets. The commandos were restlessly awaiting the coded transmission that would send them into action, while the boat owners nervously watched the time pass hoping they would not be stopped and checked by the various national patrol boats off whose territorial waters they were loitering.

In downtown Baghdad, Colonel Rousan replaced the telephone and breathed a long sigh. He was sweating profusely despite the cold and rain outside and the windows of his office being wide open. But then, he always did when speaking with his president, as did everybody else.

He had just advised Saddam Hussein that all his men were now in position and, subject to the president's final approval, was ready to launch his attacks the following night.

'Approval given!' came the flat reply and the line had gone dead.

Antigua, Leeward Islands

THE FIFTEENTH GCC Summit Meeting began at noon on 21st December, 1995. The monarchs had all fully rested after their journey and first night's reception and were now ready to do business.

Actually, their idea of 'doing business' was to exchange incessant fraternal greetings and expressions of goodwill, most of which were not that sincerely felt. The business had already been done by their ministers and minions several weeks before and the summit, as always, was really little more than a signing ceremony. However, it sent out signals of solidarity to an interested world who, for their own ease of mind and economic well-being, needed to see peace and stability in the Middle East, or at least, where the oil was.

At two o'clock, each leader was driven up to one of six magnificent villas overlooking the club where they ate sumptuously and again rested before the next meeting scheduled for five PM. The press meanwhile were given extensive briefings and duly prepared and dispatched their reports.

Beaumont, Ashman and Awaida met for a late lunch by the pool and discussed the event so far.

'I must say Lawrence, it's all going very well. You and your chaps have done a sterling job.'

'Thank you general, but it's not over yet, you know. There's still tonight's gala dinner and tomorrow's fun and games. Frankly, until they've all left the island, I'm not going to let up an inch.'

'You're quite right of course Lawrence but don't worry, things are going to be fine.' Awaida was a transformed man now that he was no longer top dog. There was no cigar wedged in his mouth, and as there was no alcohol being provided and consumed, publicly at any rate, his manner was altogether quieter and more controlled.

'Well, I hope you're right Sheikh Awaida. Will you both please excuse me now; I need to check up on the conference room.'

After he had left Awaida said, 'I'm glad you got hold of him for this. Can you imagine how Wilkinson would have managed?'

'The mind boggles,' replied the general. 'Anyway, I suppose we had better get ready for the afternoon bash. This is the important session when the major announcements will come out. Any idea what they've decided?'

'Well they still haven't agreed a common defence strategy, not that we ever thought they could. But I understand at last they have agreed on a common visa policy. Also a determination to share labour forces and so jointly clobber the expats more. Not that people like you need worry.'

'I wouldn't be too sure about that, Yaya,' replied Ashman. 'I'm useful at the moment but can easily be replaced if it seems the politically correct thing to do. Still, there's a lot of expatriates who have had a rough deal over the last few years. It wouldn't hurt to make the terminations somewhat more humane and certainly generous.'

'You're right there Paul, but my people almost seem to enjoy expat bashing. We know we'll have a less efficient replacement but we still take perverse delight in sending out our little brown envelopes. Odd bunch, aren't we?'

'Well I'm glad you said it.' They both smiled and headed their separate ways for the evening's events.

The second meeting passed predictably. That night's gala dinner went smoothly and afterwards most of the group returned to their ships. One, however, took the road back to his villa where arrangements had been made for him to indulge in his preferred and somewhat extreme sexual deviations.

The third day was the one that everybody was really looking forward to, for many different reasons.

The morning's conference was scheduled for the comparatively early start of ten o'clock and only due to last a couple of hours at the most. It was to be more a session of concluding courtesies, further expressions of goodwill and eternal thanks for a great summit and to a bountifully generous host, which for once was actually genuinely meant.

By half-past eleven they had had enough and the summit was declared over. Now it was time to party.

As host, King Abdullah took off in his helicopter first and travelled the short distance to Shirley Heights where the day's main festivities would be conducted and viewed from.

At the best of times, Shirley Heights is a magnificent place with breathtaking views over the island's southern approaches, sited for strategic superiority over English Harbour and those that would enter it. 'The Lookout', as it had been originally known, had been garrisoned and the original eighteenth century buildings nowadays served food and liquor to an insatiable crowd of locals and tourists alike.

Today the natural beauty of the setting was augmented by the billowing canvas of a massive tented structure, so designed to protect its occupants from the elements while at the same time affording them the best views Antigua had to offer.

No one could come near this canvas palace unless they had the very exclusive clearance and passes. The entire area was cordoned off by an assortment of security services from the Middle East, principally from Saudi Arabia, and the island's own defence force who, for once, were taking things very seriously.

One by one the monarchs made their brief sojourn over from the club and eventually the proceedings began. Food and drinks, non-alcoholic ostensibly but many liberally laced with rum or vodka, were there in abundance. When the last of the ministers and senior guests of honour had arrived, including half of the Fish family dynasty, a Very pistol fired a flare arcing high over English Harbour and the first of the day's races began.

Amman, Jordan

Prendergast was again finding himself on the receiving end of an exceptionally hostile and vitriolic ear bashing from his boss in London.

'If you hadn't produced such good intel in the past I'd recall you now Prendergast,' bellowed Sir William down the telephone. 'I'm the laughing stock of the intelligence community and since I'm now being cold-shouldered by Sir James bloody Parsons, I'm almost certainly for the chop. And I promise you, my friend, if I go down over this, you'll bloody well come with me; and that fucking Iraqi captain of yours will think his ex-boss was a cuddly teddy bear.'

'Sir, I'm absolutely certain on this one. Another twenty-four. . . .'

'You'd bloody well better be.'

'I am sir. Another twenty-four hours and you'll see. But are they really going to do nothing?'

'Not a bloody thing, "unless any concrete developments occur",' mimicked Sir William.

'Maybe I could drop some hints to my opposite numbers. At least then they'd be partly prepared.'

'No way, I'm afraid. The foreign secretary told me specifically after the meeting to drop it. Yet the Israelis are on amber alert and they're not even threatened. That's usually enough to shake up our people.'

'Yes, I'd heard. Well sir, we'll just have to wait and see what happens. I'll keep you informed on any developments.'

'You do that,' growled Sir William and hung up.

Prendergast, meanwhile, decided he would not 'drop it'. He therefore called colleagues in the principal areas of threat and, without giving too much away, asked if they would keep an eye and ear open and contact him directly if anything unusual happened.

When asked he described 'unusual' as simply, 'anything unexpected, old boy. Chin! Chin!'

Antigua, Leeward Islands

THE DAY'S RACING HAD BEEN SPECTACULAR. Bahrain had not managed to beat their rivals from the Emirates, even though one of the UAE Victory team powerboats had nose-dived into an Atlantic roller. Her powerful engines had driven her under without a trace and she had plunged straight to the sea-bed with the crew left to bob up a minute later in their life jackets.

Equally spectacular had been the magnificent lunch that had been prepared and by late afternoon, the racing over, the party retired to their yachts and villas for a break before the final fixture of the summit.

This was to be a presentation of thanks to the island's host, the Honourable Lester Fish, and for his people a fireworks display, the likes of which would never have been seen in the Caribbean. Huge stands had been erected on the far side of Mamora Bay to accommodate guests of honour and assorted worthies along with as many islanders who could find a slot. Those who could not sought vantage positions on the surrounding hills and waited expectantly for the proceedings to begin, scheduled for just after sundown at eight o'clock.

Arabian Peninsula

FIFTEEN LETHAL GROUPS OF MEN clad and painted fully in black, synchronised their watches. For those in the Persian Gulf and off the coast of Oman, it was 4:00 AM; and for those in the Red Sea it was 3:00 AM. Unbeknown to them all, a fanfare of trumpets had just announced the beginning of the closing ceremony for the GCC Summit meeting on an island in the Caribbean most had never heard of.

The hour was perfect. The pre-dawn: still dark, when sentries are at their most tired; when lethargy and mind-numbing dullness reign supreme over alertness; and when the sick and infirm and others, whose destiny has ordained, die quietly.

From each fleet, inflatable Zodiacs with powerful but muffled engines departed from their parent boats, packed with charges, weapons and high explosives. All ordnance for Operation Necklace was of Israeli origin, procured through the considerable resources of Colonel Rousan and designed to cause a measure of confusion and antagonism in the event of anyone being captured, something he considered to be inevitable.

The entire region was overcast but only those approaching the Omani coastline found the seas a little choppy. When each Zodiac was a mile out from its target, the engines were cut and the men began rowing hard for the shore.

Although oil is popularly considered the most important commodity in the Middle East, for those inhabiting that sparse and barren region, water has been the main resource over which they have fought.

Since the mid-seventies, the population of the region, particularly the GCC countries, had expanded beyond belief and with it the demands on the land's meagre water resources. The water table was now so low that, where accessible, major spoilage was occurring in most countries due to inevitable seepage of salt water. Huge areas that had been successfully producing dates and basic vegetables were now barren and yet the demand for fresh water increased. It was needed initially for people's domestic use, then for their farms and animals, then for industry and, finally and most extravagantly, for beautification. The roadsides were planted with shrubs and lawns; golf courses were built on open desert; parks were created with huge rolling lawns; and so the unchecked demand for water increased.

There was only one way to satisfy this insatiable need and that was with massive and exorbitantly expensive desalination plants. Saudi Arabia now had four on her Red Sea coast and three on the Persian Gulf to satisfy her thirst. Kuwait, Qatar, Bahrain and Oman each had one, while the United Arab Emirates between them possessed four. These fifteen plants provided the true life-blood for the people of this arid area and without them the consequences for the region could be catastrophic. Indeed, in just a matter of days, the sand would move back in to prove its natural supremacy.

Despite the strategic importance of the desalination plants, they were comparatively lightly policed and defended. The only exception to this was Kuwait which had learnt her lesson the hard way a few years previously.

Each attack group consisted of two inflatables. One contained scuba divers, trained in underwater demolition, while the other contained ground attack and explosives experts.

The locations of the long pipes through which the millions of gallons of salt water were sucked daily were well known to the divers, and they peeled off in twos to set their charges. Using M4, a particularly effective explosive for underwater demolition work, they fixed their charges at the huge mouths of the pipes and then at regular intervals along their lengths. The Zodiacs waited anxiously for them to return a mile offshore.

The land assault, however, was less easy. One can only kill so many sentries before an alarm is raised and the first group to encounter resistance was at the aluminium smelting plant in Dubai where over fifty percent of that Emirate's fresh water is produced. Being such a large facility, however, the attack group was one of the largest and, although some casualties were inflicted upon them, they were absorbed and the heart of the plant taken. The explosives were set and the group prepared to fight their way back to the boat.

Stiff resistance was initially encountered also in Oman. However, after a short but fierce and bloody gun fight, this too was secured and the survivors retreated to the sea.

The remainder of the attack groups were able to silence the opposition totally and had placed their explosives and retreated to their boats before an alarm had been raised. In Kuwait, though, it was a different story.

Following Prendergast's call, the local agent had tipped off the Kuwaiti Intelligence Service who had in turn warned the military that something was likely to happen. The military decided to take no chances and were waiting for their foes. The carnage was particularly gruesome, for these were the most bitter of rivals, and many were killed on both sides. A few of the Iraqi raiders were unlucky enough only to be wounded and their subsequent fate when captured did not bear thinking about.

The divers, however, had succeeded in their task and were returning to the parent fishing vessel when a Kuwaiti patrol boat picked them up. They exchanged fire but it was an uneven fight and there were no survivors. The fishing boat made a bolt for it but was quickly overhauled and taken back to Kuwait where her crew would similarly never be heard from again.

Ten minutes after the ground troops had set their charges, the detonations began. Great mushrooms of flame and smoke reached skywards and from their cores, raging infernos blazed, melting and twisting metal, incinerating and charring the bodies of defenders and retreating attackers alike. Only those who had been able to reach their inflatables and leave were spared, but in some cases this was short lived.

In Oman and by the Saudi resort region at Jeddah, patrol boats were quickly on the scene and the aggressors either killed or arrested. But any sense of accomplishment on the part of the defenders was rapidly dispelled with the later detonation of the pipe lines.

Less than an hour had passed since the commandos had left their main craft and although almost half of them had failed to return, fourteen of the Arabian Peninsula's major desalination plants had been either totally wrecked or at least seriously damaged.

And throughout the land, the drip feed and irrigation systems stopped and the desert was poised for her parching return.

Antigua, Leeward Islands

THE PEOPLE WERE THRILLED TO SEE THEIR LEADER being showered with such praise and riches. Aside from the personal endowment handled at a more private occasion through Awaida many months previously, a new hospital, school and cricket stadium were bequeathed by the generous and strange visitors. The crowds were fairly pleased to hear about the hospital, almost totally disinterested in the school and ecstatic with the news of the cricket stadium.

It was now almost nine o'clock and the speeches, prize giving and massed band entertainment were coming to an end. A spirit of restlessness pervaded the crowd.

And then with a roar, a dozen massive rockets soared one after the other into the night sky to shower great canopies of colour and heavenly patterns over the breathless onlookers. For others, the first rocket signalled the beginning of something else.

Mike Church fired his distress flares from the wheelhouse of *Paladin*, which had now been bought out by Marshall, 200 metres from the shore and just off the reef that protected the club from the big Atlantic rollers. This was also very close to the approaches to Willoughby Bay where the fleet of royal yachts and supply ships were moored. He had no engine, was showing no navigation lights and had only a small storm jib up. As he fired his last distress flare, he started broadcasting a 'Mayday' with his usual rum-soaked slur.

'Mayday! Mayday! Mayday! This is yacht *Paladin* bound for English Harbour. Have lost all power and am uncertain of present location. Mayday! Mayday! Mayday!'

Normally such a call would have met with little or no response but, because of the occasion, the island's three motor patrol boats were all cruising in the vicinity. They rarely had an opportunity to show their abilities, limited as they were and so, switching on their arc-lights, began quartering the seas. At the same time, all three radio operators starting interrogating *Paladin* at once until eventually some order was established.

'*Paladin! Paladin!* This is Patrol Boat *Hibiscus* responding to your Mayday. Can you identify any shore features? Over!'

'*Hibiscus! Hibiscus! Paladin!*' replied Church. 'There seem to be lots of big ships in a bay close to and a fireworks display by a whole lot of buildings. Also I can see waves breaking and suspect I'm about to go on the bricks. Over!'

'Christ, man, he's in Willoughby Bay by the St Peter's,' shrieked the *Hibiscus* radio operator. All formal radio speak now forgotten, the three patrol boats headed fast for the location, the first arriving within a couple of minutes. They were very close to Horseshoe Reef in the mouth of the bay, although much of this had been destroyed during Hurricane Salome.

Hibiscus crept cautiously closer to *Paladin*.

'Here, take this rope man,' invited the captain as one of his seamen threw a line over. Church made a pretence of catching it but fumbled it and dropped it back in the water. After repeating the action two more times the captain, realising Church was inebriated, told two men to board the yacht and take control. He had to manoeuvre his patrol boat carefully and did not notice that Church had quietly slipped over the side of *Paladin* into the water. He also did not notice a second man, fully clad in scuba gear, who had just set a short fuse in the Semtex-packed bows of the yacht, also go over the side.

By now the second patrol boat, *Barracuda,* had arrived and was holding station close to the first. As *Hibiscus* came slowly alongside *Paladin* to deposit the crewmen, a massive explosion ripped through the yacht and into the patrol boat. Twenty-gallon drums of petrol which were stacked on *Paladin*'s deck ignited simultaneously and a wave of flame poured over the sea, totally engulfing *Hibiscus* and spreading to *Barracuda*.

Without thought, *Barracuda*'s captain heaved his wheel round and accelerated away from the carnage and approaching flames. But in his haste, he had forgotten about Horseshoe Reef and his now rapidly moving craft ran hard aground the jagged and viscous jaws of the coral.

Paladin and *Hibiscus* were now sinking rapidly, locked together in a deathly embrace. Although the flaming inferno was burning itself out without reaching *Barracuda*, she was taking water fast in the bows and her captain was giving orders to a shocked and confused crew to abandon ship.

The third patrol boat was the *Lester Fish*, the newest and largest of Antigua's sea defence vessels. A product of the new Vosper Thornycroft yards, not far from where *Al Batross* originally emerged, she was a state-of-the-art, hugely expensive deep-sea patrol vessel. She had been patrolling farthest out and was therefore the last to arrive. Her captain and crew of six had seen the explosion and were heading to it with all speed, trying to raise her two sister ships on the radio without success. They were as yet unaware of their fates and when 200 metres off, cut speed and approached more slowly.

All hands were on deck, and so a feeble call from the water to starboard caught their attention. Lights were redirected, engines cut and within seconds a swimmer was picked out towing what appeared to be a second person. Willing hands reached down and plucked Masterson and Church from the sea.

When they were aboard, however, the two apparently exhausted swimmers sprang to life. Before the startled crew could react, Masterson was on the bridge, a small compact machine pistol, removed from its waterproof casing, pointing at the captain and first officer. Church was similarly covering the crew who were totally flat-footed.

'Everyone overboard, NOW!' barked Masterson. 'Any resistance and you will be shot dead.'

The stunned crew were too stupefied to react except for the first officer who felt he had a chance. He made a lunge at Masterson who side-stepped and hit him hard on the temple with the barrel of his machine pistol.

'Last chance. Over the side and take him with you,' he said, indicating the moaning first officer with his boot. They needed no second bidding and within seconds all were in the water and heading for the life raft of the *Barracuda*.

Everything had happened so quickly but the more efficient royal yachts were all fully alerted to a problem, however inexplicable. They had all picked up Church's initial distress call but had decided to leave it to the patrol boats. When the explosion occurred with the resultant mayhem, Captain Knowles, who, as master of the Saudi royal yacht was the senior officer of the flotilla, ordered a lifeboat and captain's launch into the water to investigate and pick up survivors. The officer commanding the launch could not make any sense of the situation but found many shocked people to collect from the water, some with nasty burns. Their stories made little sense and he radioed in to his captain what was happening. He was also surprised to see the remaining patrol boat dousing its lights and heading off out to sea towards Green Island. He called for more help.

The capture of the *Lester Fish* had gone more smoothly than Masterson and Church had dared to hope. The self-impaling of the *Barracuda* on the reef had been a sheer stroke of good fortune, saving them the risk and difficulty of having to sink the third patrol boat by firing on her. They were now headed at full speed up the coast to Green Island to collect the extra fuel for *Al Batross* that would be needed for the long trip ahead. This had been concealed there the night before and they would then rendezvous with *Al Batross* and transfer the fuel in mid-Atlantic.

Masterson's reverie was shattered by the sound of a pistol shot, followed immediately by a round of machine-gun fire. He looked down from the open fly-bridge to see a uniformed Antiguan slumped on the deck and Church lying on the deck near him, cursing loudly.

He cut the engines and jumped down to see what had happened. Church, who was nursing a wound in his chest, was swearing fluently like the old pirate he was.

'Get me some fucking rum, Jim. Bastard just came out of the engine room and fucking shot me.' Then he looked up and grinned 'Still, I cut the bugger in half, eh? Where's the frigging Pusser's?'

'Looks and sounds like you'll live, shipmate. Hold on a sec.' Despite his jocular reply, Masterson was very worried. The wound was just below the heart and as Church had been speaking, bloody bubbles of air were coming through it. He returned to the bridge and headed straight for a cabinet marked with a green cross. Apart from a few meagre medical supplies, it was as he had expected – packed with liquor. He took some of each, fixed up Church as best he could, both internally and externally, heaved the Antiguan over the side and restarted the engine. Dribbles of blood were now coming from Church's mouth and his breathing had become erratic and laboured. The ex-SBS officer had seen such wounds before and knew that the old yachtsman could not last long.

After a while, the sound of the engines obliterated the gurgling sounds from Church and when Masterson next looked, his eyes had glazed over and he was still. A cursory check confirmed that he was dead. There was no point keeping him on deck and so reluctantly, and gently, Masterson put him over the side. He drifted slowly away and then sank out of sight.

Masterson spun the wheel and resumed his course for Green Island.

The bulk of the fireworks were being launched from the top of a hill on the headland between Mamora Bay and Indian Creek. This was a great vantage point and served as a safe place to manage and present the display from. It also made ideal cover for Marshall who had concealed himself earlier amongst the scrub and vegetation and was awaiting his moment with a shoulder-held Javelin missile system.

Closely parked just below him were four Puma attack helicopters, engines turning over their great blades, active and ready to respond to any threat to the dignitaries across the bay. They were all from the Royal Saudi Arabian Air Force.

Marshall was sweating profusely. It was many years since he had seen active service and although he had had an action-packed and distinguished military career, he was nonetheless nervous. He waited until he saw the white bow wave of *Al Batross* in the mouth of Mamora Bay moving in at high speed and then fired his first missile.

The hot exhaust vents of most military helicopters are the most vulnerable and the first Javelin missile hit home with devastating effect. He was reloading when a sympathetic detonation exploded a second Puma next to the one he had hit. The third and fourth helicopters had increased their rotor revolutions, preparing to vacate the scene as rapidly as possible. The whine of their engines could clearly be heard above the explosions of the first two.

Marshall's second missile streaked down just as one of the Pumas was lifting off and it too turned into a big red fireball and crumpled to the ground. The fourth, however, managed to get airborne.

Marshall was already loading and then aiming as the surviving helicopter rose into the air seeking vengeance for its brethren like an angry hornet. It was almost at his eye level when Marshall let off his third missile which streaked home with the same effect as its two predecessors. The Puma's momentum took it into the hillside where, already on fire, it erupted in a blazing inferno.

Marshall was by now making hell-for-leather across the scrub, tearing his clothes and flesh on the numerous cacti growing in the area, and made for his pickup truck. He headed off across country to the edge of a cliff the other side of the headland overlooking Indian Creek, where he threw the Javelin and remaining missiles far out into the sea. He then struck back towards the road which he joined several miles away from the club and headed home to the Copper & Lumber Store.

Ashman had a very bad feeling. He was desperately trying to establish the Pumas' status, but the firework detonations and roars from the crowd made it impossible to hear anything. So he dispatched runners to advise the officers and guards around the VIP enclosure to be extra vigilant and alert, and proceeded there himself.

He was making his way to the VIP enclosure at a run to communicate his acute concern to King Abdullah and request that he and his guests depart the scene immediately, when the Vosper materialised at the end of the ski jetty.

At the wheel of *Al Batross,* Cooper brought the boat in fast towards the jetty bow-to. Maintaining revs he waited just long enough for Newcombe, Chater, George and Carson to leap ashore. He then reversed back out into the bay and manoeuvred the Vosper into position for a fast pick-up.

The landing party were dressed in full combat gear and each carried an MI6A2 automatic rifle with an M203 grenade launcher attached. As they landed, Chater fired off a short burst which incapacitated the three indecisive guards on the jetty while Carson and George used their grenade launchers and fired off several rounds of smoke bombs either side of the enclosure. Newcombe meanwhile had raised a small but effective megaphone to his mouth and in fluent Arabic ordered the group to remain still and the soldiers to drop their weapons.

'You are totally surrounded and any attempt to return fire will result in the immediate execution of all the GCC leaders.'

By now, all four were at the base of the stand, and climbing up through the startled guests to cover the leaders' thrones at its centre. Two other guards had been shot but any further ideas of resistance disintegrated when it was seen that Newcombe and Chater each were holding two large Mills 36 hand grenades, their pins removed and held threateningly over the royal gathering.

Switching to English, Newcombe continued, 'Everybody remain still and calm – no movement or that person dies. Tony, George – the helos, now.'

Dropping from the side of the stand, the two soldiers now fired their grenade rounds at the nearby and closely parked tender helicopters from the ships. As well as rapidly destroying them, this also caused more confusion. A further salvo of smoke bombs in a wide arc around the area completed the mayhem, reinforcing the impression that a large attack force had indeed surrounded the place. They then returned to the base of the stand and waited either side, alert for any intervention from soldiers who had not yet received the message.

Newcombe then addressed King Abdullah. 'Your Majesty, please speak into this megaphone and instruct all military personnel to keep away and make no attempt to interfere. You already know the consequences if they do not.'

Abdullah, however, was seething with rage and belligerence, distinctly contrasting some of the snivelling fear being shown by one or two of his colleagues.

'I will do nothing of the sort, you terrorist scum. . . .' he had not finished when a single shot was fired into the right shoulder of the Emir of Kuwait who was sitting on his left.

'Perhaps this will help you reconsider – now hurry,' ordered Newcombe in a quiet voice that was the more sinister and threatening in its calm and measured ruthlessness. The king made the announcement requested in both Arabic and English.

Although quiet so far, Lester Fish, who was on King Abdullah's right, now felt a need to contribute to the proceedings. He was petrified but was feeling a helpless sense of responsibility.

'You'll never get away with this. You will all be hunted and killed and. . . .'

'Shut up and count your Swiss bank accounts,' barked Newcombe. 'This is not your affair. Now King Abdullah, please be kind enough to lead your five guests down to the end of the jetty. Remember, any nonsense and you all die!'

'How do we know you will not kill us anyway?' demanded Sheikh Al Nahyan from Abu Dhabi.

'If we wanted to do that, we'd have done it already, Your Royal Highness. Now, please proceed as instructed and no one else need be hurt.' Newcombe then gestured to Sultan Qaboos from Oman. Your Majesty, please assist your colleague from Kuwait. Now, everybody, move!'

Then more loudly to the remaining guests; 'We are leaving now. Make no attempt to follow or interfere with us. Remember, you are still surrounded from behind and my men have orders to shoot to kill.' The startled onlookers had no reason to disbelieve him and remained rooted to their seats.

He prodded the Saudi Arabian king with his gun and Abdullah led the way through the ranks of appalled and stupefied ministers and guests out to the jetty. One small group of soldiers tried to rush the party but, unable to quickly select targets in the dark, fell under a barrage of fire from George.

The Vosper was now stern-to at the end of the jetty, holding station.

'Everyone aboard, quickly, and get below!'

Carson had gone ahead and was covering the group from the boat and holding a stern hatch open for the party to descend through. Sheikh Salem Al Sabah was now needing extra help and was assisted on board by two of his colleagues. Then they were off the jetty and accelerating out of the bay at full speed.

Back on land, pandemonium had broken out. Everyone was shouting and gesticulating at once but still not daring to move for fear of the unseen threat from behind. Meanwhile, high above, a glorious panoply of colour showered down on the happy and joyful crowd. The various explosions on land and all the smoke merely heightened the atmosphere of the occasion and they, along with most of the military personnel, remained blissfully ignorant of the calamity that had occurred before them.

The day before, Scott had caught a LIAT flight to the nearby island of St Bart's from where he had chartered a high-wing Cessna. Customs and immigration checks were so casual as to be non-existent and he had had no trouble in carrying his lethal cargo onto the small aircraft.

On the evening of the final ceremony on Antigua, he had filed a flight plan to St Marten's, further north up the Leeward Islands, but after take-off on schedule at 2015 hours, had soon deviated from his flight plan, dropped height to a mere fifty feet above sea level, and headed for Lester Fish International Airport on Antigua.

No international flights were listed for arrival or departure at 2100 hours and, making his silent and unannounced approach over the resort of Jumby Bay, he made his final approach.

Air traffic control was quite unaware of his existence until he pulled the Cessna up to 200 feet just at the beginning of the runway. A barrage of questions were shouted excitedly at the offending plane but Scott ignored them and concentrated on his purpose.

He had his side window open and his cargo of cluster bombs were armed and ready. A third of the way down the runway, he started dropping them out. This was no easy feat, requiring as it did controlling the aircraft with one hand while dropping the heavy ordinance with the other on a precise, and from his elevation, narrow target.

There were six bombs in all but he had only dropped five by the end of the runway. He considered circling back to drop the sixth but decided against it. Looking round as he climbed away, he could see the detonations of the first five pitting the runway with potholes that would keep the airport closed for days or even weeks. There would be no pursuit of the Brown Envelope Club from here and so he set course out to sea and his dangerous rendezvous.

London, England

T HE TELEPHONE WIRES WERE BURNING and the radios were exchanging a veritable storm of waves between the Middle East, London and the Caribbean.

Sir William Hood was in his office when the call from Prendergast came in with the news of the desalination plant attacks. There was no sense of vindication, merely clear and analytical data. While Hood had his personal assistant mobilise his department on a full emergency footing, he himself called the foreign secretary, who had been guest of honour at a formal dinner at the Savoy Hotel and was extremely displeased to be disturbed having arrived home late.

'Well, what is it?' he snapped. 'This better be important Hood or else. . . .'

'The Iraqis have attacked exactly as projected, minister. Would you be good enough to summon an emergency meeting of the OPD or would you prefer me to handle it?'

'God Almighty!' exclaimed the foreign secretary. 'I'll call the PM if you could gather the rest together. Meeting in half an hour at Number 10. I'll clear it.'

'Very good, minister,' replied Sir William calmly. He then started making the arrangements and instructed his assistant, Crispin Steele, to keep him fed with information as and when it came in. 'Also, before I go to Downing Street in ten minutes, I want information on how they're reacting in Antigua.' Then to his secretary, 'Get me Ari Diarra on the line.'

The call was connected through immediately, which surprised him not at all.

'Hello Ari, it's William Hood. How are things looking your end?'

'Well, information so far suggests a one-off strike all around the Arabian Peninsula, exactly as the Iraqi captain said would happen,' replied Ari Diarra resignedly.

'What are they trying to prove or gain d'you think?'

'My bet would be some sort of bargaining position with the threat of more grief to come if negotiations don't materialise. But what really worries me now is what the hell the reaction is going to be with all the GCC guys stuck over in Antigua. We're trying to get on to that angle now, but communications there seem completely buggered. We've got agents there naturally, but so far no sound from them and we can't reach them.'

'Okay, I'll try getting through from my side and let's keep each other posted. Got a meeting with the prime minister now which should be fun. I'll get back to you,' Hood stated bluntly as he rang off and hurried to his waiting car, Steele updating him with the last dispatches as he left. It was now 1:30 AM local time and the news from Antigua had still not come in. Quite a day lay ahead.

Baghdad, Iraq

IT WAS JUST AFTER SUNRISE when Colonel Rousan broke the news of the raids to his president. He had expected little thanks and received none. But a rare sparkle in Saddam Hussein's eyes showed his pleasure with the success of the mission. He would let them all stew for a while and strenuously deny any Iraqi involvement when the inevitable accusations came. Then the bargaining could begin.

Antigua, Leeward Islands

BY THE TIME ASHMAN HAD BROUGHT a semblance of order to the chaos around Mamora Bay, the fireworks display was over and the crowds were dispersing, oblivious to the saga unfolding beneath them.

His first efforts were spent assembling the most senior ministers and security personnel together for a crisis meeting and to arrange action. This included a much humbled Lester Fish whose security people and officers were running around like headless chickens.

Communication links had rapidly been established and news of the kidnap was now being broadcast to all home countries, as well as certain international organisations including the United Nations.

Conversely and at the same time, the recipients of the information were also trying to contact Antigua with the news of the attacks on the desalination plants. Absolute chaos and confusion reigned and the closure of the airport, effectively prolonging a feeling of incarceration on the island, merely served to make an already stressful situation intolerable.

The meeting eventually came to order and some rational thinking began to emerge. The first priority was to instruct all affected countries to remain calm and take no unilateral action. This was to be followed by arranging the rapid repatriation of all the most senior officials home. The royal yachts would take them to the nearest island where flights would be chartered. The more junior staff, journalists and military would have to wait, which in the case of the latter was probably a good thing – their welcome home would be unlikely to be gracious or friendly and hospitable. Ashman would remain on Antigua for a while and co-ordinate with the international community from an investigative point of view. Good communications equipment was already established at the club so this was a logical place from which to manage the short-term response.

The meeting dispersed and the delegates went their separate ways to issue instructions and make the arrangements as agreed. Beaumont and Ashman sat back in their chairs when the last had left; they were utterly deflated. 'I don't know about you general,' said Beaumont, 'but I need a bloody great scotch!'

North Atlantic Ocean

THE RENDEZVOUS POINT had been determined principally by the range of the Cessna. Using GPS equipment, *Al Batross* and the *Lester Fish* had linked up just three hours after the snatch due east of Antigua and were holding position awaiting the arrival of the plane. There was a clear night sky and a gentle swell, as good a set of conditions as Scott could possibly have hoped for.

The patrol boat was an hour late as Masterson had been obliged to load and secure all the fuel supplies by himself. He was exhausted and relieved to have Chater join him and take over the controls. The news of Church was met stoically and everyone now concentrated on the arrival of the small plane.

When they established shortwave radio contact, the *Lester Fish* turned on its main search-light and pointed it skywards to guide the pilot in.

From his cockpit, Scott spotted the light, fixed his height at 3,000 feet and put in a last radio call to the boat. He gave his parachute harness a quick check then opened the Cessna's door and jumped out. His canopy deployed soon after and he glided slowly down to his waiting companions, landing within fifty metres of the Vosper. He was soon aboard and the two powerful launches set off at the maximum speed allowed by the conditions. At almost thirty-five knots, this was most exhilarating for some and positively nauseating for others.

The six prisoners were locked up in the aft cabin which had been comfortably, if sparsely, prepared for their journey. Sheikh Sabah Al Salem had been patched up and given a shot of morphine which had settled him down. Aside from this, there had been no further dialogue between captors and captured. Newcombe had told them simply that all would be explained when they reached their destination.

On the bridge, Carson was tuning the powerful radio listening out for any news on the heist. He had just found the BBC World Service and called out for everyone to listen in.

To everyone's astonishment, the lead story was not of their night's activity – this was not even mentioned in the bulletin – but of the attacks in the Middle East. When the announcements were over, it was Little George who broke the stunned silence.

'Bleedin' 'eck, major, d'ya reckon we just started World War bloody three?'

New York, USA

IT WAS WITH EXACTLY THAT IN MIND that an emergency meeting of the United Nations Security Council was convening, along with the ambassadors of the respective countries involved and the British secretary general of the United Nations, Lord Douglas Styles.

The volatility of the situation escaped no one and the tension was acute. Air strikes on Baghdad were being called for as a priority and full mobilisation of all Allied armed forces was sought.

'Gentlemen, it's all very well calling for instant vengeance,' said the secretary general, 'but it is not yet clearly established that Iraq is responsible for these outrages.'

He was unable to continue in the resultant clamour that greeted this statement. The Arab ambassadors particularly were scathing in this apparently weak position being taken.

'Who else could it be?' growled the Saudi Arabian representative pointing aggressively at the full-time council members. 'Iraq has been biding its time to get even ever since you failed to properly vanquish her during the Gulf War.'

This accusation met with a storm of protest. Everyone was again hurling vitriol at everyone else and the meeting was going nowhere.

'Gentlemen, please, this meeting must come to order.' Douglas Styles rarely raised his voice, but when he did, people listened. 'This crisis will not be sorted out if we all bicker and accuse each other of considered past imperfections, whether justified or not. We have a real and current crisis to resolve and before any action can even be considered, we need much more information.'

This statement was generally accepted and it was arranged that a further meeting would take place as soon as everyone was better informed and able to make more qualitative judgements and decisions. It also gave the principal players time to consult with their intelligence sources and Styles was particularly concerned to know the score from Mossad and the SIS who, it was generally recognised, had the most effective coverage throughout the Middle East. He also wanted some time to talk to Baghdad.

For although the obvious indications pointed to the Iraqis for the outrages, he could not believe they had either the nerve or, more particularly, the capability to mount such a combined operation, without at least some indication of their intentions coming to the attention of the intelligence community. The only people the secretary general felt capable of pulling off such an enterprise, and who had the motivation, were the Israelis. They had successfully driven a wedge between the GCC and the Arab League and were now reaping the rewards of Rabin and Peres' combined initiatives with the Palestinians. Israel could now break up the GCC completely, could pick off its individual component parts at leisure and consolidate its economic, political and military dominance of the entire Middle East.

Baghdad, Iraq

S ADDAM HUSSEIN AND HIS COUNCIL of ministers were almost as mystified as the rest of the world community. Their initial reaction had been one of delight, that not only had their operation been such a success, but that also parties unknown, with apparently similar hatreds, had abducted the leadership of their rivals.

However, upon further reflection, they recognised that the Antiguan action posed a grave danger to them, for they would surely be blamed and subsequently ruthlessly punished.

Colonel Rousan was asked for his assessment but he was unable to shed any light on the affair. He was dispatched with instructions to find out urgently. The sweetness of his earlier euphoria was now distinctly soured and he set about his mission with ruthless intention.

Meanwhile, the president decided to announce a complete denial of the entire affair and publicly castigate those who would cause disharmony and strife in the region. Had not the people of Iraq suffered enough and had not the country paid to the full through the punitive United Nations sanctions imposed upon it since the Gulf War? This was clearly a Zionist plot designed to discredit Iraq and propagate the subjugation of her people. Suppression of her emergence as a responsible and important player in the region was clearly the intention.

This was the message broadcast to the world. Confusion reigned absolute.

North Atlantic Ocean

By DAWN ON THE 24TH OF DECEMBER, a full-scale air, land and sea search had been launched. Principally co-ordinated by the United States Coast Guard, the search swept the Caribbean from north to south, covering the seas and all island groups. It was not considered for a moment that the boats would be heading out into open ocean; where could they possibly be going? The weather was clear and fine and for the whole of that day and the next, the search continued.

Meanwhile, the Vosper and the patrol boat continued on their northeasterly heading. They made good progress and the powerful engines of both craft drove them through the kindly Atlantic swells at a formidable thirty knots. This was punishing both passengers and ships but the weather held good and they maintained pace and schedule.

They were still stunned by the news of the attacks in the Middle East and since both incidents, now being aired constantly on the various news media, were being linked together, Newcombe and his men were trying to assess their position. There was a feeling that they should just dump their captives and make good their escape while they could.

However, the majority agreed that having gone this far, it would be pointless to abort their plans now and they should seek to exploit the extra confusion that prevailed. They would have to be extra circumspect as to how they made contact with their proposed benefactors but their objective remained viable.

New York, USA

THE ISRAELI RESPONSE to Douglas Styles's enquiry had been predictably indignant and belligerent. The British, however, had been strangely quiet and non-committal. Styles had spoken directly with the prime minister who had promised whatever help and co-operation was needed but had otherwise remained aloof and almost disinterested in the affair.

Styles decided to call Sir William Hood, who he knew well from his time in British politics and for whom he had the greatest respect.

'Sir William? Douglas Styles here. I was wondering if we could have a chat about this Middle East fracas.'

'I've been expecting your call, Lord Styles,' replied the intelligence chief smoothly. 'How can I be of assistance?'

'Well, if I know you, you probably already know exactly who's behind it all and what's happening. Any chance of sharing the info?'

'It's very kind of you, my lord – I wish others shared your faith in our service. In point of fact, we are fairly sure the Iraqis are behind the desalinator raids but we just don't believe they have the resources to carry out the snatch in Antigua. It's either sponsored by them with a mercenary group doing the business or else a completely coinciden-tal wild card that's been played. Either way, since it appears to be a hostage situation, the best we can hope for is a lead when the kidnappers make contact with their demands.'

'Yes and the mind boggles what those are likely to be. Anyway, you don't think the Israelis are behind it at all? That's certainly the popular view over here at the moment.'

'Good God, no, absolutely not. We've been working together on this one for some weeks but unfortunately, certain politicians preferred to ignore and ridicule our warnings.'

'Yes, well, that's been known to happen before, and I daresay will again,' stated Styles resignedly. 'Look, I know this is all very off the record, but do you think you could keep me discreetly updated on what's happening from your end Sir William? We really have got to contain this before it all blows up in our faces.'

'No problem, my lord. I don't envy your position on this and I'll do all I can to help.'

'Many thanks. And, er, happy Christmas Sir William.'

'Happy Christmas to you too,' he replied with a chuckle and hung up.

Lord Styles mused over the discussion he had had. He trusted Hood but was still faced with how to defuse the situation at the next meeting with the council.

North Atlantic Ocean

THE ATMOSPHERE AT SEA on Christmas Day was hardly festive. Dawn found the patrol boat running low on fuel and so it was time to abandon her and transfer the diesel supplies over to the Vosper. This was not an easy task but when eventually completed, charges were set on the *Lester Fish,* and the boat quietly and untraceably scuttled.

Progress had been good and they were now just under halfway home. The hostages, however, were another matter. After the first shock of their abduction had passed, they became possessed of a courage that few had needed to call upon in years. They had begun by threatening their captors, then seeing that this was gaining little response, resorted to that time-tested certainty, money. 'Whatever you're being paid, we'll double it if you release us,' was the general pitch but since there was no way of providing assurances for such a proposal, this, too, had had no impact. So they speculated amongst themselves disconsolately and listened avidly to the news bulletins that Newcombe ordered should be played to them. They were well fed and, although the space was cramped, comfortably treated despite the constant buffeting of the ship through the sea.

It was 11:00 AM on Christmas Day when the Brown Envelope Club made contact with an expectant world.

Antigua, Leeward Islands

No ONE HAD HAD MUCH SLEEP as the clear-up operation around the club took place. Ashman and Beaumont became the principal co-ordinating and also investigative officers as nobody else seemed able or willing to assume the roles. This was independent Antiguan territory and the level of competence to handle such a situation was zero. Other international agencies and resources were either unwilling to become involved or were irrelevant to the issue. Only the UN maintained an interest but, with no real executive clout, there was little else it could do except make speeches.

Indeed, rhetoric was reaching new levels of bravado the world over, with everybody condemning everybody else, though attention seemed to be particularly focused on Israel and Iraq.

Christmas Day came about as festively as a flying brick with investigations having achieved nothing. Everyone at the club was under a cloud of suspicion, particularly senior managers, as it was felt that such an operation must have needed inside information. This especially applied to Marshall, whose apparent association with the group from the Vosper at the Copper & Lumber Store was attracting a high level of suspicion. But he maintained that they had been guests like any others, with a particularly interesting boat which was why so much attention and fuss was paid to them. But nothing came to light and the time drifted by depressingly.

Then, just after eight in the morning, the telephone in the main communications centre at the club rang, and a very British military accent politely asked to be connected to Mr Lawrence Beaumont. No clue was given as to the identity and location of the caller.

Beaumont and the general, who had been having breakfast, came at the run.

Beaumont took the phone and put it to speaker. 'This is Lawrence Beaumont speaking at the St Peter's Club.' (The 'Saint' had never been seriously dropped.) 'Who is speaking?'

'Happy Christmas, Mr Beaumont,' replied Mike Newcombe cheerfully, 'and to you too General Ashman. I imagine you are there too. I represent your uninvited guests from the other night and. . . .'

'Who is this?' broke in Ashman.

'You don't really think I'm going to tell you, do you general?' said Newcombe, feigning amazement. 'But you can call me Mr Brown. Anyway, we propose to conduct all our discussions and negotiations through a neutral party, specifically, Mr Beaumont.'

'May I ask why?' queried Beaumont who didn't want to be involved any more than he already had been. Being a middleman in international hostage negotiations was simply ludicrous and a role for which he was just not qualified.

'Certainly Mr Beaumont. First, you are familiar with many of the players involved. You know the region from which they hail but also, as I just said, you're neutral with no political axe to grind. Additionally, although you don't know it now, you have a clear understanding, empathy even, with our position. You're a natural choice.'

'What is the status of the GCC leaders?' asked Ashman.

'They're fine general, except Sheikh Salem Al Sabah, whose shoulder is rather painful.' Newcombe sounded almost pleased. 'But no serious damage is done.'

'Can I speak with King Abdullah?'

'''Fraid not general, at least, not for the moment. Anyway, enough natter for now. I expect you'll want to be making some calls. We'll call back soon and chat some more!' The telephone went dead.

The two men for several moments stared silently at each other. Then Ashman placed a call through to Saudi Arabia and to Sheikh Ahmad, the King's brother and next in line to the throne. He briefly recounted the discussion they had just had and was instructed to keep him informed.

'Well I must say, he didn't seem too bothered,' said the general to the hotelier.

'That fits with the rest of them too, doesn't it?' agreed Beaumont. 'I wonder if one or more of the number twos are behind the whole thing? A sort of complicated regional coup.'

'It's a thought. Anyway, we should get on to the UN.'

A contact point had been arranged for them with Douglas Styles's executive assistant, a young and very bright Harvard graduate called Chuck Campbell, and they now called him with the news of the contact.

The general spoke when the call was established and he relayed the same story to the UN executive.

'Did you manage to record the conversation?' asked Campbell.

'Yes, certainly. Every call is being taped as a matter of course.'

'Good! I'll brief Lord Styles and we'll arrange for a professional hostage negotiation team to get down to you. If they want to deal with Mr Beaumont, that's no problem but you're going to need support and advice and we're going to need on-the-spot analysis.'

'Well, you can be sure we're looking forward to their arrival,' stated Ashman. 'Anything in the meantime we should ask about if they call again or should we just be reactive and listen to their demands?'

'See if you can get any information on the desalination plant raids. We need to know whether the two events are connected. We also want to know who the hell these guys are and who they're working for, but I doubt they'll tell you.'

'Well we can always try.'

'Sure, but go easy. The first priority is the safe return of the hostages. Do nothing to aggravate the captors.'

'Okay, we'll keep in touch.' Ashman paused; 'Let us know when your chaps are expected.'

'Will do general – good luck to you both and, uh, happy Christmas!'

'Thanks Mr Campbell – you too.'

Now the waiting game began.

Arabian Peninsula

Tensions were running very high throughout the region. Each nation was threatening war on Iraq or Israel and anyone else who came to mind. It was their natural expression of belligerence and the basic tribal instincts were at the forefront of their reasoning.

However, with Iraq's continuing denial of involvement, the world community was not going to become involved until specific proof existed as to their guilt. In any case, there were still other angles to be explored and a connection, if any, to be established between the raids on the desalination plants and the snatch of the regions' leaders.

So a variety of 'experts' and 'officials', some self-appointed and others designated, shuttled around the area in a series of diplomatic efforts to defuse and lighten the tension, at least until more facts could be presented.

North Atlantic Ocean

FORTY-EIGHT HOURS AFTER HIS FIRST CALL, Newcombe had *Al Batross* heave too and once again radioed Porlock to route him through the SAS network to the St Peter's Club.

'Hello, Lawrence Beaumont, who is this please?'

Newcombe smiled to himself. Marshall has been right to suggest dealing with this man. He was businesslike and sounded unemotional. 'Good morning, Mr Beaumont, this is Mr Brown. How do you do?'

'Well, thank you,' replied Beaumont frostily. 'I hope that you are planning on being more communicative than when we last spoke. You fairly screwed up my Christmas, you know.'

Beaumont had been told by Styles's negotiators to try to build a rapport with the kidnappers. They would be nervous and highly stressed, they told him, and would need calming as much as possible. This was not how he perceived it when he spoke to Newcombe and indeed, it was not the case. They were tense, yes, but were well in control and most self-assured. Everything had been conducted with a superior military competence, and that in itself, Beaumont reasoned, must be a significant clue.

Newcombe was amused by Beaumont's reply and immediately took to the man. 'Yes, well, sorry about that but you know how things have been recently.'

'Tell me about it!' snorted Beaumont, who had hardly slept since the summit began. 'Anyway, Mr, er, Brown, what can we do for you?'

'Well, without beating about the bush, we require one hundred million dollars in ransom, to be paid equally into ten separate Swiss bank accounts, the details of which I shall now give you.'

'Petty cash or will my personal cheque do?' Although stunned, Beaumont was still trying to play it cool. The 'advisors' were not amused and were mouthing abuse at him.

'Don't antagonise them.' 'For God's sake, keep it straight.' 'No jokes!' 'Stop pissing about!' 'Cut out the fucking flippancy!'

Newcombe and his team were highly amused. 'Keep that up Mr Beaumont, and they'll think you're one of us.'

'They already do, so let's get on with it.'

'Right. I imagine this is being taped, so I'll just reel off the details,' which he proceeded to do as Gunter had earlier instructed him. Then, 'we require this to be deposited by the close of banking hours on the 3rd of January. That gives you a week.'

'Fine, I'll pass the message on. What shall I say regarding the welfare and the release of your hostages in exchange and anyway, how do we know they're safe? Can we speak with them?'

'Not for now, but soon, I promise. Anyway, they will be safe and available for collection at sea. We will contact you again nearer the time with precise co-ordinates.'

'So be it – look I've got a couple of questions and I'd like to be able to contact you if I have any. . . .'

'Forget it!' interrupted Newcombe. 'I'll contact you as and when needs be. Don't worry though, we'll keep in touch. 'Bye for now,' and he was gone, leaving only a faint hiss from the speaker at the St Peter's Club.

'Well,' he said turning to Masterson, who had just been relieved by Cooper in the wheelhouse, 'I think that went rather well. This chap Beaumont's okay. He'd have made a good member of the club.'

'He could always become a post-operation associate member,' grinned Masterson. 'Anyway, he's got his own club to look after for the moment and I doubt it's much fun there right now.'

'True. How are the worthy monarchs, George?'

Little George had just come in from checking the hostages and taking them a meal.

'Bleedin 'eck, major. They're like a bunch of flippin' children. Always bickerin' amongst themselves and arguin' about whose fault it all is. There's no love lost between that lot, I tell ya.'

'How's the Kuwaiti?'

'Oh, 'e'll live, altho' the way 'e goes on you'd think the bleedin' world was comin' to an end.'

'It probably is for him,' observed Masterson. 'Anyway, if we're ready, I'll have Brian get us on our way again.'

'Yes, go ahead Jim.' Masterson left the room and shortly after, there was a deep, throaty growl as the big engines once again sprang into life and thrust the launch onwards to its destination.

New York, USA

THE ATMOSPHERE OF THE UNITED NATIONS Security Council when it next met in private was contrastingly tranquil and unemotional.

The general view was that this was an inter-Arab tribal conflict and that they could sort it out for themselves. After the Gulf War, which had really accomplished very little, there had been a succession of UN involvements, all of which had been a nightmare and a complete waste of time and resources. Yugoslavia, Somalia, Rwanda, Korea, more damn-fool Caribbean islands – the list was endless. So much effort and money expended and no conclusive outcome or reward. Without exception, the council agreed for once to let the Arabs sort out their own back yard. As there seemed no current threat to civilian populations and the oil supply did not seem to be at risk, why become involved, they reasoned?

So the secretary general was duly advised.

Lord Styles was sympathetic from the international community's point of view. However, he still had the Arabs and the Israelis looking to him variously for solutions, action and revenge, all of which he was currently unable to satisfy. His main problem now was arranging a meeting with the acting leaders of the GCC to discuss the kidnappers' terms. Until the hostages' safe return, there could be no cohesive approach to the Iraqi question and the regional relationships with Israel.

So, soon after Chuck Campbell received the news from Antigua of the ransom demands, an emergency meeting was arranged with the ambassadors of all the concerned countries.

Their excellencies arrived in stately order, all late, with the exception of the Omani ambassador, Yousef Al Khyumi, who was meticulously punctual as always. When seated, Lord Styles opened the meeting with a summary of events since their last entanglement. This went well until he explained the Security Council's position and then bedlam broke out. Accusations of pro-Zionism/anti-Islamism rang out and for several minutes Styles allowed the fracas to take its course. When eventually peace was restored, he resumed.

'Your excellencies, are we not agreed that the first priority must be the safe return of your leaders?'

'No, Mr Secretary, we are not!' There was stunned silence and everyone turned to look at His Royal Highness, Sheikh Mohammed Al Fahd, ambassador for Saudi Arabia and first cousin of the new king.

'We agree with our colleague from Saudi Arabia.' Heads again spun, this time to look at the representative from Kuwait. Qatar, too was nodding his agreement, while the ambassadors of Bahrain, the UAE and Oman were giving nothing away.

'I am instructed by our beloved regent that no negotiations with the kidnappers should be allowed to take place. We will not deal with terrorists and extortionists.'

'This is our position too, Mr Secretary.' Sheikh Ali Althani from Qatar seemed almost to be enjoying the situation, and a malevolent sparkle shone from his predatory dark eyes.

Styles was appalled. This bunch of cutthroats didn't seem to care a damn about their leaders and all seemed to have an eye for the main chance.

'May I enquire the position of the other three countries?'

'We will convey the views of our brothers here to our government and advise you in due course of their decision,' replied the Bahraini ambassador. Other nods of agreement went round the table.

'I see,' said the secretary general, 'if this is how you wish to proceed, kindly advise me in due course if there is any way the United Nations can be of service. However, please also at the same time convey to your *acting* leaderships that the United Nations will in the meantime consider these incidents an entirely Arab affair and allow you to settle your regional differences as you see fit. Good day to you.' He stormed out of the room as an angry riposte was being delivered by Sheikh Al Fahd.

In his private office, he and Campbell reviewed the fiasco. 'It's unbelievable,' said Campbell incredulously when his boss had told him how the meeting had gone. 'Do you really think they're all going to have a coup and just leave their bosses to the kidnappers?'

'Well it seems like it, although three of them seemed pretty non-committal.' Just then there was a call from Styles' private secretary advising him that the Omani ambassador to the UN wished to see him. 'Absolutely, bring him straight in please.'

The door opened and Yousef Al Khyumi was shown into the room. Usually cheerful and vivacious, this time he look anxious and concerned. There was no idle banter.

'Mr Secretary, I cannot answer for the conduct and behaviour of my colleagues. Suffice to say that the Omani people want back their sultan. We are not Arabs and we do not behave in such treacherous ways.'

'Your excellency, I am delighted to hear this.' Styles was not surprised that this was the Omani position. 'This being the case, we need to sort out a plan of action.'

'I already have some ideas on this,' replied the ambassador. 'My deputy will remain here to liaise with you while I shall go to Antigua. This seems to be where the contact link is, so I propose to start there.'

'Very well.' Lord Styles frankly could not think of any other options at present and was quite willing to let things take their course. 'What about the Iraqi angle – do you think it's connected?'

'Frankly, no. If the Iraqis had been behind the snatch, their demands would have been very different I suspect.' Al Khyumi paused for thought. 'At the very least, I expect they would have made some mention of their need to repossess their nineteenth province.'

'Maybe, but they did shoot the Kuwaiti in Antigua remember.' This from Campbell, who otherwise had remained silent.

'True, but I suspect that was his bad luck rather than planning. I mean, they could have just shot him dead and been done with it,' said the Omani casually and standing up, continued. 'We shan't really know until we can find our leaders and their abductors. Until then, I can only urge that whatever opportunity presents itself, please do all possible, Mr Secretary, to keep my hot-headed neighbours quiet. They will try to make a lot of noise but I doubt they could agree upon any co-ordinated and combined military solution without the United Nations. I should point out, perhaps, that I am speaking with the full authority of my government in this. We want to see a rapid and peaceful solution to the affair.'

'Very well, ambassador, we will look forward to hearing from you soon. Please let me know if I can help further in any way at all.'

'Thank you, Mr Secretary.' Al Khyumi shook hands with Styles, nodded towards Campbell and left the room.

Campbell reached for a telephone. 'I had better call up Beaumont and tell him what's happening. My God, what a mess!'

Amman, Jordan

Colonel rousan was not in charge of his country's intelligence service for nothing. He was a highly intelligent, utterly ruthless individual who had built up a formidable network of agents all over the world and particularly in the Middle East. He considered that throughout the region his resources were second to none, often supported through the help of Iraq's most traditional ally, Jordan.

However, since the Gulf War he had failed to recognise a certain wind of change that had blown over his neighbour. Ostensibly, Jordan was obliged to lean increasingly towards the West and away from her Arab brother. But everyone knew that, in reality, her sympathies still lay with her vanquished friend, Iraq. So Rousan was always allowed free and easy passage in Jordan and accorded warm and sociable hospitality.

What he did not fully appreciate, though, was that part of Jordan's new accord with the West, was the almost total subjugation of her intelligence services, particularly by the British.

So in the comfort of his favourite suite at the Amman Excelsior Hotel, he spoke openly as he sought meetings and gave instructions on the telephone and conducted interviews in the privacy of his room. His single question to all his operatives and contacts was the same: 'What the hell is going on?'

In a room two floors directly below him, the big spools turned and every sound from the suite above was recorded and passed on. Prendergast's report to his chief in London was clear.

'They either really don't know what happened in Antigua or else it's a very elaborate ruse he's putting up. Frankly, I think they're as much in the dark as we are, sir.'

'What about the desalination operations?' asked Sir William. 'Has that come up at all?'

'Not mentioned once or even alluded to. Mind you, sir, there's no doubt about it as far as I'm concerned. They just can't go ahead with the next phase of their plan, whatever it was, because of the kidnapping. They're as desperate to find out about it as we are.'

'Yes, I think you're right Oswald. Anyway, keep up the surveillance and let me know everything that happens. Things seem calm enough at the moment, but it's not going to last.'

'Anything fresh I need to know about the snatch?'

'Well, keep it under your hat,' responded Sir William, 'but at least half of the GCC don't seem to want them back.'

'Bloody hell!' Even Prendergast, who was used to the vagaries of the Arab mind, was surprised by this piece of news. 'If they're all going to have coups, the mind boggles as to what will happen.'

'Quite so,' replied Hood dryly. 'It'll make our friend in Iraq look positively stable and sensible, what? Better keep an open mind on things over the coming days. Stay in close touch, Oswald.'

Antigua, Leeward Islands

Beaumont and Ashman had gone personally to meet Al Khyumi at the airport, which by this time had been repaired sufficiently to allow its use by small aircraft. Although the negotiators had insisted they stay in case of another contact from the abductors, the general had told them to get stuffed. They needed to get out of the club and its oppressive air of confinement and besides, Al Khyumi was a friend, at least of Beaumont's.

The ambassador was treated to the usual awe-inspiring welcome from the customs harridan, diplomatic passport notwithstanding, and eventually made his way out of the airport building where the two men were waiting for him. As they were climbing into the car, Bill Marshall jogged over to them. 'Morning Lawrence, general. Just been dropping Kerry off. Going to see her folks over in Trinidad. I think she's had enough of it here for a while.' He raised his eyebrows resignedly. 'How're things going with you guys?'

'Hi Bill; as well as can be expected I suppose.' Beaumont replied gloomily. 'Let me introduce you to His Excellency Yousef Al Khyumi, the Sultanate of Oman's ambassador to the UN.'

They exchanged introductions then Marshall asked, 'So, ambassador, have you come over to give a hand? Rotten business, all this, and these chaps have really been through the mill.'

'Well, I've come to give whatever support I can and act really as a liaison between the UN and the GCC. It's rather a complicated triangle really. How are you involved with the club, Mr Marshall?'

'I was helping out a bit with the summit. I own a place nearby – you must bring the ambassador round for a decent meal, mate.' He clapped Beaumont on the shoulder and grinning, turned on his heel. 'Must get back – it's Russell's day off and it'll be pandemonium soon if I'm not there. See ya.'

Later, as they were driving out of the airport, Al Khyumi grinned at Beaumont. 'Frankly Lawrence, you are looking a bit rough. Doesn't island life agree with you?'

The hotelier managed to drag up a tired smile. 'I think I've put on as many years as I've lost kilos. Honestly, Joe, I'm knackered. This certainly wasn't in the contract, I tell you.'

'I can believe it. It hasn't exactly been a picnic in New York though. Let me fill you in on the latest from our side then we'll try and work out how to wrap this problem up together.'

'But surely this is being handled at a formal international level?' Ashman asked incredulously. 'I don't know, but I presume the Security Council, UN, Interpol, that sort of thing are all involved. What are they all up to?'

Al Khyumi explained the events of the past twenty-four hours. By the time they arrived at the club, their spirits were even lower than before they left. There was actually very little they could really do except wait for 'Mr Brown' to contact them. Once he reacted to their news, they would then play things by ear and allow events to take their course. Hopefully, an opportunity would present itself.

Lyme Regis, England

THEY SIGHTED LAND LATE on the 28th, a distant smudge of craggy Cornish coastline and made their way slowly along the coast to Lyme Bay.

Newcombe wanted a night landing and well away from their base at Porlock. After much deliberation, Lyme Regis had been selected. At that time of year it was a quiet town with a good harbour, albeit small, and they could tie up at the end of the Cobb, unload their gear and passengers, drive right up in a minibus they had ready and be away before any curious customs officers or bystanders had time to even note their passing.

So that is exactly what happened and within a quarter of an hour of tying up the Vosper, she was on her way again, with Masterson and Cooper setting off to hide *Al Batross* from curious eyes. They had rented an old boathouse in a small creek well upriver from the mouth of the River Dart and it was here that they now took the launch. After thoroughly cleaning her up, refuelling her and removing all traces of the recent adventure, they would then join up with the others from the group at Porlock.

The windows of the minibus were darkened out and, much to their displeasure, the captives were handcuffed to their seats. Newcombe was not about to lose them now, having come so far.

They set off from the harbour, strained up the precipitous Cobb Road and then drove out of Lyme Regis towards their final destination at Porlock. It was just after three in the morning and they were all quite exhausted. They drove on through the night, mostly in silence, and eventually turned through the gates at Tytherleigh Manor some three hours later. The captives were taken down to the basement where they were securely locked up and the Brown Envelope Club crashed out for a much needed sleep.

Porlock, England

NEWCOMBE WOKE JUST AFTER NOON. The others all seemed dead to the world, so he fixed himself some coffee and luxuriated in a long hot bath. After finishing his ablutions, he went about waking the others. There was no sign of Major Bennett, who, he figured by now would be down at the Anchor Inn, probably oblivious to their return.

When everyone was up and about, fed and returned to the land of the living, Newcombe called a conference around the big table in the kitchen.

He started by enquiring after the captives. Little George, who had been principally responsible for their welfare, spoke.

'Well, major, they've 'ad their grub but they're feelin' pretty sorry for themselves. An' I'm not too 'appy with the Kuwaiti lad. That wound needs some proper attention.'

'Right, well it's time we had a formal chat with them all anyway. As soon as Bennett gets back, we'll have him call up Dr Morton for Al Sabah.'

'How d'you reckon it's looking Mike?' Carson asked. Of all of them, he had been the most anxious throughout and was now feeling very uneasy with the waiting game ahead.

'Everything's gone according to plan Tony. You all did a great job and we're now on the last leg. Just getting this far without getting killed is one hell of an achievement you know.'

There was a murmur of assent and rueful smiles around the table. It was true, it had been bloody marvellous. But as Newcombe then reminded them, it wasn't over yet.

'What's important now is to keep a low profile and be patient. In a way this will be harder. We're all used to action, but this next stage will be the big challenge.'

Just then, the front door opened and a moment later, Major Bennett came into the kitchen. Although initially startled, he collected himself quickly and warmly welcomed back his guests. Everyone stood respectfully and a chorus of 'Morning major' rippled around the kitchen.

'Didn't expect to see you lot for at least another day. Must say, judging by the news, you certainly seemed to hit the spot.'

'Things went exactly as planned,' said Newcombe, 'but what's all this blowing up of the desalination plants in the Middle East? We've heard the radio reports but what are the papers saying?'

'You mean it wasn't your doing?' replied Bennett. 'Tell you the truth, I thought that was you lot also. Couldn't work out how you'd done it, mind, but it was all jolly coincidental, what?'

'Well, it wasn't us, major,' said Scott. 'We have brought back some souvenirs to show where we have been though.'

They all smiled and Bennett asked, 'Got 'em in the cellar then, have you?'

'That's right; we were just going to go and have a chat with them. Incidentally, major, one of them is injured, bullet wound in the shoulder. Do you think there's any chance of Dr Morton having a look at him? We can't take him to hospital and he'll have to keep quiet about it.'

'Don't see why not. I'll give him a call. He's a good sort and since he's retired I'm sure he'll muck in.'

Bennett left for the hall to call Dr Morton and Newcombe continued. 'Nick, George, I want you to come down with me while I chat to our guests. We don't want any of them getting heroic. Then later this afternoon, we'll put a call through to Antigua and let everyone have a cosy little chat.'

In confinement terms, the cellar had been prepared luxuriously. There were two bedrooms, each with three beds, a shower and washroom with toilet and a communal room in which television could be watched and meals taken around a large table. Although there were no windows, the place was well lit and the furnishings reasonably comfortable. Unbeknown to the reluctant guests, there were also two other more Spartan rooms for the confinement of any amongst them who might become too unruly.

By the strong and heavily bolted door leading into the communal room was a bell on which the captors could be summoned. It rang now just as Newcombe descended the back stairs from the kitchen to visit them.

The bolts were pulled back and Little George and Chater moved into the room. They seemed an incongruous pair with their disparate heights but there was no mistaking their calm ruthlessness and particularly the Heckler & Koch machine pistols that each carried, cocked and ready to use. Newcombe then entered and shut the door behind them.

Four of the captives were in the room seated at the table. The Emir of Bahrain then entered from one of the bedrooms. Although a very short man and much too overweight, he was nonetheless forceful and assertive. He seemed totally unfazed by Chater and George and, storming up to Newcombe, unleashed a barrage of invective and abuse. This culminated with a demand that the Emir of Kuwait be accorded proper medical attention. 'He is becoming very weak and needs a doctor immediately. If he dies you will be his murderer and fully responsible.'

'We have already sent for a doctor, Your Majesty,' replied New-combe politely. 'Now, if you would all be so kind as to listen, I will explain to you the circumstances in which you find yourselves.'

He then described the background in broad terms which had led to the idea of kidnapping the GCC leadership and holding them to ransom. How King Abdullah's decision to hold the summit in Antigua had made wishful thinking become a viable opportunity, subsequently seized and executed. And how they were now into the final stage of the operation after which the monarchs would be released to go home and sort out the new threat to their regional security. When he had finished, Sheikh Al Nahyan said, 'Do you really think you can get away with this? Once you've been paid and we return, the world community will hunt you down. There will be nowhere you can go. Why not give up now, hand us over to the authorities and let us see if we can work out, how shall we say, an arrangement?'

'I regret, Your Majesty, that you over-estimate world opinion. Since the Gulf War and the endless aggravations that have been imposed on the UN, both before and since the war, the "world community", as you put it, is fed up with the Middle East. With respect to you all, they see you and others in the region as a group of rather spoilt despots. You can beat the hell out of each other for all that everyone cares, and I don't think you'll find a single Western country now that will lift a finger to help.'

They were all rattled by this, but it was Abdullah who started bellowing indignantly, 'Your arrogance . . .'

'. . . is exceeded only by your own, Your Majesty, so let's dispense with the abuse, shall we!' spat back Newcombe. He noted more than a couple of private smiles around the table.

'We'll see who's so clever,' hissed Abdullah. 'When the oil stops flowing and all the Western companies get kicked out – then we'll see if your precious United Nations will want to help us.'

'Unfortunately, Your Majesty, the West will be able to manage without you more easily than you without them. You have nothing but oil. If you stop your sales and rely on your local labour forces, your economies will fall apart overnight. Fundamentalists will gain control and your dynasties will be forgotten in the decay and regression in your society that will follow. I mean, just look at Iran and you'll understand what I mean.'

'Unfortunately Abdullah, Mr Brown is right.' This was the first time that Sultan Qaboos had said anything in front of his captors. Of all of them, he was perhaps the most astute and balanced. He also had less oil and was therefore not absolutely dependent on the black gold. 'We must settle this affair quickly and cleanly and return to our countries to face the higher threat from Iraq.' He turned to Newcombe. 'Tell me, Mr Brown, is it possible that we may be able to talk with your negotiators. It might help if they know firsthand that we are safe and encourage our governments to expedite the funds you speak of.'

'Our very thoughts, Your Majesty – we shall be calling them in a couple of hours and will be pleased to have you join us.' Newcombe rose from the table. 'The doctor will be here shortly for Sheikh Al Sabah. We shall keep in touch.'

With that he left the room, followed by his two silent minders.

Baghdad, Iraq

T HE NEWS, WHEN IT FINALLY ARRIVED, came not from Colonel Rousan but from Jordan's ambassador to the United Nations. Whether officially sanctioned or not, the leadership of Iraq was most pleased.

Could it really be true that the UN had had enough of these squabbling tribesmen and this time were going to leave the region alone? And the idea of the kidnappers being left stranded with the GCC monarchs was positively side-splitting. It was rare indeed for the inner cabinet to see their president in so jovial a mood, but very few of them relaxed sufficiently to share in the jocularity.

'Perhaps we may now be able to repossess our errant province at last,' said Saddam Hussein, assuming his more usual and sinister air of quiet menace. 'What are your thoughts, General Musbah?' This was addressed to the chief of staff, a puppet general who would always say and do exactly what he felt his master wanted, regardless of the merit or wisdom of the issue in question. Knowing his master's obsession with taking over Kuwait, the answer to the question was easy.

'Without outside interference, my president, we should be able to take back the province with ease. It should be even easier without the leader, the spineless dog Al Sabah.'

'Exactly so; and tell me general,' whispered Saddam so quietly they had to strain to hear him, 'should we stay there this time?'

'Where else had you in mind, my president?' asked Musbah uncertainly.

'All of them!' he snapped. 'The entire fat-cat GCC. If the interfering allies will for once mind their own business and leave us all to settle our differences without them, we could do it.'

'We would need help; other countries' support.' This from the foreign minister, Tariq Aziz, one of Iraq's longest serving ministers and tipped to fill Saddam Hussein's shoes, should they ever become empty.

'Such as?'

'Jordan and Yemen definitely, quite possibly Syria – we might even persuade Iran to play a part this time. We'd also have to talk to Oman, at least to persuade them to stay out of it. I would not be happy having to take a fight down to them.'

'Are we truly ready to supply and support the army on the move now?' The minister of information was always one of the more astute in the Cabinet. Sly and cunning, Mazen Magbul was also one of Iraq's senior survivors.

The president replied, 'Thanks to the UN we have spent our resources since the war on quietly developing a more conventional fighting force. This had not been an area in which they have been too interested, so our capability here is good. We are now faster and more mobile and, thanks to some of our old pre-Gorbachev and Yeltsin friends, have built up good supplies of anti-aircraft equipment, ammunition, fuel and spare parts, particularly for the tanks. Yes, I think we could run through the Gulf and over to Riyadh quite quickly.'

'My president, we still do not have the air support we would need,' said General Musbah. Our few planes would be no match for the Saudi Air force and our troops would be dreadfully exposed.'

'It's not like you to worry about the welfare of your troops general,' replied the president with a wicked but short-lived smile. 'However, your point is fair. This is where it will be necessary to bring in support from established and new allies.' He paused and then stood up. Both fists were balled and placed on the table in front of him over which he now leant.

'Gentlemen, our time has once again come. We must exploit our enemies' confusion and move fast against them. We already have plans for invasion but these must now be refined quickly to address the current circumstances. You Tariq, have the biggest task. Go with God's speed and blessings to make new friends and consolidate old ones. Show them how good will be the pickings for them when we have control over the entire continent. Colonel Rousan, activate your agents to cause as much trouble and insurrection as possible in the GCC nations. The time is ripe for it with water supplies cut off and no established leaders. Water will become our weapon, and with it we will bring these tribal dogs to their knees.'

Arabian Peninsula

THE LEGIONS OF DUNES WERE MASSED against the pitiful humans that would control them. These dunes would always be the ultimate victors and on many occasions over the centuries had proven it. But the stubborn little creatures kept on trying. They had built wells and canals and cities and more recently roads and gardens.

Now great highways cut through the desert, where the constantly shifting sands allowed it. The big cities were bordered by lush gardens. Rich grass, bushes of bougainvillea, palm trees; all these abounded, nourished by drip-fed irrigation and sprays. These green ribbons impudently defied the mighty desert.

But now the water had stopped. In just a matter of days, these fertile strips had withered and died. The shifting sands began advancing and reclaiming that which was theirs. Humans were faring little better. Those whose water came from wells continued much the same, but the majority of people had drawn their ever increasing requirements from the network of desalination plants surrounding their country and these needs were not being met.

There was no organised water rationing yet: it just was not coming out of the taps. The supermarkets no longer had supplies of mineral water and other soft drinks were becoming scarce. And this all in just a few days.

The people were confused. Although the news of the raids had been suppressed, communications had become far too sophisticated to muzzle such stories. And the massive expatriate work forces and their families had begun a great exodus.

The people were alarmed. Very few actually had much love for their monarchs, but they knew where they stood. Their kings had now disappeared, along with the leaders of their neighbours and rumours of coups frightened them, with unknown tyrannies lurking around the corner.

And the people were becoming thirsty. Already there had been several independent outbreaks of civil disorder, ruthlessly suppressed by the police, but all could see it was the thin end of the wedge.

Barely a week had passed and yet already the newly acquired fabric of civilisation which covered the emerging Arab nations was becoming tattered.

Nature, like a great desert leopard, motionless but for her twitching tail before falling on her prey, seemed poised to strike and regain the ascendancy amongst her most barren wastes.

Antigua, Leeward Islands

Beaumont, al khyumi and ashman had been waiting anxiously and nearly jumped on the telephone when it rang.

'Hello, gentlemen, Mr Brown calling. Anyone awake yet in your island paradise?'

'Very funny!' retorted Beaumont, 'Sleep doesn't happen to be high on our agenda yet. What can you do about it for us?'

'Well, Mr Beaumont, would it be a comfort for you all to speak to our guests?'

'Thank you, Mr Brown, that would be kind. May I speak with his Majesty, Sultan Qaboos please?'

Another voice came on the line, smooth, calm, cultured and assured. They all recognised Oman's leader instantly.

'Mr Beaumont, general, this is Qaboos. We are all well except Al Sabah whose injury from the shooting is causing some problems. We are being well treated. Can you please advise us on progress regarding our release?'

Al Khyumi replied, announcing himself formally to his monarch and then switching to English for everyone else's benefit.

'Your Majesty, there are three problems. The first is a serious threat to the region from Iraq. The second is that the regents of Saudi Arabia, Qatar and Kuwait have told the United Nations secretary general that they will not pay any ransom.'

This last news brought uproar from the room in Porlock. There was shouting and cursing, death threats, some very horrible in their ingenuity, and a general barrage of impotent abuse. The commotion not only came from the hostages, but the captors as well. Newcombe finally overrode the bedlam. His voice was unemotional.

'You mentioned, excellency, that there was a third problem. What is it?'

'Based on the first two,' replied Al Khyumi succinctly, 'the United Nations and Security Council have decided, for the time being at least, to take no action. They consider this a purely Arab affair and are willing to sit on the sidelines.'

A further round of profanity greeted this statement. Eventually order was established, again by Newcombe.

'So what do you suggest we do, ambassador? It would be a shame to have to execute everyone after so much effort.' This too brought screams of protest by the group of captives listening to the conversation. It was suddenly cut short by a bellow from Chater for silence and a quick burst of machine pistol fire.

'What's happened? Has anyone been shot?' This from Ashman.

'No general, just one of my men redecorating the ceiling,' replied Newcombe dryly. 'Next time, though, he may aim lower. So again, gentlemen, the question; what do you propose?'

'I don't believe you'd shoot them,' said Beaumont. 'They are your passport to safety. With one or more of them dead, you'd be hounded for the rest of your life, which I doubt would be all that long.'

Although not alarmed, Newcombe conceded the point. 'What a right bloody mess,' he thought. It was Qaboos who spoke next, in his balanced and reasonable way. Of all the captors he was surely the superior statesman.

'Gentlemen, it seems that we must all review our strategy. I would suggest we reconsider our positions and then talk again later.'

'Certainly, Your Majesty.'

'Before we break off, is there any information available on the Iraqi threat?'

'Not yet Your Majesty, but we will find out what we can.' Al Khyumi was back on the line. 'God be with Your Majesty and we pray to have you free and back with your people soon.'

'Inshallah,' replied the sultan and the call ended.

London, England

THE ONLY GRATIFYING ASPECT of Hood's past week had been both the prime and foreign ministers' calls to him apologising for the earlier assessments of his intelligence reports and now encouraging him to redouble his efforts. As the UN was keeping out of things, the efforts were essentially to be concentrated on fact-finding rather than any overt activity, and Prendergast and his agents throughout the Middle East were deluging him with reports.

Reports were consistent throughout the region. There was significant civil unrest, with each outbreak getting bolder and taking less regard for the vicious and punitive measures being dealt out on them by their respective authorities.

The Asian subcontinent workers, who numbered millions throughout the region, were becoming particularly active, since their Arab masters were treating them more contemptuously than before and trying to deprive them of water.

Anyone who could get out of the region was doing so. Expatriates by the thousands had decided enough was enough, and the Arabian Peninsula, starved of its manual and administrative labour forces, was rapidly falling into unorganised disarray.

All of which was a matter of significant concern to all nations. However, the stance of the United Nations and Security Council was accepted and the world watched with bated breath.

What was also particularly galling for Hood was the apparent inability of the world's various intelligence services to find any trace of the hostages or their captors. He was totally familiar with the recordings of the calls to Antigua and, along with the description of the abduction itself, all indicators pointed to a highly trained and well-financed British mercenary group.

He was chewing these thoughts over in his mind when he remembered his conversation with Renard at MI5 about the arms dealer Carson. Now, there might be a lead. He called her to find out if she had any news.

'Since our last talk, we've arranged for the police to issue "wanted" notices throughout the country.' Renard was still somewhat defensive, but since Hood's predictions had turned out so accurately, she felt somewhat awed by him and wished to co-operate fully. 'So far, though, we haven't had any luck. Do you think there's any connection with this Arab affair then?'

'Put it this way, Sarah, he's our only lead at the moment. He may be nothing at all to do with it but there's a pattern of coincidence that I don't like.'

'I see what you mean. I'll pull out all the stops and have another session with the police commissioner.'

'Thanks a lot – please keep me posted.'

After hanging up, his hand lingered on the telephone. Perhaps it was time for another chat with Mossad – see what they're up to, he thought.

Tel Aviv, Israel

T HE SITUATION IN TEL AVIV was much the same as London. Too many unanswered questions and no clear picture of intent. In fact, the feeling generally was that the two separate terrorist activities were actually linked and were simply a one-off revenge attack launched by Iraq to get even with her neighbours.

Ari Diarra had said as much to Hood the previous day and was now discussing the same with that nation's often-convened war council.

With the chaos developing throughout the area, the amber alert was still very much in place. The council was now considering an even more active state of readiness for their armed forces, just in case anyone wanted to direct attention from their own internal conflicts and attack their common enemy. With all the rhetoric emanating from Baghdad since Christmas Eve, many eyes, and not just Arab ones, were turned on Israel, wondering if the destabilisation of the area was in fact her doing.

The meeting was interrupted by a messenger with urgent dispatches for Ari Diarra. He read them quickly then addressed the council.

'Gentlemen, it would appear that Iraq may not be content with their achievements so far. These reports show large-scale military build up and activity on the Saudi and Kuwaiti borders. Also, our friend Tariq Aziz seems to be busy and has been visiting Jordan and Syria yesterday and is presently en route to Yemen. Finally, our troublesome Colonel Rousan is back in Amman playing the puppet-master and doubtless causing trouble.'

This was greeted in the usual sombre and lugubrious fashion. Peres spoke without dissent from any.

'Brigadier Diarra, thank you for this news. Please keep it coming and obtain satellite pictures from our American friends – we must also have tight liaison here with the British.'

The foreign secretary said, 'We also need to know more about Aziz's meetings. Who's he met with, what did he say and where else is he going? We need this fast, brigadier.'

'We're already on to it, sir. There's one point I'd like the council's sanction for please. In view of the escalating tensions and his current vulnerability in Jordan, I'd like to take out Rousan. He can be nothing but trouble and is a principal hatchet man overseas for Saddam. I believe the time has come for him to go."

In many parts of the world, such discussion at cabinet level would have met with horror, but here the proposal was simply considered. Peres asked, 'Do you plan to kidnap him and bring him here or just kill him?'

'We would love to kidnap him, prime minister, but I fear the logistics of such an exercise would be most complex and have a high risk of failure. He is well protected, in a country hostile to us and is constantly on the move. I think, therefore, our best interests will be served by his execution.'

'Agreed!' and a murmur of assent went round the room. 'Get to it brigadier! Meanwhile, we shall put the armed forces on full alert – please see to it, chief of staff. We shall reconvene here again tomorrow, same time. Thank you, gentlemen.'

Antigua, Leeward Islands

T WO DAYS HAD PASSED SINCE THE LAST CALL and everyone's nerves were stretched to breaking point.

The biggest concern was that the hostages had been killed and the abductors had cut their losses and vanished.

But all anyone could effectively do for the time being was wait and wait and wait. Sitting at the Docksider Café overlooking the scene of the disaster for the umpteenth time, the summit's organisers were gloomily reviewing their situation over a round of beers.

'The news from Styles wasn't very bright,' said Al Khyumi who just then joined them. 'There's an Iraqi military build up on the Saudi and Kuwaiti borders and general chaos in the GCC. There's even talk of military takeovers if things don't stabilise quickly.'

'Oh bloody marvellous!' cried Ashman. 'And what will that megalomaniac lunatic call this next bash, I wonder. "The Mother of all Battles Two!"' This brought a brief but jaded smile from the others. 'At this rate I won't be able to go home at all – I'll be permanently out to grass unless I can get Abdullah back.'

'Oh don't worry Paul, another military bash may never happen and you'll just have to content yourself with what we've been through here; a real mother of all summits!'

This time they all laughed and swallowed thirstily from their chilled Red Stripes.

'Seriously though,' Beaumont continued, 'next time you want to organise a conference, leave me out of it and keep it an all-Arab affair will you.'

Part III
About Turn

Winter 1996

Porlock Weir, England

'HAPPY NEW YEAR!' The cry was taken up by all at the Anchor Inn who were still sober enough to say it at midnight on New Year's Eve.

For most of the patrons, this was just the end of one rather dull year and the beginning of another one. There was not much excitement in their lives as common farm labourers or in the rather hopeless fishing and uninspiring tourism industries.

Still others did nothing at all. These were the local layabouts – young lads in their late teens and early twenties, who were unemployable and generally a nuisance. They were getting heavily boozed up and, inevitably for their age, were discussing what they each would like to do with Jill, the only unattached and decent-looking girl in sight. They were becoming increasingly jealous of the attention she was giving to the two elderly 'barmy boys' at the bar, and as their scrumpy soaked more and more into their brains, so did their malevolence increase and the seeds of violence grow.

Chater and Carson had come down to the pub alone. They both needed to get out of the house and Newcombe felt it would do no harm as long as they kept a low profile. The rest of the team preferred to stay put and again go over their options with the hostages. They were equally divided between just dumping the group and dispersing or trying to hold out and make a deal. They all agreed, however, to sit tight, keep quiet and see what developments occurred on the international arena. This certainly seemed to be hotting up, according to Marshall who had just called from Antigua, updating them with as-yet-unpublished inside information.

The hostages were quieter now and, except for meals, had been left alone. Al Sabah had been treated by Dr Morton, whose initial reluctance was soon overcome by Major Bennett's persuasiveness, and if not recovering speedily, he was at least in no danger.

Back at the Anchor, Bailey called over to Jill and asked her to get in some more wood for the fire. She winked at Chater mischievously saying she'd be back in a minute. Chater and Carson grinned at each other, more relaxed than they had been for weeks. But neither noticed the five yobs that got up and followed her out of the bar.

'Here Jill, me darlin', let me give you a 'and with that wood,' volunteered the eldest. 'Looks to me to be pretty heavy.'

Jill whirled round at the voice and felt a surge of alarm. She was in the woodshed at the back of the pub with three drunken youths, plus one propping up the doorway and another pacing outside in the dark, wind and drizzle. She tried to keep calm.

'I'm fine thanks Henry. You go on back to the bar and I'll bring you a round of drinks soon as I'm back, okay?'

'I don' wan' to give 'er a 'and with wood,' slurred another as he began undoing his belt, 'I wan' to give 'er another present.' They all laughed drunkenly and came closer to her, each uncertain of himself, hoping for another to make the first move.

'Now you lot get out of here or I'll scream,' cried Jill, grabbing a piece of wood as a club and now feeling really frightened.

'What you going to do with that club, Jill, me darlin'?' asked the first.

'I know wha' I'd like to do wi' it,' giggled the second.

'Nobody will hear you scream Jill. They're all making too much bleedin' noise themselves. I reckon your fancy toffs from the major's place won't 'elp you this time.'

Panic stricken, Jill swung the club at the nearest and tried to run past him. The blow caught him on the side of his head and drew blood down his cheek. He was momentarily stunned, but as he cursed, the second youth had grabbed her and was starting to grab at her cashmere sweater.

The first thug now turned and backhanded her across the mouth. 'Bitch! You'll pay for that.' She tried to scream but the fear choked her cry and she felt blood on her lips. 'Hold 'er up Alan; I've got a club 'ere she'll really like.' He pulled at her skimpy skirt which fell away while Alan finished the attack on her sweater which ripped in half to reveal her firm and untethered breasts.

She was struggling fiercely but was no match for Alan's powerful grip and still she could not cry out. She watched in horror as her tormentor lowered his trousers, ripped off her flimsy panties and violently entered her. His stinking heavy breathing revolted her, adding to the horror, while his vile organ thrust painfully inside her.

It did not last long and as he came grunting and panting, she at last found her voice.

She screamed loud and hard before his punch to her face almost knocked her senseless.

Then she was on the floor and her second attacker was rolling her over. She dimly realised he had even worse intentions as the animal came at her from behind.

"'Ere, what you guys up to?' called the youth watching outside. 'Aren't you done yet? All that screamin' will bring someone.'

'What d'you fuckin' think they're up to?' said the one on the door. 'Besides, why are you in such a hurry to go? You haven't 'ad your go yet?'

'No, an' I'm not goin' to neither. This 'as gone too far already.'

'If you've got cold feet, you better fuck off then, 'adn't you. But you'll never lose it stayin' at 'ome.' He laughed evilly and returned his attention to the scene before him. Alan too was almost done, judging by the noises he was making and Jack, the third in line was preparing himself uncertainly.

Bailey came over to Chater and Carson. He was fairly tipsy and having a grand time. 'Either of you codgers seen Jill? Sent her out for some wood about ten minutes ago and she's bloody scampered. If the fire goes out, I'll kill her.'

'I'll go and see, bring some wood back too,' said Chater.

'I'll come with you in case you get lost,' chuckled Carson. 'Besides, I could do with the fresh air and I need a pee.'

They went out together and as they rounded the back of the pub saw a shadowy figure dart inside the dimly lit woodshed and heard muffled voices mixed with an anguished cry against the wind. They looked at each other and ran to the shed door, both sensing trouble.

The door to the shed was bolted, but Chater's weight behind his foot quickly obliterated the lock and the rickety old door flew in on its hinges.

The scene that greeted them was repulsive and both men were temporarily rooted to the spot. Chater bellowed at them. 'You miserable little fuckers, you're going to regret this.' He moved towards the third youth who had been struggling to enter their hapless victim when he and Carson had crashed in. 'Get off her you bastard.' A sound to his left alerted him and he ducked just in time to avoid a blow from a log wielded by the as yet unseen 'doorman'. He pivoted round and chopped ruthlessly at his assailant's exposed throat with a flat hand, every bit as hard as the log. The boy fell to his knees and collapsed with an unhealthy sounding gargling, choking noise in his throat, then lay still.

The sentry tried to run for it but Carson caught him in the solar plexus with a bunched fist and he too crumpled. Chater by this time had Jack by his hair and lifting his head up had hit him so hard he was unconscious before he was once again prone on the floor.

Everything had so far happened in a matter of seconds but the first two, Henry and Alan, had collected their wits and a couple of ugly sheath knives. They stood their ground and beckoned to Chater.

'Come on grandpa, let's see how you handle men instead of beatin' up on boys,' taunted Henry.

'Reckon he's probably an old queer anyway,' said Alan, waving his knife from side to side, not as a good fighter would, but more as he had probably seen in the movies.

Chater relaxed and straightened up. He called to Carson. 'Tony, get Jill covered and out of here. I'll be with you in a minute as soon as I've settled with these two chummies here.'

Knowing of Chater's skills at unarmed combat, Carson almost felt sorry for the two thugs – but not quite. As he bent down to help Jill up, he saw the bruising and the bleeding and was sickened. She was whimpering and moaning quietly and very gently he covered her in his coat, picked her up uncomplainingly in his arms and carried her to the kitchen door at the back of the pub. Brigitte was there cooking up some toasted sandwiches for the revellers.

Normally pretty hardboiled, she cried out when she saw her daughter. 'For God's sake, what's happened Tony?' She asked as she opened the door and took hold of her daughter.

'She's been badly beaten and raped, Brigitte. She needs to get to hospital and we need police and an ambulance here quickly. Nick is handling her attackers. You get Charlie to make the calls and then help me with her upstairs. Now move.'

'Oh my God . . . okay Tony. . . .' she hesitated in the doorway. 'Will she. . .?'

'Go and get Charlie,' Carson shouted and she fled.

Henry lunged at Chater. To his astonishment, his thrust had completely missed the mark, and his right arm now dangled helplessly and painfully at his side, knifeless and broken in two places.

A savage growl preceded Alan's attack, which was similarly repulsed. This time, however, Chater ducked low and while grabbing the knife hand in the savage vice of one enormous paw, sprang up and rammed the heel of his other into the bridge of Alan's nose. The bone broke away from the retaining cheek bones and sank deep into Alan's brain, killing him instantly.

Chater then turned back to Henry who was trying to inch his way towards the door and a slowly recovering doorman. He grabbed him by the broken arm and pulled him violently around making him scream with the pain.

'Now my little friend, let's see how sharp your mate's knife is.'

'What, what, what're you going to do? Please, please Mister, give me a break. I'll, I'll. . . .' Henry burst into tears, begging and pleading. Chater shook him away, disgusted by him. He heard a noise at the door as the now conscious colleague tried to leave. With one great bound he was over to him and with a swift chop to the back of his neck sent him into oblivion. He then returned his attention to Henry.

'Now, where were we, you little shit? Oh, I remember, I was about to castrate you.' He moved in closer to Henry whose scream now almost drowned out the call from the door, where Carson had reappeared and was yelling at him.

'For God's sake man, ease up. Come on, Nick, ease up.'

Chater was almost crazed with rage, but slowly pulled himself together. He looked round at Carson, waved a hand and visibly relaxed. Nonetheless, he still turned and slammed a huge fist into Henry's chest, who doubled up and sank to the ground. Carson had heard the crack of ribs breaking even from the door.

The police and ambulance when they came were not amused. The senior police officer from Minehead, the nearest large town, was called and began his enquiries in the now all but deserted pub.

Carson had earlier called the manor and briefed Newcombe.

'Why do you guys have to kill people when you're pissed off? This could be really bad news for us. Now stick to your cover stories about adventure training and all that, and I'll see about a lawyer. I'll be in touch tomorrow but meantime, tell that great ape Chater to keep cool.'

'Okay, Mike, will do. And, er, sorry about all this. Just couldn't be helped really.'

'Yeah, well, it's a bit late for that isn't it? 'Night.'

They had rung off just as the first ambulance sirens were heard coming down the hill.

London, England

SIR WILLIAM HOOD PICKED UP the telephone. Although New Year's Day, it was still business as usual in MI6. It was Sarah Renard and for the first time in ages she sounded cheerful and excited.

'Sir William, great news – I think we've found Carson.'

'Capital, my dear, capital. Tell me about it.'

She relayed the events of the early morning and how Carson had come to be arrested. But it was more the other man, Nick Chater, who interested Hood. He told Renard he'd call her back shortly, then punched his intercom and asked his secretary to get hold of Crispin Steele. They had been together for years and what between them they didn't know about the intelligence community wasn't worth knowing. Steele appeared a few minutes later.

'Crispin, it's just a hunch, but I think we may have a lead in the GCC hostage saga.'

Steele was immediately alert and eager for news.

'Tell me, what've you got?'

Hood told him of his conversation with Sarah Renard some weeks earlier and the subsequent search for Carson. 'I reckon with his connections and the man he's been picked up with, it's worth following up from our side, wouldn't you think?'

'Absolutely. I'll do a check on Chater, see what we have on him. Meanwhile, can you hold them in isolation, say under prevention of terrorism or some such, till we can get down there and talk to them?'

Hood smiled. 'My thoughts exactly. I'll stay here in case something comes up, but you get on down there as soon as possible. I'll fill in Renard so there'll be no trouble.'

'Perfect – I'll call you later when I've seem them.' He left for his computers and files.

Hood called Renard and told her of their plans, to which she immediately agreed.

'Would you like me down there too?' she asked, 'or in view of the international nature of the affair, do you prefer to handle it alone?'

'Kind of you to ask, Sarah,' replied Hood smoothly. 'By all means do come along, but we'd prefer to run things ourselves from now on, if that's okay.'

'No problem, Sir William, I'll give the necessary instructions and leave you to it. Please keep me informed.'

'Will do, Sarah, and thanks. By the way, Happy New Year.' He hung up.

Baghdad, Iraq

THE SUPREME COUNCIL MEETING chaired by President Saddam Hussein was charged with a mixture of electric excitement, anxiety, fear and anticipation. No one really wanted another fight yet but the opportunity seemed God-sent.

Tariq Aziz had just returned from a whistle-stop tour of Jordan, Syria and Yemen, all of whom had pledged to keep out of any forthcoming conflict. In the case of Jordan and Yemen, they had further agreed to mobilise their troops on the borders with Saudi Arabia and Oman to keep those nation's forces fragmented and divided. He was looking tired but pleased. He would shortly be going to Tehran where he hoped to have similar success. If Iran could be seen to seriously threaten all the Gulf States, there was a real chance that this time Iraq could move through the area and vanquish her foes.

Saddam seemed pleased with the progress. The army was massing along the Saudi and Kuwaiti borders and tension in the region was rising. More importantly, the West seemed to be playing a far less interfering role, which was most gratifying even if a little surprising.

'Tariq, Douglas Styles in the UN is trying to contact you. I suggest you call him on your return from Tehran and see what he wants. That will give us another twenty-four hours to strengthen our armies and prepare for the great onslaught.'

'Certainly, my president. On another subject, should we, do you think, issue an ultimatum to the GCC before our attack or should our terms follow a military action?'

'I think we should spill some blood first, to show them how serious we are. They have fully co-operated with the West over the past few years and I have a need for a little revenge. But tell me Tariq, what terms would you dictate when the time is right?'

'Well to begin with, a total write-off of all debts and a lifting of all trade embargoes. This they can easily afford and will not hurt them unduly.'

'This seems very reasonable,' put in Mazen Magbul. 'Other ideas, my president, could include membership of OPEC and a multi-billion dollar package to revitalise our economy and those of our allies.'

'Good, gentlemen, good, but two things above all else must be. Our errant province must be publicly proclaimed a part of Iraq. Kuwait must no longer exist.'

He paused, looking round the table. Not surprisingly, there was no dissent. He continued now more softly than before. 'And then must follow the founding of the Great Arab Republic, consisting of all Arab nations, beginning with the GCC and led by Baghdad. We shall then become the next truly great world force, and with our shared resources, will then be able to dictate terms to the West. This land shall once again be the heart of an empire which will last for generations and be remembered forever.'

Saddam Hussein's eyes shone with passion and all those who heard him felt swept along by his aura of power and persuasiveness. They now had the means to achieve this dream and as long as the West stayed out of their business and the GCC monarchs remained lost, the confusion that reigned would make for easy pickings.

This time, they all felt, it just might work.

Porlock Weir, England

'WE MOVE OUT IMMEDIATELY THEN,' stated Newcombe. The group had been discussing the events of the night since Carson's call in the early hours and had now agreed a plan of action. However, the extrication of Chater and Carson from police custody seemed to be more of a problem. New Year's Day was not a good time to find competent and sympathetic lawyers.

'Ian, after the first task we discussed, you, Jim and George go to Shoreham and get a plane. George, you'll need all your contacts and influence today, but get it and make sure it'll get all of us on board. We'll meet the three of you in Jersey on the third as agreed.'

'Will do, Mike,' replied Scott quietly and confidently. 'Come on chaps, let's go.'

'Don' you want an 'and wiv the prisoners, major? They might try somefink stupid.'

'No problem George, we'll manage fine. Now get going.' Newcombe turned to Cooper. 'Brian, you get the prisoners up and into the van one at a time. Be careful though, especially with that Saudi bastard, okay? Chain them all into position and I'll join you as soon as I've called Antigua again. Qaboos should be brought up last and left with me.'

They all went their separate ways leaving Newcombe to put in a call to Marshall and get an update on the situation from his end. There was little fresh information, so he went to find Bennett and bid him farewell. 'Well major, I reckon this is "cheerio" for the time being. Sorry it's had to end in such a rush.'

'My dear boy, it's been the best time I've had in years. Can't think what I'm going to do for a laugh, though, after you chaps have gone.' Bennett sounded very morose. Newcombe felt an affectionate concern for the pain-racked old soldier.

'Are you going to be okay? Just play innocent, remember, and stick to the adventure training story.'

'I'll be fine – just you make sure you get your money and stay out of prison, all right? After all this effort, it'd be a shame not to get anything back for it. Now I'm going off down to the pub. Wonder if they'll be open after last night's trouble?'

He pottered off out of the room muttering to himself. Newcombe was about to go after him when the first of the prisoners appeared, handcuffed and escorted by a particularly malevolent looking Cooper. One by one they were put in to the minivan and finally, Sultan Qaboos came out, unfettered and bearing his dignity with his usual regal grace.

Newcombe stood and addressed him.

'Your Majesty, perhaps we could have a few words before joining the others.'

Qaboos raised a questioning eyebrow and sat down. 'Yours to command!' he said with an unusual hint of sarcasm.

Newcombe, ignoring the barb, continued. 'We have a dilemma. . . .'

'I should have thought that's putting it mildly,' interrupted Qaboos. 'If I remember the expression correctly from my Sandhurst days, you're up a creek without a paddle.'

'Well, actually, Your Majesty, it's more your problem than ours. We have a fairly straightforward plan to separate ourselves safely from you, with or without the ransom. The bigger issue now, though, appears to be the imminent invasion of the Arabian Peninsula by Iraq and the internal strife in your various countries due to water shortages.'

'Well, I hope you're satisfied with yourselves. If the GCC crumbles and there is war in the Middle East, it will be principally your fault.'

'Bullshit, sir, it will be fully deserved and you know it. Your spoilt and morally deprived neighbours have had this coming to them for years. Anyway, this is neither the time nor the place to argue the subject. I have a proposal for you, after which you may wish to make a telephone call.'

Amman, Jordan

ALL OVER THE WORLD, PEOPLE were nursing headaches and suffering from an excess of partying and inadequate sleep. The staff in the Amman Excelsior Hotel were no exception.

They did not notice the two purposeful middle-aged men, each carrying a baggy hold-all enter the lobby and head straight for the bank of elevators. The duty clerk on the executive floor did not notice them come out of the lifts and head with determination towards the Royal Suite. The housekeeping supervisor did not notice them ring the doorbell and be admitted by a particularly fat and unpleasant character, Mahmoud Kanaan, the hotel's director of sales, who had been taking Turkish coffee with his guest, Colonel Rousan, and providing him with information, damning to everyone and everything except Iraq.

But Kanaan noticed them, or more particularly, their Uzi machine pistols now pointed at his chest. They pushed him inside towards the suite's large and spacious lounge, where they were confronted by Aziz's two personal security guards. A silenced burst from the Uzis stopped them in their tracks as they were reaching for their weapons and they fell back, dead before they hit the floor.

Kanaan was shaking uncontrollably as he backed into the lounge. He had soiled himself at the shooting of the guards and the foul smell of his excrement, blending with that of sweat and fear, now pervaded the room.

Although it had been only a matter of seconds since the doorbell had first rung, Rousan was alerted to danger and had his own automatic pistol in his hand. The two intruders heard it being cocked and, pushing Kanaan aside, each let off a long and devastating burst of gunfire at their target, who seemed almost to disappear in a fountain of shredded upholstery, cushion feathers and blood. They then turned their weapons on the remaining, and by now snivelling witness, and Kanaan's obese frame fell apart in a storm of bullets.

Placing on the door as they left the DO NOT DISTURB sign, the two Mossad agents left as unnoticed as they had arrived.

Minehead, England

THE AFTERNOON FOUND A VERY HARASSED and overloaded local police chief on the north Cornish coast. New Year's Eve was always a problem night but usually drunk and disorderly, bar brawls and motoring offences were the limit. Keep everyone locked up for twenty-four hours to sober up and then discharge them, that was his usual policy.

But last night had left one girl badly beaten and raped, two of her attackers killed and three others in intensive care – and that was from just one pub. Added to which was that one of the girl's saviours had 'Most Wanted' status and now both MI5 and MI6 were getting in on the act; whatever next? He had been told by his superior officer that the two men being held in connection with the events in Porlock were to be kept in isolation and under no circumstances should anyone have access to them at all until officers representing the intelligence services arrived. Yes, that also included lawyers, he was told.

His reverie was interrupted by his deputy who came into his office to announce the arrival of not one but three lawyers to see the two prisoners.

'You heard the orders,' he roared at his hopeless assistant. 'Nobody bloody goes in there, all right? Tell 'em they're being held under the Prevention of Terrorism Act.'

'Yes sir, but they are being most insistent. They say they want to speak with you immediately or else they'll be calling the press – infringement of civil liberties and all that, sir.'

'Bloody hell, where are those London spooks anyway? I want to get shot of all this . . . okay, you better send them in.'

The chief inspector's first thought as the three men were shown in was that a less-likely looking trio of lawyers he had never seen, especially the short stocky one.

His second thought confirmed his first as he and his deputy both found themselves staring at two machine pistols and an automatic. The door was closed quietly and with great economy of movement and with chilling calmness, the three men positioned themselves around the room before the leader, Jim Masterson, spoke.

'We wish no harm to you or your men but we are familiar with these weapons and willing and able to use them. Please believe me.'

The two policemen did believe him and nodded their assent. They were not trained for this and were badly frightened.

'Good,' continued Masterson quietly. 'Now, I understand you are holding in custody two men involved in rescuing a girl last night in Porlock. I would like you both to take us to them and release them. We shall then leave you here and quietly depart. Any problems?'

'You're the man with the gun,' said the chief inspector as he rose and headed round his desk for the door.

They left in an orderly line for the back of the police station where the cells were. A junior officer on duty looked up at the procession and was reaching for an alarm bell when there was a spit from Masterson's silenced automatic and the young policeman crumpled to the ground, a bullet through the thigh ensuring his New Year would begin in hospital. He lay on the floor groaning as Little George bent over him and started patching him up. 'Next time, try not to be a bleedin' 'ero mate, it can damage yer 'elth.'

They quickly found Chater and Carson. Chater said, 'Well you guys are a sight for sore eyes. Thanks for coming lads. What's happening to. . . .'

'Shut up!' snapped Masterson. 'No talking from anybody. Right chief inspector, let's move. George, lock up the boy hero here along with these two officers.'

The group then left quietly through the back of the station, and piled into a Range Rover and drove off.

An hour later, Steele and two colleagues from MI6 arrived and asked to see the chief inspector immediately. Within two minutes the alarm was raised and a full police alert was being posted throughout the region.

Enquiries with Bailey the previous night had revealed where the prisoners were living and so Steele instructed that firearms be issued to the region's Special Response Group and they proceeded with all haste to Tytherleigh Manor.

They arrived at the old house and approached cautiously, some officers skirting around the back and sides of the building, a few with Steele advancing from the front. There seemed no signs of life, but they were extremely cautious.

When no one answered the bell or their louder knocking, they forced their way in and began searching the house.

Old Bennett sat by the fireplace, the logs now hardly glowing. The pink gin from the broken glass at his side had stained the threadbare carpet but it didn't really matter. The note beside him simply read, *After so much fun, I'll cash in now that I'm ahead,* and the empty pot of distalgesic pain-killing tablets were testimony to his intentions.

The cells in the basement and the recent signs of occupation were all Steele needed to see and so he left the police to sort it out and returned to London.

Antigua, Leeward Islands

BEAUMONT STOOD UP AND LOOKED around at the others. Incredulity was on all their faces.

One of the negotiators asked: 'Is this guy Brown for real? I mean, after everything he's caused so far, he's now proposing this. He's out of his tree!' ·

'That's as may be,' replied Al Khyumi, 'but it sounds like a good idea and no one else has got any others.'

'Yes, but. . . .' the first negotiator was interrupted by Beaumont.

' "Yes but" nothing. I reckon we should go along with it and fast. General, what do you think?'

'As his excellency says, there seems to be no choice. Anyway, it is a good plan and we should go for it. Sitting around here certainly isn't getting us anywhere.'

'Right then,' declared Beaumont, more decisively than he had done anything in days, 'let's get off this bloody island and sort this nonsense out.'

Baghdad, Iraq

'TARIQ, YOU HAVE DONE WELL,' praised Saddam Hussein. 'Tehran becoming a partner in this enterprise is indeed a bonus. Are they ready to engage our enemies immediately?'

'Yes, my president. Even now they are mobilising their forces. Two to three days and they will be ready.'

'General Musbah, what is the status of our army?'

'Our forces are prepared and ready to strike, my president. However, we need a couple of days to have the back-up and support services ready.'

'Very well. What news from the international community? Will everyone leave us alone this time?'

Tariq Aziz answered cautiously. 'My president, we received another message this morning from the United Nations. Lord Styles wishes to meet with me in Oman in two days from now. I believe we should wait until I have had this meeting and get a clear picture of the international position.'

Saddam was displeased. 'I don't like waiting. If we are ready, we should move. However, Tariq, you are right, especially if the Iranians need two days to mobilise. We will wait until your return, but unless there is any reason to the contrary, we attack in three days.'

River Dart, England.

THE JOURNEY TO THE OLD BOATHOUSE was uneventful and hostages and captors arrived without incident in the early hours of the 2nd of January.

Cooper drove while Newcombe kept an eye on the prisoners. Although handcuffed to their seats, he did not want to take chances at this stage. He had also agreed with Qaboos not to share their plan with the others for the time being. After all, the solution they had agreed upon was non-negotiable.

They found the Vosper in good order, if a bit damp and cold, and piled aboard. Newcombe ensured that the hostages were well and safely secured below, while Cooper prepared the vessel for sea. He and Masterson had fully fuelled, victualled and prepared the boat when they had left it, so they had little to do before their forthcoming trip. They quietly slipped their lines and made for open water, a course set for Jersey in the Channel Islands.

Shoreham, England

LITTLE GEORGE WAS WELL KNOWN at Shoreham Airport. He had been a parachute instructor there for some years, and was one of the more colourful characters at the flying club. Even so it took him several calls and considerable bullying tactics to charter an appropriate sized plane.

Eventually, they had to settle on a Navajo, which was suitable enough but not an aircraft Scott was familiar with. It was mid-morning before he was happy with it, not to mention the lessees, and eventually they took off, a flight plan filed for Fort William in Scotland. Their nerves were raw by the time they left the ground as news of their escapade in Minehead was being broadcast on all radio, TV and media channels.

Once the other side of the South Downs, however, they changed direction and headed first west, then southwest and soon they were flying low, headed for a rendezvous with their colleagues in Jersey.

Fortunately, the scale of the police search had not yet extended to private aircraft charter and they were soon lost to the authorities and air traffic control.

The Brown Envelope Club had once again left England, embarked upon a bigger and more incongruous adventure than they had ever at first conceived.

Qatar

FOR A COUNTRY SO WELL RENOWNED for ruthlessly keeping law and order, it was doubly surprising to all observers how severe and extreme the riot was. The authorities insisted it was the work of fundamentalist Islamic extremists, stirring up both the indigenous population and the expatriate labour force. Oswald Prendergast's agents were able to confirm that, to an extent, this was true and Iranian provocateurs were also almost certainly involved. However, they were using natural influences as their main weapon and that most basic of human needs – water.

The people were thirsty and dirty. Not just in Qatar, but throughout the Arabian Peninsula. There was tension and disquiet everywhere. The continued absence of their leaders, the uncertainty of the people and the mixed loyalties of the police forces and armies were making for a volatile and explosive scenario.

In every country of the GCC there had been increasing incidents of 'civil commotion', as it was euphemistically described, small riots ruthlessly suppressed along with any media coverage. But the events in Qatar on the 2nd of January amounted almost to civil war. By the time the authorities had regained control throughout the country, over two thousand people had died, both civilian and military.

The generals in Iraq and the Mullahs in Iran rubbed their hands in glee. Their strange alliance looked as though it would bear good fruit and certainly the GCC was now looking ripe for plucking.

London, England

THE CHIEFS OF MOSSAD AND MI6 had just finished a telephone conversation. Whilst there was inevitable disappointment at having been so close to finding the hostages, the news from Antigua was truly amazing.

With Lord Style persuading Tariq Aziz to go to Oman, now all the pieces seemed in place for settling the entire affair.

Steele was less optimistic, however. 'Suppose the whole thing's a red herring. I mean, why the hell should they do what they proposed? It doesn't make any sense.'

'I agree,' replied Hood dryly, 'but they've now got nothing to lose. Anyway, they may have struck a deal with the royals – probably had to because of their own fiasco. Otherwise they'll get nothing, be hounded until captured and probably killed in the process.'

'I suppose you're right, chief. These Arabs are nothing if not vindictive. Anyway, I'll get over to Jersey and co-ordinate things from there. Better hurry or I'll miss the flight.'

'Too true; anyway, I think the best I can do for the moment is watch and listen, see what Prendergast can come up with and, perhaps most important, see what Styles can manage in Muscat. That's where the fun and games are really going to happen. Keep in touch.'

Jersey, Channel Islands

GOREY CASTLE ROSE OUT of the morning mist like some ghostly monster from ancient mythology. The sea was unusually flat calm and the Vosper cautiously entered the small fishing harbour below the ramparts, inching its way slowly and carefully through the fog. Newcombe had chosen this quiet fishing village harbour in preference over the bigger and better equipped port of St Helier, for there would be fewer prying eyes and less attention paid to them.

To his great relief, he spotted the other members of the group waiting for them on the quay beside a large Bedford van. Chater's huge bulk loomed out of the mist, looking almost as sinister as the castle above him, and he reached down to grab their lines as the Vosper slid gently up to the harbour wall. Fortunately it was high tide, so they were able to unload their protesting passengers quickly and easily and bundle them unceremoniously into the van.

There was a cold chill in the air and no harbour master or customs officers were around. This suited the resilient group of soldiers perfectly but their captives, used to a more equable climate, were grumbling mightily at the bitter conditions.

'Cheer up, gen'lmen, you'll feel better soon,' quipped Little George who hovered happily over his charges on the floor in the back of the Bedford, his machine pistol resting comfortably in his hands.

'Where are you taking us now?' asked King Abdullah savagely. 'I promise you, you will all pay for this outrage.'

'No, actually Your Majesty,' replied Newcombe, 'you're the one who's going to pay; anyway, enough talk. Brian – you fix up the boat for sea again, get through the harbour formalities and then join us at the airport as soon as you can. If everything's as scheduled, we'll be leaving at about midday.'

They drove off quickly along the quay and out of town on almost deserted roads. Everything seemed so quiet it was as if the Channel Island residents didn't really want the New Year to get started. Half an hour later they arrived at the airport.

Here too everything seemed tired and slow and sluggish. There appeared to be no commercial traffic of any sort with one very sizeable and noticeable exception. Jersey airport was accustomed to a wide variety of aircraft, mostly small ones, so the huge, white, stretch-top Boeing 747-400 parked close by the departure building was something of a curiosity.

'Ian, you come with me,' ordered Newcombe. 'The rest of you stay here and keep this lot quiet and out of sight. If we're not back in thirty minutes, get the hell out of here.'

They entered the departure terminal and, as arranged during the last telephone call from Tytherleigh with Qaboos, approached the information desk and asked for Colonel Kenwright. The receptionist reached for a telephone.

Newcombe whispered under his breath to Scott. 'This is when we see just how much diplomatic clout these guys really have. If it's not stratospheric, we've had it.'

After a few brief words, the receptionist hung up and pointed to a door marked STRICTLY NO ADMITTANCE – AUTHORISED PERSONNEL ONLY. 'Take these two passes, go through that door and you'll be taken to Colonel Kenwright, sir.'

'Thank you!'

They pushed at the door and entered a small office from which led a corridor lined with plain, unmarked doors. Colonel Kenwright emerged from one, followed by two very tough and capable looking armed Omani soldiers, two uniformed British policemen, also armed, and another civilian, Crispin Steele.

Kenwright recognised Scott straight away. 'Why commander, I hadn't expected to see you again. Fancy you being involved in this little escapade.' He turned offering his hand. 'And you must be the master strategist, Major Newcombe I presume.' They shook hands and he continued. 'As you've gathered, I'm Colonel Kenwright and this is Mr Steele who's come to help out. Why don't we go into the office and have a little chat.'

Both Newcombe and Scott felt uneasy but they were committed now. Newcombe replied, 'Fine but we need to check back with our associates in twenty minutes or the deal's off. So let's make it quick.'

'No problem at all,' Kenwright replied. 'Mr Steele, can you outline the details please.'

'Certainly colonel – I assume that the hostages are close by. They should be brought here through the door you have just entered by and they will then be taken directly to the plane waiting just outside. You and your men will then. . . .'

'You'll have to do better than that Mr Steele,' interrupted Newcombe. 'After coming this far, we don't propose to get picked off by your sharpshooters on our way. No, let me tell you how we'll board up. Each of my men will accompany one monarch at a time to the aircraft. I shall accompany Sultan Qaboos last.' He noticed the two Omanis flinch and made a point to keep a special eye on them. 'Wing Commander Scott, here, will go ahead of us, check out the aircraft and remain on the flight deck for the duration. When he is satisfied that all is in order he will signal us and only then will we commence embarkation.'

'Well, it's all very well you coming and dictating terms to us,' replied Steele somewhat haughtily, 'but. . . .'

'But nothing Mr Steele. This is non-negotiable and we're wasting time. I suggest we proceed and, as instructed, there had better be no police or other, shall we say "services" waiting to play games with us outside.' He raised an eyebrow towards Kenwright. 'All right with you colonel?'

'Okay, okay! There's no need to worry about our previous requirement. No one else is involved.' Steele sounded somewhat disappointed as he confirmed this.

'I'm sure we'll all manage just fine.' Kenwright issued instructions to the two Omanis and Scott followed them on to the tarmac towards the flagship of the Sultanate of Oman's Royal Flight. Newcombe also left the room, retraced his steps to the van and briefed his team. He then returned to await Scott's signal.

The first couple to make their tentative and cautious way to the plane were the Emir of Kuwait and Carson. Although still weak from his wound, the ministrations of Doctor Morton had done its work and at least he was now walking wounded. There was also a doctor on the plane and the sooner further medical supervision began the better.

Despite Steele's assurances, Newcombe kept an anxious lookout for signs of a trap, both on the apron and the departure terminal car park. However, there were still no signs of activity and the embarkation continued.

Masterson took the Emir of Qatar aboard next. Newcombe wanted his ruthlessness and skills to protect their position before he himself arrived on board. Little George came next then Chater, with the rulers of Bahrain and Saudi Arabia respectively. A brief delay then followed while Newcombe, supervising both Al Nahyan and Qaboos, waited for Cooper to arrive. This did not take long however, and as soon as he came, Cooper took Al Nahyan out to the Jumbo. Newcombe and Qaboos sedately took up the rear, pausing at the bottom of the steps to the big aircraft to take their leave of Steele.

'I don't know how you fixed all this Newcombe but you've certainly caused a ton of grief.'

'Well, sorry and all that. Incidentally, you won't forget that full pardon we discussed, will you? Have a happy new year!' Sultan Qaboos smiled to himself as he boarded his own aeroplane to head home.

Muscat, Oman

IN A COUNTRY MORE USED TO A SEDATE PACE, the buzz of behind-the-scenes activity was remarkable. Although advance warning had been given, it had not been until Al Khyumi had arrived, accompanied by Ashman and Beaumont, that the stops were really pulled out.

The Al Bustan Palace Hotel was turned into something more closely resembling a fortress. The redoubtable Nadine had been called and told to begin evacuating and relocating all guests to other hotels. 'So sorry sir,' the helpless management would say to infuriated tourists, 'the government is taking over the hotel – it's beyond our control.' Which indeed it was.

By the time Beaumont arrived and started throwing his weight about, grumpy and jetlagged, much had already been prepared. The royal court were supervising the preparations of the six exquisite suites on the ninth floor of the hotel and the fabulous conference rooms were being similarly attended to. Normally GCC head-of-state gatherings took six months and more to prepare for. This extraordinary general meeting had given less than forty-eight hours notice.

Unusually, but as instructed, the arrival of the Royal Flight from Jersey received no pomp or ceremony. Anyway, it was four o'clock in the morning, so there were few about. The 747 merely taxied to the VIP terminal and, under the pre-dawn cover of darkness, disembarked its passengers. They travelled in convoy with the minimum of fuss in the same configuration they had first boarded the aircraft and arrived at the hotel where for the first time in over a week, they bathed in the luxury that they were accustomed to, rested and slept.

The journey from Jersey had been an interesting one to say the least. The captives' initial and startled realisation that they were almost free had been quickly followed by cries for blood, particularly from King Abdullah. However, Newcombe's assurance that any nonsense from them would lead to the instant detonation of the many pounds of Semtex strategically placed on the aircraft quickly dispelled ideas of heroics. As he argued, they had nothing now to lose. The fact that he was bluffing was not even considered by his captives.

In any case, after some extremely heated discourse, Qaboos explained the details of the plan and the deal he had struck with Newcombe. Although somewhat bizarre, they all finally accepted that, after what they had been through, the plan was a sound one, and so they quietly acquiesced. The Brown Envelope Club breathed a huge but silent sigh of relief.

As well as the GCC leaders and their previous wardens, there were at the grand dinner that night many others. The ambassadors of each concerned nation were present along with certain relevant ministers and senior military and intelligence personnel from Oman. But the most intriguing guest of all was Lord Douglas Styles, the United Nations secretary general. None of the guests had been advised the purpose of the summons to the dinner and their anxiety and worry over the region's current affairs were dispelled when they saw their host and principal guests of honour.

After the meal, Sultan Qaboos spoke to his assembled company. He explained to them the ordeal they had all been through and then introduced the group of abductors in their midst. This caused some consternation but Qaboos called for silence. He then discussed the current threat pitted against them all, both internally and externally.

And finally, he presented the solution agreed upon on the flight from the Channel Islands.

The dinner ended in the early hours of the 4th of January as the Royal Jordanian flight carrying Tariq Aziz made its final approach into Seeb International Airport in Oman.

He was met by his ambassador and taken without delay to the Al Bustan. By arrangement, there was nobody in the lobby and he was shown to his room by a duty manager without delay. As informed, the Iraqi ambassador confirmed to him Lord Styles's slightly earlier arrival and that a meeting was scheduled for noon later that day. Such a delay aggravated Aziz but he was sufficiently familiar with the nuances of the diplomatic service not to be rattled or distracted by it.

He was, however, startled beyond words when, at the appointed time, he and his ambassador were led into the conference room to meet with Lord Styles. Instead of finding just a few United Nations representatives, he was confronted by a hostile, aggressive and more importantly, united GCC leadership, their closest advisors and a strange group of Europeans. These latter, he thought, were more sinister than the rest put together. There was no chair for him on which to sit.

Sultan Qaboos greeted him coldly. 'Your excellency. Forgive us if we do not rise but we have become somewhat tired of your country's bothersome antics, along with those of your most recently found and troublesome allies. In any event, we shall not keep you long. You may then return to your master, if you still wish, and consider your position.'

Lord Styles spoke next. 'Unfortunately for you Aziz, your country has once again misinterpreted the international response to your leader's greedy and megalomaniacal aspirations. Quite simply, you will not be allowed an inch. Any sign of aggression or warlike military activity of any nature will result in the total obliteration of your capital, its leadership and those armies of participating allies. Is that clear?'

'Lord Styles, your words are certainly clear, but the capability of the international community and, more importantly, their collective inclination to react as you suggest strikes me as unlikely.' Aziz felt he could do little else other than try to brazen out this awful encounter and gain from it what intelligence he could. He was surprised, however, that it was the English major who quietly and in fluent Arabic responded to him.

'Who said anything about the international community your excellency? Since your last escapade, the GCC have been preparing itself to fully meet and confront a similar act of aggression without recourse to external support. The GCC now possesses the technology, training and will to eradicate Iraq. Please believe me when I tell you that this time the forces against you will not stop in the south but continue north until you are totally vanquished.' He paused for a moment and leant forward, continuing in a voice barely above a whisper. 'You should further believe me that there are those of us who also know the way and are itching for the excuse to go.'

It was not so much the words that convinced Tariq Aziz but the quiet intensity of the ice blue eyes. The hostility against him from all round was almost tangible but it was Newcombe's quiet forceful-ness that persuaded him.

He bowed a curt nod of his head towards Qaboos and Styles, turned on his heel and left the room, his ambassador following like a terrified puppy at his heel. This would certainly not please Saddam.

In a private audience with Sultan Qaboos later that afternoon, the Brown Envelope Club waited anxiously to hear the results of their proposals. Lord Styles was also present.

Qaboos opened the proceedings. 'Well, gentlemen, do you think they will buy it?'

'We clearly won't know for a day or two, Your Majesty,' replied Newcombe, 'but I don't see why not. With the announcements to the world news media and the press conference at lunch-time today, a fully unified position will be seen in the GCC for the first time ever. Stability will be required in the more volatile of the countries and with the leaders returning home, I'd just hate to be some of their regents.'

Qaboos laughed at this. 'In fact,' he predicted, 'our new found unity will frighten everyone so much, the USA will probably declare war on us. What do you think, Lord Styles?'

'Well, Your Majesty, the US certainly does not like competition, and that's a fact. I must say, I am rather inclined to agree with Major Newcombe's assessment.

'But suppose they call our bluff?' persisted Qaboos. 'We'll be quite unable to stop them you know, even though our entire collective armed forces have been mobilised.

'Quite so, sir, but they don't know that. Neither do the Iranians, come to that,' predicted Styles, 'and since they just wanted to leap on any old bandwagon that would make trouble for the West, they'll be easily discouraged.'

'Well, gentlemen, I hope you are right. In the meantime, Lord Styles, you are returning to New York to brief the Security Council and the United Nations as appropriate. As for you all,' he paused dramatically, 'in the short term, you will be retained as agreed to advise on immediate developments. If the invasion does not materialise, your brief will be to co-ordinate, as a neutral authority, the combined GCC armed services to prepare itself independently along the very lines of our statement to Mr Aziz earlier. With such an arrangement, you will also receive one tenth of your original, er, ransom demand and an appropriate working package as yet to be arranged.'

'This is most gracious of you, sir, and we are all most grateful – thank you.' Newcombe was about to continue, when Little George spoke up.

'Er, 'scuse me Your Majesty, but what 'appens to us if the Iraqis do invade?'

'Well, Mr George, since you will have been one of the principal reasons for their aggression, I do not imagine you and your colleagues will have a very nice time. But we are providing you with this somewhat unusual opportunity because you came up with such an ingenious resolution to the potential catastrophe in which we all found ourselves. Do I make myself clear?'

'Absolutely, sir,' cut in Newcombe before George could respond. 'Once again, thank you. We shall now leave you and wait until we hear from you.'

He rose and left the room, the others following him. Out in the hotel gardens, they strolled and exchanged a few words. As always, the waiting game was the hardest for these men of action and it did not come easily.

They walked to the end of a small rocky promontory at the end of the beach and stared out of the rich blue waters of the Gulf of Oman. A pair of courting eagle rays broke surface and flipped in mid-air before slipping once again noiselessly beneath the mirror-like sea. So beautiful was it and so preoccupied their thoughts, that they did not notice the arrival of Beaumont behind them.

'Mr Brown, I presume. I'm Lawrence Beaumont.'

'Mr Beaumont, it's a pleasure. He introduced the group, ending with himself. 'And my name's actually Newcombe, Mike Newcombe. How are you bearing up? Hope we didn't cause you too much personal grief.'

'Frankly, you're the biggest bunch of pains in the ass I've ever come across and, yes, you caused a whole ton of grief. Anyway, if you can now direct it against Saddam, I'll buy you all a beer.'

They grinned and headed for the beach bar.

Epilogue
Seeds Resown

Baghdad, Iraq

FEW HAD EVER SEEN SADDAM HUSSEIN in such a violent temper and lived to speak of it. The cabinet sat in awe around him, each trying to distance himself from one another, and prayed quietly to whichever God gave them sustenance to be delivered from this meeting alive.

The principal targets of Saddam's wrath were his chief of staff and foreign minister. The latter had just delivered his extraordinary message from Muscat and described his encounter. The chief of staff had then back-pedalled and stated that if the foreign minister's report was correct, then it would be truly suicidal for an attack at this time, even with the untrustworthy Iranians on side. 'Who knows,' he declared, 'they may even change sides when they see the stakes and attack us instead.'

'Well, general,' whispered Saddam, 'since you clearly have no stomach for a fight, your services are redundant. Leave us.'

General Musbah rose cautiously and almost backed his way from the room, the sweat cascading down his terrified face despite the air conditioning. As he turned to negotiate the door, a loud explosion echoed throughout the room, dazing and numbing everyone.

Saddam had replaced his still smoking revolver in its holster before the lifeless remains of General Musbah had slumped to the floor. No one dared look or move and they all sat around the table in abject misery. This was not the first time such a spectacle had been seen and no one wished to add to the statistics.

'So it seems that we are out-manoeuvred and unable to risk an attack, is that it Tariq?'

'Yes, my president, so it would seem.'

'But suppose they're bluffing. What if this is just an elaborate hoax made out of desperation by a group of bickering old sheiks, Tariq. Think of the prize and opportunity we will have lost – rather, you will have lost.' He fingered the butt of his pistol distractedly, an insane gleam in his eyes.

'My president, I have served you from the beginning and my loyalty to you and the Iraqi nation is beyond dispute. I would be failing you now if I simply advocated war to please you. I truly believe that if we attacked the GCC, it would be our downfall and that is why I implore you to reconsider.'

'Very well, Tariq, so be it. But we must now seek the alliances and technologies once again to crush these desert upstarts and establish Iraq as the absolute power in the region. We will be patient, Tariq, for I know how careful and discreet we must be.' He paused, as if considering his apparent new-found enlightenment. 'But we will not be too patient.'

ABOUT THE AUTHOR

CHARLES BARKER IS AN HOTELIER who spent much of his career in the Middle East. He became well acquainted with all of the key players on both sides of the first Gulf War and was uniquely positioned to see at first hand the issues and manoeuvrings of this troubled region.

He has worked in eight countries on five continents and enjoys immersing himself in the cultures and regions in which he finds himself. Having already written a collection of short stories, *Capital Tales*, and a children's book, *The Adventures of Godfrey and Oliver*, *The Brown Envelope Club* is his first novel.

He now lives in Hong Kong with his wife and keeps a home in England.

Please see *http://www.charlesbarker.org* for updates on forthcoming books.

CPSIA information can be obtained
at www.ICGtesting.com
Printed in the USA
BVHW061035190820
586812BV00013B/904